DEAD WATER

DEAD WATER

Ngaio Marsh

FELONY & MAYHEM PRESS • NEW YORK

All the characters and events portrayed in this work are fictitious.

DEAD WATER

A Felony & Mayhem mystery

PRINTING HISTORY
First U.S. edition (Little, Brown): 1963
First U.K. edition (Collins): 1964
Felony & Mayhem edition: 2015

ISBN: 978-1-63194-024-8

Manufactured in the United States of America

Printed on 100% recycled paper

Library of Congress Cataloging-in-Publication Data

Marsh, Ngaio, 1895-1982.
Dead water / Ngaio Marsh. -- Felony & Mayhem edition.
    pages cm. -- (A Felony & Mayhem mystery)
ISBN 978-1-63194-024-8
1. Alleyn, Roderick (Fictitious character)--Fiction. 2. Police--England--
Fiction. I. Title.
PR9639.3.M27D38 2015
823'.912--dc23
                          2014042120

For Alister and Doris McIntosh with love

CONTENTS

Other "Vintage" titles from

FELONY&MAYHEM

CAST OF CHARACTERS

DEAD WATER

CHAPTER ONE

Prelude

A BOY STUMBLED up the hillside, half-blinded by tears. He fell and, for a time, choked and sobbed as he lay in the sun but presently blundered on. A lark sang overhead. Farther up the hill he could hear the multiple chatter of running water. The children down by the jetty still chanted after him:

> *Warty-hog, warty-hog*
> *Put your puddies in the bog*
> *Warty Walter, Warty Walter*
> *Wash your warties in the water.*

The spring was near the top. It began as a bubbling pool, cascaded into a miniature waterfall, dived under pebbles, earth and bracken and at last, loquacious and preoccupied, swirled mysteriously underground and was lost. Above the pool stood a boulder, flanked by briars and fern, and above that the brow of the hill and the sun in a clear sky.

He squatted near the waterfall. His legs ached and a spasm jolted his chest. He gasped for breath, beat his hands on the ground and looked at them. Warty-hog. Warts clustered all over his fingers like those black things that covered the legs of the jetty. Two of them bled where he'd cut them. The other kids were told not to touch him.

He thrust his hands under the cold pressure of the cascade. It beat and stung and numbed them, but he screwed up his blubbered eyes and forced them to stay there. Water spurted icily up his arms and into his face.

"Don't cry."

He opened his eyes directly into the sun or would have done so if she hadn't stood between: tall and greenish, above the big stone and rimmed about with light like something on the telly so that he couldn't see her properly.

"Why are you crying?"

He ducked his head, and stared like an animal that couldn't make up its mind to bolt. He gave a loud, detached sob and left his hands under the water.

"What's the matter? Are you hurt? Tell me."

"Me 'ands."

"Show me."

He shook his head and stared.

"Show me your hands."

"They'm mucky."

"The water will clean them."

"No, t'won't, then."

"Show me."

He withdrew them. Between clusters of warts his skin had puckered and turned the colour of dead fish. He broke into a loud wail. His nose and eyes ran salt into his open mouth.

From down below a voice, small and distant, halfheartedly chanted: "Warty Walter. Warty Walter. Stick your warties in the water." Somebody shouted: "Aw *come* on." They were going away.

He held out his desecrated hands towards her as if in explanation. Her voice floated down on the sound of the waterfall.

"Put them under again. If you believe: they will be clean."

"Uh?"

"They will be clean. Say it. Say 'Please take away my warts.' Shut your eyes and do as I tell you. Say it again when you go to bed. Remember. Do it."

He did as she told him. The sound of the cascade grew very loud in his ears. Blobs of light swam across his eyeballs. He heard his own voice very far away, and then nothing. Ice-cold water was bumping his face on drowned pebbles.

When he lifted his head up there was no one between him and the sun.

He sat there letting himself dry and thinking of nothing in particular until the sun went down behind the hill. Then, feeling cold, he returned to the waterfront and his home in the bay.

For about twenty-four hours after the event, the affair of Wally Trehern's warts made very little impression on the island. His parents were slugabeds: the father under the excuse that he was engaged in night-fishing and the mother without any excuse at all unless it could be found in the gin bottle. They were not a credit to the Island. Wally, who slept in his clothes, got up at his usual time, and went out to the pump for a wash. He did this because somehow or another his new teacher had fixed the idea in his head and he followed it out with the sort of behaviourism that can be established in a domestic animal. He was still little better than half-awake when he saw what had happened.

Nobody knows what goes on in the mind of a child: least of all in a mind like Wally Trehern's where the process of thought was so sluggish as to be no more than a reflex of simple emotions: pleasure, fear or pride.

He seemed to be feeling proud when he shambled up to his teacher and, before all the school, held out his hands. "Why—!" she said. "Why—why—*Wally!*" She took both his hands in hers and looked and pressed and looked again. "I can't believe it," she said. "It's not true."

"Be'ant mucky," he said. "All gone," and burst out laughing.

The school was on the mainland but the news about Wally Trehern's warts returned with him and his teacher to the Island. The Island was incorrectly named: it was merely a rocky blob of land at the end of an extremely brief, narrow and low-lying causeway which disappeared at full tide and whenever the seas along that coast ran high. The Island was thus no more than an extension of the tiny fishing village of Portcarrow and yet the handful of people who lived on it were accorded a separate identity as if centuries of tidal gestures had given them an indefinable status. In those parts they talked of "islanders" and "villagers," making a distinction where none really existed.

The Portcarrow school-mistress was Miss Jenny Williams, a young New Zealander who was doing postgraduate research in England, and had taken this temporary job to enrich her experience and augment her bursary. She lodged on the Island at The Boy-and-Lobster, a small Jacobean pub, and wrote home enthusiastically about its inconveniences. She was a glowing, russet-coloured girl and looked her best that afternoon, striding across the causeway with the wind snapping at her hair and moulding her summer dress into the explicit simplicity of a shift. Behind her ran, stumbled and tacked poor Wally, who gave from time to time a squawking cry not unlike that of a seagull.

When they arrived on the Island she told him she would like to see his mother. They turned right at the jetty, round a point and into Fisherman's Bay. The Treherns lived in the least prepossessing of a group of cottages. Jenny could feel nothing but dismay at its smell and that of Mrs. Trehern who sat on the doorstep and made ambiguous sounds of greeting.

"She'm sozzled," said Wally, and indeed, it was so.

Jenny said: "Wally: would you be very kind and see if you can find me a shell to keep. A pink one." She had to repeat this carefully and was not helped by Mrs. Trehern suddenly roaring out that if he didn't do what his teacher said, she'd have the hide off of him.

Wally sank his head between his shoulders, shuffled down to the foreshore and disappeared behind a boat.

"Mrs. Trehern," Jenny said, "I do hope you don't mind me coming: I just felt I must say how terribly glad I am about Wally's warts and—and—I did want to ask about how it's happened. I mean," she went on, growing flurried, "it's so extraordinary. Since yesterday. I mean—well—it's— *Isn't* it?"

Mrs. Trehern was smiling broadly. She jerked her head and asked Jenny if she would take a little something.

"No, thank you," She waited for a moment and then said: "Mrs. Trehern, haven't you noticed? Wally's hands? Haven't you seen?"

"Takes fits," said Mrs. Trehern. "Our Wally!" she added with an air of profundity. After several false starts she rose and turned into the house. "You come on in," she shouted bossily. "Come on."

Jenny was spared this ordeal by the arrival of Mr. Trehern who lumbered up from the foreshore where she fancied he had been sitting behind his boat. He was followed at a distance by Wally.

James Trehern was a dark, fat man with pale eyes, a slack mouth and a manner that was both suspicious and placatory. He hired out himself and his boat to visitors, fished and did odd jobs about the village and the Island.

He leered uncertainly at Jenny and said it was an uncommonly brave afternoon and he hoped she was feeling pretty clever herself. Jenny at once embarked on the disappearance of the warts and found that Trehern had just become aware of it. Wally had shown him his hands.

"Isn't it amazing, Mr. Trehern?"

"Proper flabbergasting," he agreed without enthusiasm.

"When did it happen exactly, do you know? Was it yesterday, after school? Or when? Was it—sudden? I mean his hands were in such a state, weren't they? I've asked him, of course, and he says—he says it's because of a lady. And something about washing his hands in the spring up there. I'm sorry to pester you like this but I felt I just *had* to know."

It was obvious that he thought she was making an unnecessary to-do about the whole affair, but he stared at her with a sort of covert intensity that was extremely disagreeable. A gust of wind snatched at her dress and she tried to pin it between her knees. Trehern's mouth widened. Mrs. Trehern advanced uncertainly from the interior.

Jenny said quickly: "Well, never mind, anyway. It's grand that they've gone, isn't it? I mustn't keep you. Good evening."

Mrs. Trehern made an ambiguous sound and extended her clenched hand. "See yurr," she said. She opened her hand. A cascade of soft black shells dropped on the step.

"Them's our Wally's," she said. "In 'is bed."

"All gone," said Wally.

He had come up from the foreshore. When Jenny turned to him, he offered her a real shell. It was broken and discoloured but it was pink. Jenny knelt down to take it. "Thank you very much," she said. "That's just what I wanted."

It seemed awful to go away and leave him there. When she looked back he waved to her.

That evening in the private tap at The Boy-and-Lobster Wally Trehern's warts were the principal topic of conversation. It was a fine evening and low-tide fell at eight o'clock. In addition to the regular Islanders, there were patrons who had strolled across the causeway from the village: Dr. Maine of the Portcarrow Convalescent Home; the Rector, the Rev. Mr. Adrian Carstairs, who liked to show, as was no more than the case, that he was human; and a visitor to the village, a large pale young man with

a restless manner and a general air of being on the look-out
for something. He was having a drink with Patrick Ferrier, the
stepson of the landlord, down from Oxford for the long vacation. Patrick was an engaging fellow with a sensitive mouth,
pleasant manners and a quick eye which dwelt pretty often
upon Jenny Williams. There was only one other woman in the
private besides Jenny. This was Miss Elspeth Cost, a lady with
vague hair and a tentative smile who, like Jenny, was staying
at The Boy-and-Lobster and was understood to have a shop
somewhere and to be interested in handicrafts and the drama.

The landlord, Major Keith Barrimore, stationed between
two bars, served both the public and the private taps: the
former being used exclusively by local fishermen. Major
Barrimore was well-set-up and of florid complexion. He
shouted, rather than spoke, had any amount of professional
bonhomie and harmonised perfectly with his background of
horse-brasses, bottles, glasses, tankards and sporting prints. He
wore a check coat, a yellow waistcoat and a signet ring and kept
his hair very smooth.

"Look at it whichever way you choose," Miss Cost said,
"it's astounding. Poor little fellow! To think!"

"Very dramatic," said Patrick Ferrier, smiling at Jenny.

"Well it was," she said. "Just that."

"One hears of these cases," said the restless young man,
"Gipsies and charms and so on."

"Yes, I know one does," Jenny said. "One *hears* of them
but I've never met one before. And who, for heaven's sake, was
the green lady?"

There was a brief silence.

"Ah," said Miss Cost. "Now that *is* the really rather
wonderful part. The green lady!" She tipped her head to one
side and looked at the Rector. "M-m—?" she invited.

"Poor Wally!" Mr. Carstairs rejoined. "All a fairytale, I
daresay. It's a sad case."

"The cure isn't a fairytale," Jenny pointed out.

"No, no, no. Surely not. Surely not," he said in a hurry.

"A *fairy* tale. I wonder. Still pixies in these yurr parts, Rector, d'y'm reckon?" asked Miss Cost, essaying a roughish burr.

Everyone looked extremely uncomfortable.

"All in the poor kid's imagination, I should have thought," said Major Barrimore and poured himself a double Scotch.

"Still: damn' good show, anyway."

"What's the medical opinion?" Patrick asked.

"Don't ask me!" Dr. Maine ejaculated, throwing up his beautifully kept hands. "There is no medical opinion as far as I know." But seeing perhaps that they all expected more than this from him, he went on half-impatiently, "You do, of course, hear of these cases. They're quite well-established. I've heard of an eminent skin-specialist who actually mugged up an incantation or spell or what have-you and used it on his patients with marked success."

"There! You see!" Miss Cost cried out, gently clapping her hands. She became mysterious. "You wait!" she said. "You jolly well wait!"

Dr. Maine glanced at her distastefully.

"The cause of warts is not known," he said. "Probably viral. The boy's an epileptic," he added. "*Petit mal.*"

"Would that predispose him to this sort of cure?" Patrick asked.

"Might," Dr. Maine said shortly. "Might predispose him to the right kind of suggestibility." Without looking at the Rector, he added: "There's one feature that sticks out all through the literature of reputed cures by some allegedly supernatural agency. The authentic cases have emotional or nervous connotations."

"Not all, surely," the Rector suggested.

Dr. Maine shot a glance at him. "I shouldn't talk," he said. "I really know nothing about such matters. The other half, if you please."

Jenny thought: "The Rector feels he ought to nip in and speak up for miracles and he doesn't like to because he doesn't want to be parsonic. How tricky it is for them! Dr. Maine's the same, in his way. He doesn't like talking shop for fear of showing off. English reticence," thought Jenny, resolving to make the point in her next letter home. "Incorrigible amateurs."

The restless young man suddenly said, "The next round's on me," and astonished everybody.

"Handsome offer!" said Major Barrimore. "Thank you, sir."

"Tell me," said the young man expansively and at large. "Where is this spring or pool or whatever it is?"

Patrick explained. "Up the hill above the jetty."

"And the kid's story is that some lady in green told him to wash his hands in it? And the warts fell off in the night. Is that it?"

"As far as I could make out," Jenny agreed. "He's not at all eloquent, poor Wally."

"Wally Trehern, did you say? Local boy?"

"That's right."

"Were they bad? The warts?"

"Frightful."

"Mightn't have been just kind of ripe to fall off? Coincidence?"

"Most unlikely, I'd have thought," said Jenny.

"I see," said the young man, weighing it up. "Well, what's everybody having? Same again, all round?"

Everybody murmured assent and Major Barrimore began to pour the drinks.

Jenny said: "I could show you a photograph."

"No? Could you, though? I'd very much like to see it. I'd be very interested, indeed. Would you?"

She ran up to her room to get it: a colour-slide of the infant-class with Wally in the foreground, his hands dangling. She put it in the viewer and returned to the bar. The young man looked at it intently, whistling to himself. "Quite a thing," he said. "Quite something. Nice sharp picture, too."

Everybody wanted to look at it. While they were handing it about, the door from the house opened and Mrs. Barrimore came in.

She was a beautiful woman, very fine-drawn with an exquisite head, of which the bone-structure was so delicate and the eyes so quiet in expression that the mouth seemed like a vivid accident. It was as if an artist, having started out to paint an ascetic, had changed his mind and laid down the lips of a voluptuary.

With a sort of awkward grace that suggested shyness, she moved into the bar, smiling tentatively at nobody in particular. Dr. Maine looked quickly at her and stood up. The Rector gave her good-evening and the restless young man offered her a drink. Her husband, without consulting her, poured a glass of lager.

"Hallo, Mum. We've all been talking about Wally's warts," Patrick said.

Mrs. Barrimore sat down by Miss Cost. "Have you?" she said. "Isn't it strange? I can't get over it." Her voice was charming: light and very clear. She had the faintest hesitation in her speech and a trick of winding her fingers together. Her son brought her drink to her and she thanked the restless young man rather awkwardly for it. Jenny, who liked her very much, wondered, not for the first time, if her position at The Boy-and-Lobster was distasteful to her and exactly why she seemed so alien to it.

Her entrance brought a little silence in its wake. Dr. Maine turned his glass round and round and stared at the contents. Presently Miss Cost broke out in a fresh spate of enthusiasm.

"...Now, you may all laugh as loud as you please," she cried with a reckless air. "I shan't mind. I daresay there's some clever answer explaining it all away or you can, if you choose, call it coincidence. But I don't care. I'm going to say my little say." She held up her glass of port in a dashing manner and gained their reluctant attention. "I'm an asthmatic!" she declared vain-gloriously. "Since I came here, I've had my usual go, regular as clockwork, every evening at half past eight. I daresay some of you have heard me sneezing and wheezing away in my corner. Very well. Now! This evening, when I'd heard about Wally, I walked up to the spring and while I sat there, it came into my mind. Quite suddenly. *I wonder.* And I dipped my fingers in the waterfall—" She shut her eyes, raised her brows and smiled. The port slopped over on her hand. She replaced the glass. "I wished my wee wish," she continued. "And I sat up there, feeling ever so light and unburdened, and then I came down." She pointed dramatically to the bar clock. "Look at the time!" she exulted. "Five past ten!" She slapped her chest. "Clear as a bell! And I *know*, I just *know* it's happened. To ME."

There was a dead silence during which, Jenny thought, everyone listened nervously for asthmatic manifestations from Miss Cost's chest. There were none.

"Miss Cost," said Patrick Ferrier at last. "How perfectly splendid!" There were general ambiguous murmurs of congratulation. Major Barrimore, looking as if he would like to exchange a wink with somebody, added: "Long may it last!" They were all rather taken aback by the fervency with which she ejaculated. "Amen! Yes, indeed. Amen!" The Rector looked extremely uncomfortable. Dr. Maine asked Miss Cost if she'd seen any green ladies while she was about it.

"N-n-o!" she said and darted a very unfriendly glance at him.

"You sound as if you're not sure of that, Miss Cost."

"My eyes were closed," she said quickly.

"I see," said Dr. Maine.

The restless young man who had been biting at his nails said loudly, "Look!" and having engaged their general attention, declared himself. "Look!" he repeated, "I'd better come clean and explain at once that I take a—well, a professional interest in all this. On holiday: but a newshound's job's never done, is it? It seems to me there's quite a story here. I'm sure my paper would want our readers to hear about it. London *Sun* and I'm Kenneth Joyce. 'K.J.'s Column.' You know? 'What's The Answer?' Now, what do you all say? Just a news item. Nothing spectacular."

"Oh, *no!*" Mrs. Barrimore ejaculated and then added: "I'm sorry. It's simply that I really do so dislike that sort of thing."

"Couldn't agree more," said Dr. Maine. For a second they looked at each other.

"I really think," the Rector said, "*not*. I'm afraid I dislike it too, Mr. Joyce."

"So do I," Jenny said.

"*Do* you?" asked Mr. Joyce. "I'm sorry about that. I was going to ask if you'd lend me this picture. It'd blow up quite nicely. My paper would pay—"

"No," said Jenny.

"Golly, how fierce!" said Mr. Joyce, pretending to shrink. He looked about him. "Now *why* not?" he asked.

Major Barrimore said: "I don't know why not. I can't say I see anything wrong with it. The thing's happened, hasn't it, and it's damned interesting. Why shouldn't people hear about it?"

"Oh, I *do* agree," cried Miss Cost. "I'm sorry but I *do* so agree with the Major. When the papers are full of such dreadful things *shouldn't* we welcome a lovely, lovely true story like Wally's. O, yes!"

Patrick said to Mr. Joyce: "Well, at least you declared yourself," and grinned at him.

"He wanted Jenny's photograph," said Mrs. Barrimore quietly. "So he had to."

They looked at her with astonishment. "Well, honestly Mama!" Patrick ejaculated. "What a very crisp remark!"

"An extremely cogent remark," said Dr. Maine.

"I don't think so," Major Barrimore said loudly and Jenny was aware of an antagonism that had nothing to do with the matter under discussion.

"But, of course I had to," Mr. Joyce conceded with a wide gesture and an air of candour. "You're dead right. I *did* want the photograph. All the same, it's a matter of professional etiquette, you know. My paper doesn't believe in pulling fast ones. That's not *The Sun*'s policy, at all. In proof of which I shall retire gracefully upon a divided house."

He carried his drink over to Miss Cost and sat beside her. Mrs. Barrimore got up and moved away. Dr. Maine took her empty glass and put it on the bar.

There was an uncomfortable silence, induced perhaps by the general recollection that they had all drunk at Mr. Joyce's expense and a suspicion that his hospitality had not been offered entirely without motive.

Mrs. Barrimore said: "Good night, everybody," and went out.

Patrick moved over to Jenny. "I'm going fishing in the morning if it's fine," he said. "Seeing it's a Saturday, would it amuse you to come? It's a small, filthy boat and I don't expect to catch anything."

"What time?"

"Dawn. Or soon after. Say half past four."

"Crikey! Well, yes, I'd love to if I can wake myself up."

"I'll scratch on your door like one of the Sun King's courtiers. Which door is it? Frightening, if I scratched on Miss Cost's!"

Jenny told him. "Look at Miss Cost now," she said. "She's having a whale of a time with Mr. Joyce."

"He's getting a story from her."

"Oh, no!"

"Oh, yes! And tomorrow, betimes, he'll be hunting up Wally and his unspeakable parents. With a camera."

"He won't!"

"Of course he will. If they're sober they'll be enchanted. Watch out for K.J.'s 'What's The Answer?' column in *The Sun*."

"I do think the gutter-press in this country's the rock bottom."

"Don't you have a gutter-press in New Zealand?"

"Not as low."

"Well done, you. All the same, I don't see why K.J.'s idea strikes you as being so very low. No sex. No drugs. No crime. It's as clean as a whistle, like Wally's hands." He was looking rather intently into Jenny's face. "Sorry," he said. "You didn't like that, either, did you?"

"It's just—I don't know, or yes, I think I do. Wally's so vulnerable. I mean, he's been jeered at and cowed by the other children. He's been puzzled and lonely and now he's a comparatively happy little creature. Quite a hero, in a way. He's not attractive: his sort aren't, as a rule, but I've got an affection for him. Whatever's happened ought to be private to him."

"But he won't take it in, will he? All the ballyhoo, if there *is* any ballyhoo? He may even vaguely enjoy it."

"I don't want him to. All right," Jenny said crossly, "I'm being bloody-minded. Forget it. P'raps it won't happen."

"I think you may depend upon it," Patrick rejoined. "It will."

And, in the event, he turned out to be right.

WHAT'S THE ANSWER?

Do You Believe in Fairies?
Wally Trehern does. Small boy of Portcarrow Island had crop of warts that made life a misery.
Other Kids Shunned Him Because of his Disfigurement. So Wally washed his hands in the Pixie Falls and—you've guessed it.
This is what they looked like before.

And here they are now.
Wally, seen above with parents, by Pixie Falls, says mysterious green lady "told me to wash them off."
Parents say no other treatment given.
Miss Elspeth Cost (inset) cured of chronic asthma?
Local doctor declines comment.
(Full story on Page 9.)

Dr. Maine read the full story, gave an ambiguous ejaculation and started on his morning round.

The Convalescent Home was a very small one: six single rooms for patients, and living quarters for two nurses and for Dr. Maine who was a widower. A veranda at the back of the house looked across a large garden and an adjacent field towards the sea and the Island.

At present he had four patients, all convalescent. One of them, an elderly lady, was already up and taking the air on the veranda. He noticed that she, like the others, had been reading *The Sun.*

"Well, Mrs. Thorpe," he said, bending over her, "this is a step forward, isn't it? If you go on behaving nicely we'll soon have you taking that little drive."

Mrs. Thorpe wanly smiled and nodded. "So unspoiled," she said, waving a hand at the prospect. "Not many places left like it. No horrid trippers."

He sat down beside her, laid his fingers on her pulse and looked at his watch. "This is becoming pure routine," he said cheerfully.

It was obvious that Mrs. Thorpe had a great deal more to say. She scarcely waited for him to snap his watch shut before she began.

"Dr. Maine, *have* you see *The Sun?"*

"Very clearly. We're in for a lovely day."

She made a little dab at him. "Don't be provoking! You know what I mean. The paper. *Our* news! The *Island!"*

"Oh, that. Yes, I saw that."

"Now, *what* do you think? Candidly. Do tell me."

He answered her as he had answered Patrick Ferrier. One heard of such cases. Medically there could be no comment.

"But you don't pooh-pooh?"

No, no. He didn't altogether do that. And now he really must—

As he moved away she said thoughtfully, "My little nephew is dreadfully afflicted. They *are* such an eyesore, aren't they? And infectious, it's thought. One can't help wondering—"

His other patients were full of the news. One of them had a first cousin who suffered abominably from chronic asthma.

Miss Cost read it over and over again: especially the bit on page nine where it said what a martyr she'd been and how she had perfect faith in the waters. She didn't remember calling them the Pixie Falls but now she came to think of it, the name was pretty. She wished she'd had time to do her hair before Mr. Joyce's friend had taken the snapshot and it would have been nicer if her mouth had been quite shut. But still, at low tide she strolled over to the newsagent's shop in the village. All their copies of *The Sun*, unfortunately, had been sold. There had been quite a demand. Miss Cost looked with a professional and disparaging eye at the shop. Nothing really at all in the way of souvenirs and the postcards were very limited. She bought three of the Island and covered the available space with fine writing. Her friend with arthritic hands would be interested.

Major Barrimore finished his coffee and replaced the cup with a slightly unsteady hand. His immaculately shaven jaws wore their morning purple tinge and his eyes were dull.

"Hasn't been long about it," he said, referring to his copy of *The Sun*. "Don't waste much time, these paper wallahs. Only happened day-before-yesterday."

He looked at his wife. "Well. Haven't you read it?" he asked.

"I looked at it."

"I don't know what's got into you. Why've you got your knife into this reporter chap? Decent enough fellah of his type."

"Yes, I expect he is."

"It'll create a lot of interest. Enormous circulation. Bring people in, I wouldn't wonder. Quite a bit about The Boy-and-Lobster." She didn't answer and he suddenly shouted at her. "Damn it, Margaret, you're about as cheerful as a dead fish. You'd think there'd been a death on the Island instead of a cure. God knows we could do with some extra custom."

"I'm sorry, Keith. I know."

He turned his paper to the racing page. "Where's that son of yours?" he said presently.

"He and Jenny Williams were going to row round as usual to South Bay."

"Getting very thick, aren't they?"

"Not alarmingly so. She's a dear girl."

"If you can stomach the accent."

"Hers is not so very strong, do you think?"

"P'raps not. She's a fine strapping filly, I will say. Damn' good legs. Oughtn't he to be swotting?"

"He's working quite hard, really."

"Of course *you'd* say so." He lit a cigarette and returned to the racing notes. The telephone rang.

"I will," said Mrs. Barrimore.

She picked up the receiver. "Boy-and-Lobster. Yes. Yes." There was a loud crackle and she said to her husband, "It's from London."

"If it's Mrs. Winterbottom," said her husband, referring to his suzerain, "I'm out."

After a moment or two the call came through. "Yes," she said. "Certainly. Yes, we can. A single room? May I have your name?"

There were two other long-distance calls during the day. By the end of the week the five rooms at The Boy-and-Lobster were all engaged.

A correspondence had got under way in *The Sun* on the subject of faith-healing and unexplained cures. On Friday there were inquiries from a regular television programme.

The school holidays had started and Jenny Williams had come to the end of her job at Portcarrow.

While the Barrimores were engaged in their breakfast discussion, the Rector and Mrs. Carstairs were occupied with the same topic. The tone of their conversation was, however, dissimilar.

"There!" Mr. Carstairs said, smacking *The Sun* as it lay by his plate. "There! Wretched creature! He's gone and done it!"

"'T, yes, so he has. I saw. Now for the butcher," said Mrs. Carstairs who was worrying through the monthly bills.

"No, Dulcie, but it's too much. I'm furious," said the Rector uncertainly. "I'm livid."

"Are you? Why? Because of the vulgarity or what? And *what*," Mrs. Carstairs continued, "does Nankivell mean by saying '2 lbs best fil.' when we never order fillet, let alone best? Stewing steak at the utmost. He must be mad."

"It's not only the vulgarity, Dulcie. It's the effect on the village."

"What effect? And threepence ha'penny is twelve, two, four. It doesn't even begin to make sense."

"It's not that I don't rejoice for the boy. I do. I rejoice like anything and remember it in my prayers."

"Of course you do," said his wife.

"That's my whole point. One should be grateful and not jump to conclusions."

"I shall speak to Nankivell. What conclusions?"

"Some ass," said the Rector, "has put it into the Treherns' heads that—O dear!—that there's been a—a—"

"Miracle?"

"Don't! One shouldn't. It's not a word to be bandied about. And they are bandying it about, those two."

"So much for Nankivell and his rawhide," she said, turning to the next bill. "No, dear, I'm sure it's not. All the same it *is* rather wonderful."

"So are all recoveries. Witnesses to God's mercy, my love."

"Were the Treherns drunk?"

"Yes," he said shortly. "As owls. The Romans know how to deal with these things. Much more talk and we'll be in need of a devil's advocate."

"Don't fuss," said Mrs. Carstairs, "I expect it'll all simmer down."

"I hae me doots," her husband darkly rejoined. "Yes, Dulcie. I hae me doots."

"How big is the Island?" Jenny asked, turning on her face to brown her back.

"Teeny. Not more than fourteen acres, I should think."

"Who does it belong to?"

"To an elderly lady called Mrs. Fanny Winterbottom who is the widow of a hairpin king. He changed over to bobby-pins at the right moment and became a millionaire. The Island might be called his Folly."

"Pub and all?"

"Pub and all. My mother," Patrick said, "has shares in the pub. She took it on when my stepfather was axed out of the Army."

"It's Heaven: the Island. Not too pretty. This bay might almost be at home. I'll be sorry to go."

"Do you get homesick, Jenny?"

"A bit. Sometimes. I miss the mountains and the way people think. All the same, it's fun trying to get tuned-in. At first, I was all prickles and antipodean prejudice, bellyaching away about living conditions like the Treherns' cottage and hidebound attitudes and so on. But now—" She squinted up at Patrick. "It's funny," she said, "but I resent that rotten thing in the paper much more than you do and it's not only because of Wally. It's a kind of insult to the Island."

"It made me quite cross too, you know."

"English understatement. Typical example of."

He gave her a light smack on the seat.

"When I think," Jenny continued, working herself into a rage, "of how that brute winkled the school group out of the Treherns and when I think how he had the damned impertinence to put a ring round *me*—"

"'Red-headed Jennifer Williams says warts were frightful,'" Patrick quoted.

"How he dared!"

"It's not red, actually. In the sun it's copper. No, gold almost."

"Never you mind what it is. O Patrick—"

"Don't say 'Ow Pettruck'."

"Shut up."

"Well, you asked me to stop you. And it is my name."

"All right. Ae-oh, Pe-ah-trick, then."

"What?"

"Do you suppose it might lead to a ghastly invasion? People smothered in warts and whistling with asthma bearing down from all points of the compass?"

"Charabancs."

"A Giffte Shoppe."

"Wire-netting round the spring."

"And a bob to get in."

"It's a daunting picture," Patrick said. He picked up a stone and hurled it into the English Channel. "I suppose," he muttered, "it would be profitable."

"No doubt." Jenny turned to look at him and sat up. "Oh, no doubt," she repeated. "If that's a consideration."

"My dear, virtuous Jenny, of course it's a consideration. I don't know whether, in your idyllic antipodes, you've come across the problem of constant hard-upness. If you haven't I can assure you it's not much cop."

"Well, but I have. And, Patrick, I'm sorry. I didn't know."

"I'll forgive you. I'll go further and tell you that unless things look up a bit at The Boy-and-Lobster or, alternatively, unless my stepfather can be moved to close his account with his bookmaker and keep his hands off the whisky bottle you'll be outstaying us on the Island."

"Patrick!"

"I'm afraid so. And the gentlemen of the Inns of Court will be able to offer their dinners to some more worthy candidate. I shan't eat them. I shall come down from Oxford and sell plastic combs from door to door. Will you buy one for your red-gold hair?" Patrick began to throw stones as fast as he could pick them up. "It's not only that," he said presently. "It's my mama. She's in a pretty dim situation, anyway, but here, at least, she's—" He stood up. "Well, Jenny," he said. "There's a sample of the English reticence that strikes you as being so comical." He walked down to the boat and hauled it an unnecessary inch or two up the beach.

Jenny felt helpless. She watched him and thought that he made a pleasing figure against the sea as he tugged back in the classic posture of controlled energy.

"What am I to say to him?" she wondered. "And does it matter what I say?"

He took their luncheon basket out of the boat and returned to her.

"Sorry about all that," he said. "Shall we bathe before the tide changes and then eat? Come on."

She followed him down to the sea and lost her sensation of inadequacy as she battled against the incoming tide. They swam, together and apart, until they were tired and then returned to the beach and had their luncheon. Patrick was well-mannered and attentive and asked her a great many questions about New Zealand and the job she hoped to get, teaching English in Paris. It was not until they had decided to row back to their own side of the Island and he had shipped his oars, that he returned to the subject that waited, Jenny felt sure, at the back of both their minds.

"There's the brow of the hill," he said. "Just above our beach. And below it, on the far side, is the spring. Did you notice that Miss Cost, in her interview, talked about the Pixie Falls?"

"I did. With nausea."

He rowed round the point into Fisherman's Bay.

"Sentiment and expediency," he said, "are uneasy bedfellows. But, of course, it doesn't arise. It's quite safe to strike an attitude and say you'd rather sell plastic combs than see the prostitution of the place you love. There won't be any upsurge of an affluent society on Portcarrow Island. It will stay like this—as we both admire it, Jenny. Only we shan't be here to see. Two years from now and everybody will have forgotten about Wally Trehern's warts."

He could scarcely have been more at fault. Before two years had passed everybody in Great Britain who could read a newspaper knew all about Wally Trehern's warts and because of them the Island had been transformed.

CHAPTER TWO

Miss Emily

"THE TROUBLE WITH my family," said Miss Emily Pride, speaking in exquisite French and transferring her gaze from Alleyn to some distant object, "is that they go too far."

Her voice was pitched on the high didactic note she liked to employ for sustained narrative. The sound of it carried Alleyn back through time on a wave of nostalgia. Here he had sat, in this very room that was so much less changed than he or Miss Emily. Here, a candidate for the Diplomatic Service, he had pounded away at French irregular verbs and listened to entrancing scandals of the days when Miss Emily's papa had been chaplain at the British Embassy in Paris. How old could she be now? Eighty? He pulled himself together and gave her his full attention.

"My sister, Fanny Winterbottom," Miss Emily announced, "was not free from this fault. I recall an informal entertainment at our Embassy in which she was invited to take part. It was a burlesque. Fanny was grotesquely attired and carried a vegetable bouquet. She was not without talent of a farouche sort and made something of a hit. *Verb. sap.:* as you shall hear. Inflamed by success she improvised a short equivocal speech at the end of which she flung her bouquet at H.E. It struck him in the diaphragm and might well have led to an incident."

Miss Emily recalled her distant gaze and focused it upon Alleyn. "We are none of us free from this wild strain," she said, "but in my sister Fanny its manifestations were extreme. I cannot help but think there is a connection."

"Miss Emily, I don't quite see what you mean."

"Then you are duller than your early promise led me to expect. Let me elaborate." This had always been an ominous threat with Miss Emily. She resumed her narrative style.

"My sister Fanny," she said, "married. A Mr. George Winterbottom who was profitably engaged in Trade. So much for him. He died, leaving her a childless widow with a more than respectable fortune. Included in her inheritance was the *soi-disant* island which I mentioned in my letter."

"Portcarrow?"

"Precisely. You cannot be unaware of recent events on this otherwise characterless promontory."

"No, indeed."

"In that case I shall *not* elaborate. Suffice it to remind you that within the last two years there has arisen, fructified and flourished, a cult of which I entirely disapprove and which is the cause of my present concern and of my calling upon your advice."

She paused. "Anything I can do, of course—" Alleyn said.

"Thank you. Your accent has deteriorated. To continue: Fanny, intemperate as ever, encouraged her tenants in their wart-claims. She visited the Island, interviewed the child in question, and, having at the time an infected outbreak on her thumb, plunged it in the spring whose extreme coldness possibly caused it to burst. It was no doubt ripe to do so but Fanny darted about talking of miracles. There were other cases of an equally hysterical character. The thing had caught on and my sister exploited it. The inn was enlarged, the spring was enclosed, advertisements appeared in the papers. A shop was erected on the island. The residents, I understand, are making money hand-over-fist."

"I should imagine so."

"Very well. My sister Fanny (at the age of 87) has died. I have inherited her estates. I need hardly tell you that I refuse to countenance this unseemly charade, still less to profit by it."

"You propose to sell the place?"

"Certainly not. Do," said Miss Emily sharply, "pull yourself together, Roderique. This is not what I expect of you."

"I beg your pardon, Miss Emily."

She waved her hand. "To sell would be to profit by its spurious fame and allow this nonsense full play. No, I intend to restore the Island to its former state. I have instructed my solicitors to acquaint the persons concerned."

"I see," said Alleyn. He got up and stood looking down at his old tutoress. How completely Miss Emily had taken on the character of a certain type of elderly Frenchwoman. Her black clothes seemed to disclaim, clear-sightedly, all pretence to allure. Her complexion was grey: her jewellery of jet and gold. She wore a general air of disassociated fustiness. Her composure was absolute. The setting was perfectly consonant with the person: pieces of buhl; formal, upholstered, and therefore dingy, chairs; yellowing photographs, among which his own young, thin face stared back at him; and an unalterable arrangement of dyed pampas plumes in an elaborate vase. For Miss Emily, her room was absolutely *comme-il-faut*. Yes, after all, she must be—

"At the age of eighty-three," she said, with uncanny prescience, "I am not to be moved. If that is in your mind, Roderique."

"I'm much too frightened of you, Miss Emily, to attempt any such task."

"Ah, no!" she said in English. "Don't say that! I hope not."

He kissed her dry little hand as she had taught him to do. "Well," he said, "tell me more about it. What *is* your plan?"

Miss Emily reverted to the French language. "In effect, as I have told you, to restore the *status quo*. Ultimately I shall remove the enclosure, shut the shop and issue a general announcement disclaiming and exposing the entire affair."

Alleyn said: "I've never been able to make up my mind about these matters. The cure of warts by apparently irrational means is too well-established to be questioned. And even when you admit the vast number of failures, there *is* a pretty substantial case to be made out for certain types of faith-healing. Or so I understand. I can't help wondering why you are so very fierce about it all, Miss Emily. If you are repelled by the inevitable vulgarities, of course—"

"As, of course, I am. Still more, by the exploitation of the spring as a business concern. But most of all by personal experience of a case that failed: a very dear friend who suffered from a malignancy and who was absolutely—but I assure you, *absolutely*—persuaded it would be cured by such means. The utter cruelty of her disillusionment, her incredulity, her agonised disappointment and her death: these made a bitter impression upon me. I would sooner die myself," Miss Emily said with the utmost vigour, "than profit in the smallest degree from such another tragedy."

There was a brief silence. "Yes," Alleyn said. "That does, indeed, explain your attitude."

"But not my reason for soliciting your help. I must tell you that I have written to Major Barrimore who is the incumbent of the inn, and informed him of my decision. I have announced my intention of visiting the Island to see that this decision is carried out. And, since she will no doubt wish to provide for herself, I have also written to the proprietress of the shop, a Miss Elspeth Cost. I have given her three months' notice, unless she chooses to maintain the place as a normal establishment and refrain from exploiting the spring or mounting a preposterous anniversary festival which, I am informed, she has put in hand and which has been widely advertised in the Press."

"Major Barrimore and Miss Cost must have been startled by your letters."

"So much so, perhaps, that they have lost the power of communication. I wrote a week ago. There has been no *formal* acknowledgment."

She said this with such a meaning air that he felt he was expected to take it up. "Has there been an informal one?" he ventured.

"Judge for yourself," said Miss Emily, crisply.

She went to her desk, and returned with several sheets of paper which she handed to him.

Alleyn glanced at the first, paused, and then laid them all in a row on an occasional table. There were five. "Hell!" he thought, "this means a go with Miss Emily." They were in the familiar form of newsprint pasted on ruled paper which had been wrenched from an exercise book. The first presented an account of several cures effected by the springs and was headed with unintentional ambiguity, "Pixie Falls Again." It was, he recognised, from the London *Sun*. Underneath the cutting was an irregularly assembled sentence of separated words, all in newsprint.

"Do not Attempt THREAT; to close you are WARNED." The second read, simply: "DANGER keep OUT"; the third, "Desecration will be prevented all costs"; the fourth: "Residents are prepared interference will prove FATAL," and the last, in one strip, "DEATH OF ELDERLY WOMAN," with a piece-meal addendum: "this could be you."

"Well," Alleyn said, "that's a pretty collection, I must say. When did they come?"

"One by one, over the last five days. The first must have been posted immediately after the arrival of my letter."

"Have you kept the envelopes?"

"Yes. The postmark is Portcarrow."

"May I see them?"

She produced them: five cheap envelopes. The address had been built up from newsprint.

"Will you let me keep these? And the letters?"

"Certainly."

"Any idea who sent them?" he asked.

"None."

"Who has your address?"

"The landlord. Major Barrimore."

"It's an easy one to assemble from any paper. Thirty-seven Forecast Street. Wait a moment though. This one wasn't built up piece-meal. It's all in one. I don't recognise the type."

"Possibly a local paper. At the time of my inheritance."

"Yes. Almost certainly."

He asked her for a larger envelope and put the collection into it.

"When do you plan to go to Portcarrow?"

"On Monday," said Miss Emily composedly. "Without fail."

Alleyn thought for a moment and then sat down and took her hand in his. "Now, my dear Miss Emily," he said. "Please do listen to what I'm going to say—in English, if you don't mind."

"Naturally, I shall listen carefully since I have invited your professional opinion. As to speaking in English—very well, if you prefer it. *Enfin, en ce moment, on ne donne pas une leçon de français.*"

"No. One gives, if you'll forgive me, a lesson in sensible behaviour. Now, I don't suggest for a minute that these messages mean, literally, what they seem to threaten. Possibly they are simply intended to put you off and if they fail to do that, you may hear no more about it. On the other hand they do suggest that you have an enemy at Portcarrow. If you go there you will invite unpleasant reactions."

"I am perfectly well aware of that. Obviously. And," said Miss Emily on a rising note, "if this person imagines that I am to be frightened off—"

"Now, wait a bit. There's no real need for you to go, is there? The whole thing can be done, and done efficiently, by your solicitors. It would be a—a dignified and reasonable way of settling."

"Until I have seen for myself what goes on in the Island I cannot give explicit instructions."

"But you can. You can get a report."

"That," said Miss Emily, "would not be satisfactory."

He could have shaken her.

"Have you," he asked, "shown these things to your solicitors?"

"I have not."

"I'm sure they would give you the same advice."

"I should not take it."

"Suppose this person means to do exactly what the messages threaten? Offer violence? It might well be, you know."

"That is precisely why I have sought your advice. I am aware that I should take steps to protect myself. What are they? I am not," Miss Emily said, "proficient in the use of small-arms and I understand that, in any case, one requires a permit. No doubt in your position, you could obtain one and might possibly be so very kind as to give me a little instruction."

"I shall not fiddle a small-arms permit for you and nor shall I teach you to be quick on the draw. The suggestion is ridiculous."

"There are, perhaps, other precautions," she conceded, "such as walking down the centre of the road, remaining indoors after dark and making no assignations at unfrequented rendezvous."

Alleyn contemplated his old instructress. Was there or was there not a remote twinkle in that dead-pan eye?

"I think," he said, "you are making a nonsense of me."

"Who's being ridiculous now?" asked Miss Emily tartly.

He stood up. "All right," he said. "As a police officer it's my duty to tell you that I think it extremely unwise for you to go to Portcarrow. As a grateful, elderly, ex-pupil, I assure you that I shall be extremely fussed about you if you're obstinate enough to persist in your plan. Dear Miss Emily," said Alleyn, with a change of tone, "do, for the love of Mike, pipe down and stay where you are."

"You would have been successful," she said, "if you had continued in the Corps Diplomatique. I have never comprehended why you elected to change."

"Obviously, I've had no success in this instance."

"No. I shall go. But I am infinitely obliged to you, Roderique."

"I suppose this must be put down to the wild strain in your blood."

"Possibly." Indicating that the audience was concluded, she rose and reverted to French. "You will give my fondest salutations to your wife and son?"

"Thank you. Troy sent all sorts of messages to you."

"You appear to be a little fatigued. When is your vacation?"

"When I can snatch it. I hope, quite soon," Alleyn said and was at once alarmed by a look of low cunning in Miss Emily. "Please *don't* go," he begged her.

She placed her hand in the correct position to be kissed. "*Au revoir*," she said, "*et mille remerciements.*"

"*Mes hommages, madame,*" said Alleyn crossly. With the profoundest misgivings he took his leave of Miss Emily.

It was nine o'clock in the evening when the London train reached Dunlowman where one changed for the Portcarrow bus. On alighting, Jenny was confronted by several posters depicting a fanciful Green Lady across whose image was superimposed a large notice advertising "The Festival of the Spring." She had not recovered from this shock when she received a second one in the person of Patrick Ferrier. There he was, looking much the same after nearly two years, edging his way through the crowd, quite a largish one, that moved towards the barrier. "Jenny!" he called. "Hi! I've come to meet you."

"But it's miles and miles!" Jenny cried, delighted to see him.

"A bagatelle. Hold on. Here I come."

He reached her and seized her suitcases. "This *is* fun," he said. "I'm so glad."

Outside the station a number of people had collected under a sign that read "Portcarrow Bus." Jenny watched them as she waited for Patrick to fetch his car. They looked, she thought, a singularly mixed bunch and yet there was something about them—what was it?—that gave them an exclusive air, as if they belonged to some rather outlandish sect. The bus drew up and as these people began to climb in, she saw that among them there was a girl wearing a steel brace on her leg. Further along the queue a man with an emaciated face and terrible eyes quietly waited his turn. There was a plain, heavy youth with a bandaged ear and a woman who laughed repeatedly—it seemed without cause—and drew no response from her companion, an older woman, who kept her hand under the other's forearm and looked ahead. They filed into the bus and although there were no other outward signs of the element that united them, Jenny knew what it was.

Patrick drove up in a two-seater. He put her luggage into a boot that was about a quarter of the size of the bonnet and in a moment they had shot away down the street.

"This is very handsome of you, Patrick," Jenny said. "And what a car!"

"Isn't she pleasant?"

"New, I imagine."

"Yes. To celebrate. I'm eating my dinners, after all, Jenny. Do you remember?"

"Of course. I do congratulate you."

"You may not be so polite when you see how it's been achieved, however. Your wildest fantasies could scarcely match the present reality of the Island."

"I did see the English papers in Paris and your letters were fairly explicit."

"Nevertheless you're in for a shock, I promise you."

"I expect I can take it."

"Actually, I rather wondered if we ought to ask you."

"It was sweet of your mama and I'm delighted to come. Patrick, it's wonderful to be back in England. When I saw the Battersea power-station, I cried. For sheer pleasure."

"You'll probably roar like a bull when you see Portcarrow and not for pleasure, either. You haven't lost your susceptibility for places, I see. By the way," Patrick said after a pause, "you've arrived for a crisis."

"What sort of crisis?"

"In the person of an old, old angry lady called Miss Emily Pride, who has inherited the Island from her sister (Winterbottom, deceased). She shares your views about exploiting the Spring. You ought to get on like houses on fire."

"What's she going to do?"

"Shut up shop unless the combined efforts of interested parties can steer her off. Everybody's in a frightful taking-on about it. She arrives on Monday, breathing restoration and fury."

"Like a wicked fairy godmother?"

"Very like. Probably flourishing a black umbrella and emitting sparks. She's flying into a pretty solid wall of opposition. Of course," Patrick said abruptly, "the whole thing has been fantastic. For some reason the initial story caught on. It was the silly season and the papers, as you may remember, played it up. Wally's warts became big news. That led to the first lot of casual visitors. Mrs. Winterbottom's men of business began to make interested noises and 'the gold-rush,' to coin a phrase, set in. Since then it's never looked back."

They had passed through the suburbs of Dunlowman and were driving along a road that ran out towards the coast.

"It was nice getting your occasional letters," Patrick said, presently. "Operative word: 'occasional.'"

"And yours."

"I'm glad you haven't succumbed to the urge for black satin and menacing jewellery that seems to overtake so many girls who get jobs in France. But there's a change, all the same."

"You're not going to suggest I've got a phoney foreign accent?"

"No, indeed. You've got no accent at all."

"And that, no doubt, makes the change. I expect having to speak French has cured it."

"You must converse with Miss Pride. She is, or was, before she succeeded to the Winterbottom riches, a terrifically high-powered coach for chaps entering the Foreign Service. She's got a network of little spokes all round her mouth from making those exacting noises that are required by the language."

"You've seen her, then?"

"Once. She visited with her sister about a year ago and left in a rage."

"I suppose," Jenny said after a pause, "this is really very serious, this crisis?"

"It's hell," he rejoined with surprising violence.

Jenny asked about Wally Trehern and was told that he had become a menace. "He doesn't know where he is but he knows he's the star-turn," Patrick said. "People make little pilgrimages to the cottage which has been tarted up in a sort of Peggotty-style *Kitsch*. Seaweed round the door almost, and a boat in a bottle. Mrs. Trehern keeps herself to herself and the gin bottle but Trehern is a new man. He exudes a kind of honest-tar sanctity and sells Wally to the pilgrims."

"You appal me."

"I thought you'd better know the worst. What's more, there's an Anniversary Festival next Saturday, organised by Miss Cost. A choral procession to the Spring and Wally, dressed up like a wee fisherlad, reciting doggerel if he can remember it, poor little devil."

"Don't!" Jenny exclaimed. "Not true!"

"True, I'm afraid."

"But Patrick—about the cures? The people that come? What happens?"

Patrick waited for a moment. He then said in a voice that held no overtones of irony: "I suppose, you know, it's what always happens in these cases. Failure after failure until one thinks the whole thing is an infamous racket and is bitterly ashamed of having any part of it. And then, for no apparent reason, one, perhaps two, perhaps a few more, people do exactly what the others have done but go away without their warts or their migraine or their asthma or their chronic diarrhoea. Their gratitude and sheer exuberance! You can't think what it's like, Jenny. So then, of course, one diddles oneself— or is it diddling?—into imagining these cases wipe out all the others and all the ballyhoo, and my fees and this car, and Miss Cost's Giffte Shoppe. She really has called it that, you know. She sold her former establishment and set up another on the Island. She sells tiny plastic models of the Green Lady and pamphlets she's written herself, as well as handwoven jerkins and other novelties that I haven't the face to enumerate. Are you sorry you came?"

"I don't think so. And your mother? What does she think?"

"Who knows?" Patrick said, simply. "She has a gift for detachment, my mama."

"And Dr. Maine?"

"Why he?" Patrick said sharply, and then: "Sorry: Why not? Bob Maine's nursing home is now quite large and invariably full."

Feeling she had blundered, Jenny said: "And the Rector? How on earth has he reacted?"

"With doctrinal *léger de main*. No official recognition on the one hand. Proper acknowledgments in the right quarter on the other. Jolly sensible of him, in my view."

Presently they swept up the downs that lie behind the coastline, turned into a steep lane and were, suddenly, on the cliffs above Portcarrow.

The first thing that Jenny noticed was a red neon sign, glaring up through the dusk: "Boy-and-Lobster." The tide was almost full and the sign was shiftingly reflected in dark water. Next, she saw that a string of coloured lights connected the Island with the village and that the village itself must now extend along the foreshore for some distance. Lamps and windows, following the convolutions of bay and headland, suggested a necklace that had been carelessly thrown down on some night-blue material. She supposed that in a way the effect must be called pretty. There were a number of cars parked along the cliffs with people making love in them or merely staring out to sea. A large, prefabricated, multiple garage had been built at the roadside. There was also a café.

"There you have it," Patrick said. "We may as well take the plunge."

They did so literally, down a precipitous and narrow descent. That at least had not changed and nor at first sight had the village itself. There was the old post-office-shop and, farther along, the Portcarrow Arms with a new coat of paint. "This is now referred to as the Old Part," said Patrick. "Elsewhere there's a rash of boarding establishments and a multiple store. Trehern, by the way, is Ye Ancient Ferryman. I'll put you down with your suitcase at the jetty, dig him out of the pub and park the car. O.K.?"

There was nobody about down by the jetty. The high tide slapped quietly against wet pylons and whispered and dragged along the foreshore. The dank smell of it was pleasant and familiar. Jenny looked across the narrow gap to the Island. There was a lamp now, at the landing and a group of men stood by it. Their voices sounded clear and tranquil. She saw that the coloured lights were strung on metal poles mounted in concrete, round whose bases seawater eddied and slopped, only just covering the causeway.

Patrick returned and with him Trehern who was effusive in salutations and wore a peaked cap with "Boy-and-Lobster" on it.

"There's a motor launch," Patrick said, pointing to it. "For the peak hours. But we'll row over, shall we?" He led the way down the jetty to where a smart dinghy was tied up. She was called, inevitably, *The Pixie*.

"There were lots of people in the bus," said Jenny.

"I expect so," he rejoined, helping her into the dinghy. "For the Festival, you know."

"Ar, the por souls!" Trehern ejaculated. "May the Heavenly Powers bring them release from their afflictions."

"Cast off," said Patrick.

The gurgle of water and rhythmic clunk of oars in their rowlocks carried Jenny back to the days when she and Patrick used to visit their little bay.

"It's a warm, still night, isn't it?" she said.

"Isn't it?" Patrick agreed. He was beside her in the stern. He slipped his arm round her. "Do you know," he said in her ear, "it's extraordinarily pleasant to see you again."

Jenny could smell the Harris tweed of his coat. She glanced at him. He was staring straight ahead. It was very dark but she fancied he was smiling.

She felt that she must ask Trehern about Wally and did so.

"He be pretty clever, Miss, thank you. You'll see a powerful change in our little lad, no doubt, him having been the innocent means of joy and thanksgiving to them as seeked for it."

Jenny could find nothing better to say than: "Yes, indeed."

"Not that he be puffed up by his exclusive state, however," Trehern added. "Meek as a mouse but all-glorious within. That's our Wally."

Patrick gave Jenny a violent squeeze.

They pulled into the jetty and went ashore. Trehern begged Jenny to visit her late pupil at the cottage and wished them an unctuous good night.

Jenny looked about her. Within the sphere of light cast by the wharf lamp, appeared a shop-window which had been injected into an existing cottage front. It was crowded with small indistinguishable objects. "Yes," Patrick said. "That's Miss Cost. Don't dwell on it."

It was not until they had climbed the steps, which had been widened and re-graded, and came face-to-face with The Boy-and-Lobster that the full extent of the alterations could be seen. The old pub had been smartened but not altered. At either end of it, however, there now projected large two-storied wings which completely dwarfed the original structure. There was a new and important entrance and a "lounge" into which undrawn curtains admitted a view of quite an assemblage of guests, some reading, others playing cards or writing letters. In the background was a ping-pong table and beyond that, a bar.

Patrick said, "There you have it."

They were about to turn away when someone came out of the main entrance and moved uncertainly towards them. He was dressed in a sort of Victorian smock over long trousers and there was a jellybag cap on his head. He had grown much taller. Jenny didn't recognise him at first but as he shambled into a patch of light she saw his face.

"Costume," Patrick said, "by Maison Cost."

"Wally!" she cried. "It's Wally."

He gave her a sly look and knuckled his forehead. "'Evening, 'evening," he said. His voice was still unbroken. He held out his hands. "I'm Wally," he said. "Look. All gone."

"Wally, do you remember me? Miss Williams? Do you?"

His mouth widened in a grin. "No," he said.

"Your teacher."

"One lady gave me five bob, she done. One lady done."

"You mustn't ask for tips," Patrick said.

Wally laughed. "I never," he said and looked at Jenny. "You come and see me. At Wally's place."

"Are you at school, still?"

"At school. I'm in the fustivell." He showed her his hands again, gave one of his old squawks and suddenly ran off.

"Never mind," Patrick said. "Come along. Never mind, Jenny."

He took her in by the old door, now marked "Private," and here everything was familiar. "The visitors don't use this," he said. "There's an office and reception desk in the new building. You're *en famille*, Jenny. We've put you in my room. I hope you don't mind."

"But what about you?"

"I'm all right. There's an emergency bolt-hole."

"Jenny!" said Mrs. Barrimore, coming into the little hall. "How lovely!"

She was much more smartly dressed than she used to be and looked, Jenny thought, very beautiful. They kissed warmly. "I'm so glad," Mrs. Barrimore said. "I'm so very glad."

Her hand trembled on Jenny's arm and, inexplicably, there was a blur of tears in her eyes. Jenny was astounded.

"Patrick will show you where you are and there's supper in the old dining-room. I—I'm busy at the moment. There's a sort of meeting. Patrick will explain," she said hurriedly. "I hope I shan't be long. You can't think how pleased we are, can she, Patrick?"

"She hasn't an inkling," he said. "I forgot about the emergency meeting, Jenny. It's to discuss strategy and Miss Pride. How's it going, Mama?"

"I don't know. Not very well. I don't know."

She hesitated, winding her fingers together in the old way. Patrick gave her a kiss. "Don't give it a thought," he said. "What is it they say in Jenny's antipodes? 'She'll be right'? She'll be right, Mama, never you fear."

But when his mother had left them, Jenny thought for a moment he looked very troubled.

In the old bar-parlour Major Barrimore, with Miss Pride's letter in his hand and his double-Scotch on the chimneypiece, stood on the hearthrug and surveyed his meeting. It consisted of the Rector, Dr. Maine, Miss Cost and Mr. Ives Nankivell, who was the newly-created Mayor of Portcarrow, and also its leading butcher. He was an undersized man with a look of perpetual astonishment.

"No," Major Barrimore was saying, "apart from yourselves I haven't told anyone. Fewer people know about it, the better. Hope you all agree."

"From the tone of her letter," Dr. Maine said, "the whole village'll know by this time next week."

"Wicked!" Miss Cost cried out in a trembling voice, "that's what she must be. A wicked woman. Or mad," she added, as an afterthought. "Both, I expect."

The men received this uneasily.

"How, may I inquire, Major, did you frame your reply?" the Mayor asked.

"Took a few days to decide," said Major Barrimore, "and sent a wire: 'Accommodation reserved, will be glad to discuss matter outlined in your letter.'"

"Very proper."

"Thing is, as I said when I told you about it: we ought to arrive at some sort of agreement among ourselves. She gives your names, as the people she wants to see. Well, we've all had a week to think it over. What's our line going to be? Better be consistent, hadn't we?"

"But can we be consistent?" the Rector asked. "I think you all know my views. I've never attempted to disguise them. In the pulpit or anywhere else."

"But you don't," said Miss Cost, who alone had heard the Rector from the pulpit, "you *don't* deny the truth of the cures, now, *do* you?"

"No," he said. "I thank God for them but I deplore the— excessive publicity."

"Naow, naow, naow," said the Mayor excitedly. "Didn't we ought to take a wider view? Didn't we ought to think of the community as a whole? In my opinion, sir, the remarkable properties of our Spring has brought nothing but good to Portcarrow: nothing but good. And didn't the public at large ought to be made aware of the benefits we offer? I say it did and it ought, which is what it has and should continue to be."

"Jolly good, Mr. Mayor," said Barrimore. "Hear, hear!"

"Hear!" said Miss Cost.

"Would she sell?" Dr. Maine asked suddenly.

"I don't think she would, Bob."

"Ah well, naow," said the Mayor, "Naow! Suppose—and mind, gentlemen, I speak unofficially. Private— But, suppose she would. There might be a possibility that the borough itself would be interested. As a spec—" He caught himself up and looked sideways at the Rector. "As a civic duty. Or maybe a select group of right-minded residents—"

Dr. Maine said dryly: "They'd find themselves competing in pretty hot company, I fancy. If the Island came on the open market."

"Which it won't," said Major Barrimore. "If I'm any judge. She's hell-bent on wrecking the whole show."

Mr. Nankivell allowed himself a speculative grin. "Happen she don't know the value, however," he insinuated.

"Perhaps she's concerned with other values," the Rector murmured.

At this point Mrs. Barrimore returned.

"Don't move," she said and sat down in a chair near the door. "I don't know if I'm still—?"

Mr. Nankivell embarked on a gallantry but Barrimore cut across it. "You'd better listen, Margaret," he said, with a restless glance at his wife. "After all, she may talk to you."

"Surely, surely!" the Mayor exclaimed. "The ladies understand each other in a fashion that's above the heads of us mere chaps, be'ant it, Miss Cost?"

Miss Cost said, "I'm sure I don't know," and looked very fixedly at Mrs. Barrimore.

"We don't seem to be getting anywhere," Dr. Maine observed.

The Mayor cleared his throat. "This be'ant what you'd call a formal committee," he began, "but if it was and if I was in occupation of the chair, I'd move we took the temper of the meeting."

"Very good," Barrimore said. "Excellent suggestion. I propose His Worship be elected chairman. Those in favour?" The others muttered a disjointed assent and the Mayor expanded. He suggested that what they really had to discover was how each of them proposed to respond to Miss Pride's onslaught. He invited them to speak in turn, beginning with the Rector who repeated that they all knew his views and that he would abide by them.

"Does that mean," Major Barrimore demanded, "that if she says she's going to issue a public repudiation of the Spring, remove the enclosure and stop the Festival, you'd come down on her side?"

"I shouldn't try to dissuade her."

The Mayor made an explosive ejaculation and turned on him: "If you'll pardon my frankness, Mr. Carstairs," he began, "I'd be obliged if you'd tell the company what you reckon would have happened to your Church Restoration Fund if Portcarrow hadn't benefited by the Spring to the extent it has done. Where'd you've got the money to repair your tower? You *wouldn't* have got it, no, nor anything like it."

Mr. Carstairs's normally sallow face reddened painfully. "No," he said, "I don't suppose we should."

"Hah!" said Miss Cost, "there you are!"

"I'm a Methodist myself," said the Mayor in triumph.

"Quite so," Mr. Carstairs agreed.

"Put it this way. Will you egg the woman on, sir, in her foolish notions? Will you do that?"

"No. It's a matter for her own conscience."

The Mayor, Major Barrimore and Miss Cost all began to expostulate. Dr. Maine said with repressed impatience: "I really don't think there's any future in pressing the point."

"Nor do I," said Mrs. Barrimore unexpectedly.

Miss Cost, acidly smiling, looked from her to Dr. Maine and then, fixedly, at Major Barrimore.

"Very good, Doctor," Mr. Nankivell said, "What about yourself, then?"

Dr. Maine stared distastefully at his own hands and said: "Paradoxically, I find myself in some sort of agreement with the Rector. I, too, haven't disguised my views. I have an open mind about these cases. I have neither encouraged nor discouraged my patients to make use of the Spring. When there has been apparent benefit I have said nothing to undermine anyone's faith in its permanency. I am neutral."

"And from that impregnable position," Major Barrimore observed, "you've added a dozen rooms to your bloody nursing home. Beg pardon, Rector."

"Keith!"

Major Barrimore turned on his wife. "Well, Margaret?" he demanded. "What's *your* objection?"

Miss Cost gave a shrill laugh.

Before Mrs. Barrimore could answer, Dr. Maine said very coolly, "You're perfectly right. I have benefited like all the rest of you. But as far as my practice is concerned, I believe Miss Pride's activities will make very little difference, in the long run. Either to it or to the popular appeal of the Spring. Sick people who are predisposed to the idea will still think they know better. Or hope they know better," he added. "Which is, I suppose, much the same thing."

"That's all damn' fine but it won't be the same thing to the community at large," Barrimore angrily pointed out. "Tom, Dick and Harry and their friends and relations, swarming all over the place. The Island, a tripper's shambles, and the Press making a laughing-stock of the whole affair." He emptied his glass.

"And the Festival!" Miss Cost wailed. "The Festival! All our devotion! The response! The disappointment. The humiliation!" She waved her hands. A thought struck her: "And Wally! He has actually memorised! After weeks of patient endeavour, he has memorised his little verses. Only this afternoon. One trivial slip. The choir is *utterly* committed."

"I'll be bound!" said Mr. Nankivell heartily. "A credit to all concerned and a great source of gratification to the borough if looked at in the proper spirit. We'm all waiting on the doctor, however," he added. "Now, Doctor, what is it to be? What'll you say to the lady?"

"Exactly what I said two minutes ago to you," Dr. Maine snapped. "I'll give my opinion if she wants it. I don't mind pointing out to her that the thing will probably go on after a fashion, whatever she does."

"I suppose that's something," said the Mayor gloomily. "Though not much, with an elderly female so deadly set on destruction."

"I," Miss Cost intervened hotly, "shall not mince my words. I shall tell her— No," she amended with control. "I shall plead with her. I shall appeal to the nobler side. Let us hope that there is one. Let us hope so."

"I second that from the chair," said Mr. Nankivell. "Though with reservations prejudicial to an optimistic view. Major?"

"What'll I do? I'll try and reason with her. Give her a straight picture of the incontrovertible cures. If the man of science," Major Barrimore said with a furious look at Dr. Maine, "would come off his high horse and back me up, I might get her to listen. As it is"—he passed his palm over his hair and gave a half-smile—"I'll do what I can with the lady. I want another drink. Anyone join me?"

The Mayor and, after a little persuasion, Miss Cost, joined him. He made towards the old private bar. As he opened the door, he admitted sounds of voices and of people crossing the flagstones to the main entrance.

Patrick looked in. "Sorry to interrupt," he said to his mother. "The busload's arrived."

She got up quickly. "I must go," she said. "I'm sorry."

His stepfather said: "Damn! All right." And to the others, "I won't be long. Pat, look after the drinks, here, will you? Two double Scotches and a glass of the sweet port."

He went out, followed by his wife and Patrick and could be heard welcoming his guests. "Good evening! Good evening to you! Now, come along in. You must all be exhausted. Awfully glad to see you—"

His voice faded.

There was a brief silence.

"Yes," said the Mayor. "Yes. Be-the-way, we didn't get round to axing the lady's view, did we? Mrs. Barrimore?"

For some reason they all looked extremely uncomfortable. Miss Cost gave a shrill laugh.

"'—and I'd take it as a personal favour,'" Alleyn dictated, "'if you could spare a man to keep an eye on the Island when Miss Pride arrives there. Very likely nothing will come of these communications but, as we all know, they can lead to trouble. I ought to warn you that Miss Pride, though eighty-three, is in vigorous possession of all her faculties and if she drops to it that you've got her under observation, she may cut up rough. No doubt, like all the rest of us, you're under-staffed and won't thank me for putting you to this trouble. If your chap does notice anything out of the way, I would be very glad to hear of it. Unless a job blows up to stop me, I'm grabbing an overdue week's leave from tomorrow and will be at the above address.

"'Again—sorry to be a nuisance,
Yours sincerely,'

"All right. Got the name? Superintendent A. F. Coombe, Divisional H.Q., wherever it is—at Portcarrow itself, I fancy. Get it off straightaway, will you?"

When the letter had gone he looked at his watch. Five minutes past midnight. His desk was cleared and his files closed. The calendar showed Monday. He flipped it over. "I should have written before," he thought. "My letter will arrive with Miss Emily." He was ready to leave, but, for some reason, dawdled there, too tired, suddenly, to make a move. After a vague moment or two he lit his pipe, looked round his room and walked down the long corridor and the stairs, wishing the P.C. on duty at the doors good night.

It was his only superstition. "By the pricking of my thumbs."

As he drove away down the Embankment he thought: "Damned if I don't ring that Super up in the morning: be damned if I don't."

CHAPTER THREE

Threats

MISS EMILY ARRIVED at noon on Monday. She had stayed overnight in Dorset and was as fresh as paint. It was agreeable to be able to command a chauffeur-driven car and the man was not unintelligent.

When they drew up at Portcarrow jetty she gave him a well-considered tip, asked his name and told him she would desire, particularly, that he should be deputed for the return journey.

She then alighted, observed by a small gang of wharf loiterers.

A personable young man came forward to meet her.

"Miss Pride? I'm Patrick Ferrier. I hope you had a good journey."

Miss Emily was well-disposed towards the young and, she had good reason to believe, a competent judge of them. She inspected Patrick and received him with composure. He introduced a tall, glowing girl who came forward, rather shyly, to shake hands. Miss Emily had less experience of girls but she liked the look of this one and was gracious.

"The causeway is negotiable," Patrick said, "but we thought you'd prefer the launch."

"It is immaterial," she rejoined. "The launch, let it be."

Patrick and the chauffeur handed her down the steps. Trehern stowed away her luggage and was profuse in cap-touching. They shoved off from the jetty, still watched by idlers among whom, conspicuous in his uniform, was a police sergeant. "'Morning, Pender!" Patrick called cheerfully as he caught sight of him.

In a motor launch, the trip across was ludicrously brief but even so Miss Emily, bolt upright in the stern, made it portentous. The sun shone and against it she displayed her open umbrella as if it were a piece of ceremonial plumage. Her black kid gloves gripped the handle centrally and her handbag, enormous and vice-like in its security, was placed between her feet. She looked, Patrick afterwards suggested, like some Burmese female deity. "We should have arranged to have had her carried, shoulder-high, over the causeway," he said.

Major Barrimore, with a porter in attendance, awaited her on the jetty. He resembled, Jenny thought, an illustration from an Edwardian sporting journal. "Well-tubbed" was the expression. His rather prominent eyes were a little bloodshot. He had to sustain the difficult interval that spanned approach and arrival and decide when to begin smiling and making appropriate gestures. Miss Emily gave him no help. Jenny and Patrick observed him with misgivings. "Good morning!" he shouted, gaily bowing, as they drew alongside. Miss Emily slightly raised and lowered her umbrella.

"That's right, Trehern. Easy does it. Careful, man," Major Barrimore chattered. "Heave me that line. Splendid!" He dropped the loop over a bollard and hovered, anxiously solici-tous, with extended arm. "Welcome! Welcome!" he cried.

"Good morning, Major Barrimore," Miss Emily said. "Thank you. I can manage perfectly." Disregarding Trehern's outstretched hand, she looked fixedly at him. "Are you the father?" she asked.

Trehern removed his cap and grinned with all his might. "That I be, ma-am," he said. "If you be thinking of our Wally, ma-am, that I be, and mortal proud to own up to him."

"I shall see you, if you please," said Miss Emily, "later." For a second or two everyone was motionless.

She shook hands with her host.

"This *is* nice," he assured her. "And what a day we've produced for you! Now, about these steps of ours. Bit stiff, I'm afraid. May I—?"

"No, thank you. I shall be sustained in my ascent," said Miss Emily, fixing Miss Cost's shop and then the hotel façade in her gaze, "by the prospect."

She led the way up the steps.

"'Jove!" the Major exclaimed when they arrived at the top. "You're too good for me, Miss Pride. Wonderful going! Wonderful!"

She looked briefly at him. "My habits," she said, "are abstemious. A little wine or cognac only. I have never been a smoker."

"Jolly good! Jolly good!" he applauded. Jenny began to feel acutely sorry for him.

Margaret Barrimore waited in the main entrance. She greeted Miss Emily with no marked increase in her usual diffidence. "I hope you had a pleasant journey," she said. "Would you like to have luncheon upstairs? There's a small sitting-room we've kept for you. Otherwise, the dining-room is here." Miss Emily settled for the dining-room but wished to see her apartment first. Mrs. Barrimore took her up. Her husband, Patrick and Jenny stood in the hall below and had nothing to say to each other. The Major, out of forgetfulness, it seemed, was still madly beaming. He caught his stepson's eye, uttered an expletive and without further comment, made for the bar.

Miss Emily, when she had lunched, took her customary siesta. She removed her dress and shoes, loosened her stays, put on a grey cotton peignoir and lay on the bed. There were several illustrated brochures to hand and she examined them. One contained a rather elaborate account of the original cure. It displayed a fanciful drawing of the Green Lady, photographs of the Spring, of Wally Trehern and a number of people passing through a sort of turnstile. A second gave a long list of subsequent healings with names and personal tributes. Miss Emily counted them up. Nine warts, five asthmas (including Miss Cost), three arthritics, two migraines and two chronic diarrhoeas (anonymous). "And many, many more who have experienced relief and improvement," the brochure added. A folder advertised the coming Festival and, inset, Elspeth Cost's Giffte Shoppe. There was also a whimsical map of the Island with boats, fish, nets and pixies and, of course, a Green Lady.

Miss Emily studied the map and noted that it showed a direct route from The Boy-and-Lobster to the Spring.

A more business-like leaflet caught her attention:

THE TIDES AT PORTCARROW

The tides running between the village and the island show considerable variation in clock times. Roughly speaking, the water reaches its peak level twice in 24 hours and its lowest level at times which are about midway between those of high water. High and dead water times may vary from day to day with a lag of about 1-1¾ hours in 24 hours. Thus if high water falls at noon on Sunday it may occur somewhere between 1 and 2:45 p.m. on Monday afternoon. About a fortnight may elapse before the cycle is completed and high water again falls between noon and 1:45 on Sunday.

Visitors will usually find the causeway is negotiable for 2 hours before and after low water. The hotel launch and dinghies are always available and all the jetties reach into deep water at low tide.

Expected times for high tide and dead water will be posted up daily at the Reception Desk in the main entrance.

Miss Emily studied this information for some minutes. She then consulted the whimsical map.

At five o'clock she caused tea to be brought to her. Half an hour later, she dressed and descended, umbrella in hand, to the vestibule.

The hall-porter was on duty. When he saw Miss Emily he pressed a bell-push on his desk and rose with a serviceable smirk. "Can I help you, madam?" he asked.

"Insofar as I require admission to the enclosure, I believe you may. I understand that entry is effected by means of some plaque or token," said Miss Emily.

He opened a drawer and extracted a metal disc. "I shall require," she said, "seven," and laid two half-crowns and a florin on the desk. The hall-porter completed the number.

"No, no, no!" Major Barrimore expostulated, bouncing out from the interior. "We can't allow this. Nonsense!" He waved the hall-porter away. "See that a dozen of these things are sent up to Miss Pride's suite," he said and bent gallantly over his guest. "I'm so sorry! Ridiculous!"

"You are very good," she rejoined, "but I prefer to pay." She opened her reticule, swept the discs into it and shut it with a formidable snap. "Thank you," she said dismissing the hall-porter. She prepared to leave.

"I don't approve," Major Barrimore began, "I—really, it's very naughty of you. Now, may I—as it's your first visit since— may I just show you the easiest way—?"

"I have, I think, discovered it from the literature provided and need not trespass upon your time, Major Barrimore. I am very much obliged to you." Something in her manner, or perhaps a covert glance from his employer, had caused the hall-porter to disappear. "In respect of my letter," Miss Emily said, with a direct look at the Major, "I would suggest that we postpone any discussion until I have made myself fully conversant with prevailing conditions on my property. I hope this arrangement is convenient?"

"Anything!" he cried. "Naturally. Anything! But I do hope—"

"Thank you," said Miss Emily and left him.

The footpath from the hotel to the Spring followed, at an even level, the contour of an intervening slope. It was wide and well-surfaced and, as she had read in one of the brochures, amply provided for the passage of a wheeled chair. She walked along it at a steady pace, looking down as she did so at Fisherman's Bay, the cottages, the narrow strip of water and a not very distant prospect of the village. A mellow light lay across the hillside; there was a prevailing scent of sea and of bracken. A lark sang overhead. It was very much the same sort of afternoon as that upon which, two years ago, Wally Trehern had blundered up the hillside to the Spring. Over the course he had so blindly taken there was now a well-defined, tar-sealed, and tactfully graded route which converged with Miss Emily's footpath at the entrance to the Spring.

The Spring itself, its pool, its modest waterfall and the bouldered slope above it, were now enclosed by a high wire-netting fence. There were one or two rustic benches outside this barricade. Entrance was effected through a turnpike of tall netted flanges which could be operated by the insertion into a slot-machine of one of the discs with which Miss Emily was provided.

She did not immediately make use of it. There were people at the Spring: an emaciated man whose tragic face had arrested Jenny Williams's attention at the bus stop and a young woman with a baby. The man knelt by the fall and seemed only by an effort to sustain his thin hands against the pressure of the water. His head was downbent. He rose, and, without looking at them, walked by the mother and child to a one-way exit from the enclosure. As he passed Miss Emily his gaze met hers and his mouth hesitated in a smile. Miss Emily inclined her head and they said "Good evening" simultaneously. "I have great hopes," the man said rather faintly. He lifted his hat and moved away downhill.

The young woman, in her turn, had knelt by the fall. She had bared the head of her baby and held her cupped hand above it. A trickle of water glittered briefly. Miss Emily sat down abruptly on a bench and shut her eyes.

When she opened them again, the young woman with the baby was coming towards her.

"Are you all right?" she asked. "Can I help you? Do you want to go in?"

"I am not ill," Miss Emily said and added, "thank you, my dear."

"Oh, excuse me. I'm sorry. That's all right, then."

"Your baby. Has your baby—?"

"Well, yes. It's a sort of deficiency, the doctor says. He just doesn't seem to thrive. But there've been such wonderful reports—you can't get away from it, can you? So I've got great hopes."

She lingered on for a moment and then smiled and nodded and went away.

"Great hopes!" Miss Emily muttered. "*Ah, Mon Dieu!* Great hopes indeed."

She pulled herself together and extracted a nickel disc from her bag. There was a notice by the turnstile saying that arrangements could be made at the hotel for stretcher cases to be admitted. Miss Emily let herself in and inspected the terrain. The freshet gurgled in and out of its pool. The waterfall prattled. She looked towards the brow of the hill. The sun shone full in her eyes and dazzled them. She walked round to a ledge above the Spring and found a flat rock upon which she seated herself. Behind her was a bank, and, above that, the boulder and bracken where Wally's green lady was generally supposed to have appeared. Miss Emily opened her umbrella and composed herself.

She presented a curious figure, motionless, canopied and black and did indeed resemble, as Patrick had suggested, some outlandish presiding deity; whether benign or inimical must be a matter of conjecture. During her vigil seven persons visited the Spring and were evidently much taken aback by Miss Emily.

She remained on her perch until the sun went down behind the hill and, there being no more pilgrims to observe, descended and made her way downhill to Fisherman's Bay, and thence, round the point, to Miss Cost's shop. On her way she overtook the village police sergeant who seemed to be loitering. Miss Emily gave him good evening.

It was now a quarter to seven. The shop was open and, when Miss Emily went in, deserted. There was a bell on the counter but she did not ring it. She examined the welter of objects for sale. They were as Patrick had described them to Jenny: fanciful reconstructions in plastic of the Spring, the waterfall and "Wally's Cottage"; badly printed rhyme-sheets; booklets, calendars and postcards, all of which covered much the same ground. Predominant amongst all these wares, cropping up everywhere, in print and in plastic, smirking, even, in the form of doll and cut-out, was the Green Lady. The treatment was consistent—a verdigris-coloured garment, long yellow hair, upraised hand and a star on the head. There was a kind of madness in the prolific insistence of this effigy. Jostling each other in a corner were the products of Miss Cost's handloom: scarves, jerkins and cloaks of which the prevailing colours were sad blue and mauve. Miss Emily turned from them with a shudder of incredulity.

A door from the interior opened and Miss Cost entered on a wave of cottage-pie and wearing one of her own jerkins.

"I thought I heard—" she began and then she recognised her visitor. "Ae-oh!" she said. "Good evening. Hem!"

"Miss Cost, I believe. May I have a dozen threepenny stamps, if you please."

When these had been purchased Miss Emily said: "There is possibly no need for me to introduce myself. My name is Pride. I am your landlord."

"So I understand," said Miss Cost. "Quite."

"You are no doubt aware of my purpose in visiting the Island but I think perhaps I should make my position clear."

Miss Emily made her position very clear indeed. If Miss Cost wished to renew her lease of the shop in three months' time, it could only be on condition that any object which directly or indirectly advertised the Spring was withdrawn from sale.

Miss Cost listened to this with a fixed stare and a clasp-knife smile. When it was over she said that she hoped Miss Pride would not think it out of place if she, Miss Cost, mentioned that her little stock of fairings had been highly praised in discriminating quarters and had given pleasure to thousands. Especially, she added, to the kiddies.

Miss Emily said she could well believe it but that was not the point at issue.

Miss Cost said that each little novelty had been conceived in a spirit of reverence.

Miss Emily did not dispute the conception. The distribution, however, was a matter of commercial enterprise, was it not?

At this juncture a customer came in and bought a plastic Green Lady.

When she had gone, Miss Cost said she hoped that Miss Pride entertained no doubts about the efficacy of the cures.

"If I do," said Miss Emily, "it is of no moment. It is the commercial exploitation that concerns us. That, I cannot tolerate." She examined Miss Cost for a second or two and her manner changed slightly. "I do not question your faith in the curative properties of the Spring," she said. "I do not suggest, I assure you, that in exploiting public credulity, you do so consciously and cynically."

"I should hope not!" Miss Cost burst out. "I! I! My asthma—! I, who am a living witness! Ae-oh!"

"Quite so. Moreover, when the Island has been restored to its former condition, I shall not prevent access to the Spring any more than I shall allow extravagant claims to be canvassed. It will not be closed to the public. Quite on the contrary."

"They will ruin it! The vandalism! The outrages! Even now with every precaution. The desecration!"

"That can be attended to."

"Fairy ground," Miss Cost suddenly announced, "is holy ground."

"I am unable to determine whether you adopt a pagan or a Christian attitude," said Miss Emily. She indicated a rhyme-sheet which was clothes-pegged to a line above the counter.

Ye olde wayes, *it read*, were wise old wayes
(Iron and water, earthe and stone)
Ye Hidden Folke of antient dayes
Ye Greene Companions' Runic Layes
Wrought Magick with a Bone.

Ye plashing Falles ther Secrette holde.
(Iron and water, earthe and stone)
On us as on those menne of olde
Their mighte of healing is Bestowed
And wonders still are showne.

O, thruste your handes beneath the rille
(Iron and water, earthe and stone)
And itte will washe awaye your ille
With neweborn cheere your bodie fille
That antient Truth bee knowne.

"Who," asked Miss Emily, fixing her gaze upon Miss Cost, "is the author of this doggerel?"

"It is unsigned," she said loudly. "These old rhymes—"

"The spelling is spurious and the paper contemporary. Does it express your own views, Miss Cost?"

"Yes," said Miss Cost, shutting her eyes. "It does. A thousand times, yes."

"So I imagined. Well, now," Miss Emily briskly continued, "you know mine. Take time to consider. There is one other matter."

Her black kid forefinger indicated a leaflet advertising the Festival. "This," she said.

A spate of passionate defiance broke from Miss Cost. Her voice was pitched high and she stared at some object beyond Miss Emily's left shoulder. "You can't stop us!" she cried. "You can't! You can't prevent people walking up a hill. You can't prevent them singing. I've made inquiries. We're not causing a disturbance and it's all authorised by the Mayor. He's part of it. Ask him! Ask the Mayor! Ask the Mayor. We've got hundreds and hundreds of people coming and you can't stop them. You can't. *You can't!*"

Her voice cracked and she drew breath. Her hands moved to her chest.

Into the silence that followed there crept a very small and eerie sound: a faint, rhythmic squeak. It came from Miss Cost.

Miss Emily heard it. After a moment she said, with compassion: "I am sorry. I shall leave you. I shall not attempt to prevent your Festival. It must be the last but I shall not prevent it."

As she prepared to leave, Miss Cost, now struggling for breath, gasped after her.

"You wicked woman! This is your doing." She beat her chest. "You'll suffer for it. More than I do. Mark my words! You'll suffer."

Miss Emily turned to look at her. She sat on a stool behind the counter. Her head nodded backwards and forwards with her laboured breathing.

"Is there anything I can do?" Miss Emily asked. "You have an attack—"

"I haven't! *I haven't! Go away.* Wicked woman! Go away."

Miss Emily, greatly perturbed, left the shop. As she turned up from the jetty, a boy shambled out of the shadows, stared at her for a moment, gave a whooping cry and ran up the steps. It was Wally Trehern.

The encounter with Miss Cost had tired her. She was upset. It had, of course, been a long day and there were still those steps to be climbed. There was a bench half way up and she decided to rest there for a few minutes before making the final ascent. Perhaps she would ask for an early dinner in her room and go to bed afterwards. It would never do to let herself get overdone. She took the steps slowly, using her umbrella as a staff, and was rather glad when she reached the bench. It was a relief to sit there and observe the foreshore, the causeway and the village.

Down below, at the end of the jetty, a group of fishermen stood talking. The police-sergeant, she noticed, had joined them. They seemed to be looking up at her. "I daresay it's got about," she thought, "who I am and all the rest of it. Bah!"

She stayed on until she was refreshed. The evening had begun to close in and she was in the lee of the hill. There was a slight coolness in the air. She prepared, after the manner of old people, to rise.

At that moment she was struck between the shoulder blades, on the back of her neck and head and on her arm. Stones fell with a rattle at her feet. Above and behind her there was a scuffling sound of retreat and of laughter.

She got up, scarcely knowing what she did. She supposed afterwards that she must have cried out. The next thing that happened was that the sergeant was running heavily uphill towards her.

"Hold hard, now, ma'am," he was saying. "Be you hurt, then?"

"No. Stones. From above. Go and look."

He peered at her for a moment and then scrambled up the sharp rise behind the bench. He slithered and skidded, sending down a cascade of earth. Miss Emily sank back on the bench. She drew her glove off and touched her neck with a trembling hand. It was wet.

The sergeant floundered about overhead. Unexpectedly two of the fishermen had arrived and, more surprisingly still, the tall bronze girl. What was her name?

"Miss Pride," she was saying, "you're hurt. What happened?" She knelt down by Miss Emily and took her hands.

The men were talking excitedly and presently the sergeant was there again, swearing and breathing hard.

"Too late," he was saying. "Missed 'im."

Miss Emily's head began to clear a little.

"I am perfectly well," she said rather faintly and more to herself than to the others. "It is nothing."

"You've been hurt. Your neck!" Jenny said, also in French. "Let me look."

"You are too kind," Miss Emily murmured. She suffered her neck to be examined. "Your accent," she added more firmly, "is passable though not entirely *d'une femme du monde*. Where did you learn?"

"In Paris," said Jenny. "There's a cut in your neck, Miss Pride. It isn't very deep but I'm going to bind it up. Mr. Pender, could I borrow your handkerchief? And I'll make a pad of mine. Clean, luckily."

While Miss Emily suffered these ministrations the men muttered together. There was a scrape of boots on the steps and a third fisherman came down from above. It was Trehern. He stopped short. "Hey!" he ejaculated. "What's amiss, then?"

"Lady's been hurt, poor dear," one of the men said.

"Hurt!" Trehern exclaimed. "How? Why, if it be'ant Miss Pride. Hurt! What way?"

"Where would you be from then, Jim?" Sergeant Pender asked.

"Up to pub as usual, George," he said. "Where else?" A characteristic parcel protruded from his overcoat pocket. "Happen she took a fall? Them steps be treacherous going for females well-gone into the terrors of antiquity."

"Did you leave the pub this instant-moment?"

"Surely. Why?"

"Did you notice anybody up-along, off of the steps, like? In the rough?"

"Are you after them courting couples again, George Pender?"

"No," said Mr. Pender shortly. "I be'ant."

"I did *not* fall," said Miss Emily loudly. She rose to her feet and confronted Trehern. "I was struck," she said.

"Lord forbid, ma'am! Who'd take a fancy to do a crazy job like that?"

Jenny said to Pender: "I think we ought to get Miss Pride home."

"So we should, then. Now, ma'am," said Pender with an air of authority, "you'm not going to walk up them steps, if you please, so if you've no objection us chaps'll manage you, same as if we was bringing you ashore in a rough sea."

"I assure you, officer—"

"Very likely, ma'am, and you with the heart of a lion as all can see, but there'd be no kind of sense in it. Now then, souls. Hup!"

And before she knew what had happened, Miss Emily was sitting on a chair of woollen-clad arms with her own arms neatly disposed by Mr. Pender round a pair of slightly fishy shoulders and her face in close association with those of her bearers.

"Pretty as a picture," Pender said. "Heave away, chaps. Stand aside, if you please, Jim."

"My umbrella."

"I've got it," said Jenny. "And your bag."

When they reached the top Miss Emily said: "I am extremely obliged. If you will allow me, officer, I would greatly prefer it if I might enter in the normal manner. I am perfectly able to do so and it will be less conspicuous." And to Jenny: "Please ask them to put me down."

"I think she'll be all right," Jenny said.

"Very good, ma'am," said Pender. "Set 'er down, chaps. That's clever. Gentle as a lamb."

They stood round Miss Emily, and grinned bashfully at her.

"You have been very kind," she said. "I hope you will be my guests, though it will be wiser perhaps if I do not give myself the pleasure of joining you. I will leave instructions. Thank you very much."

She took her umbrella and handbag from Jenny, bowed to her escort and walked quite fast towards the entrance. Jenny followed her. On the way they passed Wally Trehern.

Patrick was in the vestibule. Miss Emily inclined her head to him and made for the stairs. Her handbag was bloody and conspicuous. Jenny collected her room key from the desk.

"What on earth—?" Patrick said, coming up to her.

"Get Dr. Maine, could you? Up to her room. And Patrick—there are two fishermen and Mr. Pender outside. She wants them to have drinks on her. Can you fix it? I'll explain later."

"Good lord! Yes, all right."

Jenny overtook Miss Emily on the landing. She was shaky and, without comment, accepted an arm. When they had reached her room she sat on her bed and looked at Jenny with an expression of triumph.

"I am not surprised," she said. "It was to be expected, my dear," and fainted.

❀ ❀ ❀

"Well," said Dr. Maine, smiling into Miss Emily's face, "there's no great damage done. I think you'll recover."

"I have already done so."

"Yes, I daresay, but I suggest you go slow for a day or two, you know. You've had a bit of shock. How old are you?"

"I'm eighty-three and four months."

"Good God!"

"Ours is a robust family, Dr. Maine. My sister, Fanny Winterbottom, whom I daresay you have met, would be alive today if she had not, in one of her extravagant moods, taken an excursion in a speedboat."

"Did it capsize?" Jenny was startled into asking.

"Not at all. But the excitement was too much and the consequent depression exposed her to an epidemic of Asiatic influenza. From which she died. It was quite unnecessary and the indirect cause of my present embarrassment."

There was a short silence. Jenny saw Dr. Maine's eyebrows go up.

"Really?" he said. "Well, now, I don't think we should have any more conversation tonight. Some hot milk with a little whisky or brandy, if you like it, and a couple of aspirins. I'll look in tomorrow."

"You do not, I notice, suggest that I bathe my injuries in the Spring."

"No," he said, and they exchanged a smile.

"I had intended to call upon you tomorrow with reference to my proposals. Have you heard of them?"

"I have. But I'm not going to discuss them with you tonight."

"Do you object? To my proposals?"

"No. Good night, Miss Pride. Please don't get up until I've seen you."

"And yet they would not, I imagine, be to your advantage."

There was a tap on the door and Mrs. Barrimore came in. "Miss Pride," she said. "I'm so sorry. I've just heard. I've come to see if there's anything—" She looked at Dr. Maine.

"Miss Pride's quite comfortable," he said. "Jenny's going to settle her down. I think we'll leave her in charge, shall we?"

He waited while Mrs. Barrimore said another word or two, and then followed her out of the room. He shut the door and they moved down the passage.

"Bob," she said, "what is it? What happened? Has she been attacked?"

"Probably some lout from the village."

"You don't think—?"

"No." He looked at her. "Don't worry," he said. "Don't worry so, Margaret."

"I can't help it. Did you see Keith?"

"Yes. He's overdone it tonight. Flat out in the old bar parlour. I'll get him up to bed."

"Does Patrick know?"

"I've no idea."

"He wasn't flat out an hour ago. He was in the ugly stages. He—he—was talking so wildly. What he'd do to her—to Miss Pride. You know?"

"My dear girl, he was plastered. Don't get silly ideas into your head, now, will you? Promise?"

"All right," she said. "Yes. All right."

"Good night," he said and left her there with her fingers against her lips.

On the next day, Tuesday, Miss Emily kept to her room, where in the afternoon she received, in turn, Mr. Nankivell (the Mayor of Portcarrow), Dr. Maine and the Rev. Mr. Carstairs. On Wednesday she called at Wally's Cottage. On Thursday she revisited the Spring, mounted to her observation post and remained there, under her umbrella, for a considerable time, conscientiously observed by Sergeant Pender to whom she had taken a fancy, and by numerous visitors as well as several of the local characters, including Miss Cost, Wally Trehern and his father.

On Friday she followed the same routine, escaping a trip-wire which had been laid across her ascent to the ledge and removed by Mr. Pender two minutes before she appeared on the scene.

An hour later, this circumstance having been reported to him, Superintendent Alfred Coombe rang up Roderick Alleyn at his holiday address.

Alleyn was mowing his host's tennis court when his wife hailed him from the terrace. He switched the machine off.

"Telephone," she shouted. "Long distance."

"Damnation!" he said and returned to the house.

"Where's it from, darling?"

"Portcarrow. District Headquarters. That'll be Miss Emily, won't it?"

"Inevitably, I fear."

"Might it only be to say there's nothing to report?" Troy asked doubtfully.

"*Most* unlikely."

He answered the call, heard what Coombe had to say about the stone-throwing and turned his thumb down for Troy's information.

"Mind you," Coombe said, "it might have been some damned Ted larking about. Not that we've had a trouble of that sort on the Island. But she's raised a lot of feeling locally. Seeing what you've told us, I thought I ought to let you know."

"Yes, of course. And you've talked to Miss Pride?"

"I have," said Coombe with some emphasis. "She's a firm old lady, isn't she?"

"Gibraltar is as butter compared to her."

"What say?"

"I said: Yes, she is."

"I asked her to let me know what her plans might be for the rest of the day. I didn't get much change out of her. The doctor persuaded her to stay put on Tuesday but ever since, she's been up and about, worse luck. She's taken to sitting on this shelf above the Spring and looking at the visitors. Some of them don't like it."

"I bet they don't."

"The thing is, with this Festival coming along tomorrow the place is filling up and we're going to be fully extended. I mean, keeping observation, as you know, takes one man all his time."

"Of course. Can you get reinforcements?"

"Not easily. But I don't think it'll come to that. I don't reckon it's warranted. I reckon she'll watch her step after this. But she's tricky. You've got to face it: she is tricky."

"I'm sorry to have landed you with this, Coombe."

"Well, I'd rather know. I'm glad you did. After all she's in my district—and if anything did happen—"

"*Has* there been anything else?"

"That's why I'm ringing. My chap, Pender, found a trip-wire stretched across the place where she climbs up to her perch. He was hanging about waiting for her to turn up and noticed it. Workman-like job. Couple of iron pegs and a length of fine clothes-line. Could have been nasty. There's a five-foot drop to the pond. And rocks."

"Did you tell her?"

"Yes. She said she'd have spotted it for herself."

"When was this?"

"This morning. About an hour ago."

"Damn."

"Quite so."

"Does she suspect anyone?"

"Well, yes. She reckons it's a certain lady. Yes, Mr. Mayor. Good morning, sir. I won't keep you a moment."

"Has your Mayor just walked in?"

"That's right."

"Did you, by any chance, mean the shop-keeper? Miss Cost, is it?"

"That's right."

"I'll ring up Miss Pride. I suppose she knocks off for lunch, does she? Comes off her perch?"

"That's right. Quite so."

"What's the number of the pub?"

"Portcarrow 1212."

"You'll keep in touch?"

"That'll be quite all right, sir. We'll do that for you."

"Thank you," Alleyn said. "No matter what they say I've got great faith in the police. Good-bye."

He heard Coombe give a chuckle and hung up.

"Oh, Rory!" his wife said. "Not again? Not this time? It's been such fun, our holiday."

"I'm going to talk to her. Come here to me and keep your fingers crossed. She's hell when she's roused. Come here."

He kept his arm round her while he waited for the call to go through. When at last Miss Emily spoke from her room at The Boy-and-Lobster, Troy could hear her quite clearly, though she had some difficulty in understanding since Miss Emily spoke in French. So did Alleyn.

"Miss Emily, how are you getting on?"

"Perfectly well, I thank you, Roderique."

"Have there been unpleasantnesses of the sort that were threatened?"

"Nothing of moment. Do not disarrange yourself on my account."

"You have been hurt."

"It was superficial."

"You might well have been hurt again."

"I think not."

"Miss Emily, I must ask you to leave the Island."

"In effect: you have spoken to the good Superintendent Coombe. It was kind but it was not necessary. I shall not leave the Island."

"Your behaviour is, I'm afraid, both foolish and inconsiderate."

"Indeed? Explain yourself."

"You are giving a great deal of anxiety and trouble to other people. You are being silly, Miss Emily."

"That," said Miss Emily distinctly, "was an improper observation."

"Unfortunately not. If you persist I shall feel myself obliged to intervene."

"Do you mean, my friend," said Miss Emily with evident amusement, "that you will have me arrested?"

"I wish I could. I wish I could put you under protective custody."

"I am already protected by the local officer who is, for example, a man of intelligence. His name is Pender."

"Miss Emily, if you persist you will force me to leave my wife."

"That is nonsense."

"Will you give me your word of honour that you will not leave the hotel unaccompanied?"

"Very well," said Miss Emily after a pause. "Understood."

"And that you will not sit alone on a shelf? Or anywhere? At any time?"

"There is no room for a second occupant on the shelf."

"There must be room somewhere. Another shelf. Somewhere."

"It would not be convenient."

"Nor is it convenient for me to leave my wife and come traipsing down to your beastly Island."

"I beg that you will do no such thing. I assure you—" Her voice stopped short. He would have thought that the call had been cut off if he hadn't quite distinctly heard Miss Emily catch her breath in a sharp gasp. Something had fallen.

"Miss Emily!" he said. "Hallo! Hallo! Miss Emily!"

"Very well," her voice said. "I can hear you. Perfectly."

"What happened?"

"I was interrupted."

"Something's wrong. What is it?"

"No, no. It is nothing. I knocked a book over. Roderique, I beg that you do not break your holiday. It would be rather ridiculous. It would displease me extremely, you understand. I assure you that I will do nothing foolish. Good-bye, my dear boy."

She replaced the receiver.

Alleyn sat with his arm still round his wife. "Something happened," he said. "She sounded frightened. I swear she was frightened. Damn and blast Miss Emily for a pigheaded old effigy. What the hell does she think she's up to!"

"Darling: she promised to be sensible. She doesn't want you to go. Does she, now?"

"She was frightened," he repeated. "And she wouldn't say why."

At the same moment Miss Emily, with her hand pressed to her heart, was staring at the object she had exposed when she had knocked the telephone directory on its side.

This object was a crude plastic image of a Green Lady. A piece of ruled paper had been jammed down over the head and on it was pasted a single word of newsprint.

"Death."

Miss Emily surveyed the assembled company.

There were not enough chairs for them all in her sitting-room. Margaret Barrimore, the Rector and the Mayor were seated. Jenny and Patrick sat on the arms of Mrs. Barrimore's chair. Major Barrimore, Superintendent Coombe and Dr. Maine formed a rather ill-assorted group of standees.

"That then," said Miss Emily, "is the situation. I have declared my purpose. I have been threatened. Two attempts have been made upon me. Finally, this object"—she waved her hand in the direction of the Green Lady which, with its unlovely label still about its neck, simpered at the company "—this object has been placed in my room by someone who evidently obtained possession of the key."

"Now, my dear Miss Pride," Barrimore said. "I do assure you that I shall make the fullest possible investigation. Whoever perpetrated this ridiculous—" Miss Emily raised her hand. He goggled at her, brushed up his moustache and was silent.

"I have asked you to meet me here," she continued exactly as if she had not been interrupted, "in order to make it known, first, that I am not, of course, to be diverted by threats of any sort. I shall take the action I have already outlined. I have particularly invited you, Mr. Mayor, and the Rector and Dr. Maine because you are persons of authority in Portcarrow and also because each of you will be affected in some measure by my decision. As perhaps more directly, will Major Barrimore and his family. I regret that Miss Cost finds she is unable to come. I have met each of you independently since I arrived and I hope you are all convinced that I am not to be shaken in my intention."

Mr. Nankivell made an unhappy noise.

"My second object in trespassing upon your time is this. I wish, with the assistance of Superintendent Coombe, to arrive at the identity of the person who left this figurine, with its offensive label, on my desk. It is presumably the person who is responsible for the two attempts to inflict injury. It was—I believe 'planted' is the correct expression—while I was at luncheon. My apartment was locked. My key was on its hook on a board in the office. It is possible to remove it without troubling the attendant and without attracting attention. That is what must have been done, and done by a person who was aware of my room number. Unless, indeed, this outrage was performed by somebody who is in possession of, or has access to, a duplicate or master key." She turned with splendid complacency to Superintendent Coombe. "That is my contention," said Miss Emily. "Perhaps you, Mr. Coombe, will be good enough to continue the investigation."

An invitation of this sort rested well outside the range of Superintendent Coombe's experience. Under the circumstances, he met the challenge with good sense and discretion. He kept his head.

"Well, now," he said. "Miss Pride, Mr. Mayor and ladies and gentlemen, I'm sure we're all agreed that this state of affairs won't do. Look at it whatever way you like, it reflects no credit on the village or the Island."

"Yurr-yurr," said the Mayor who was clearly fretted by the minor role for which he seemed to be cast. "Speak your mind, Alfred. Go ahead."

"So I will, then. Now. As regards the stone-throwing and the trip-wire incidents. Inquiries have been put in hand. So far, from information received, I have nothing to report. As regards this latest incident: in the ordinary course of events, it having been reported to the police, routine inquiries would be undertaken. That would be the normal procedure."

"It has been reported," said Miss Emily. "And I have invited you to proceed."

"The method, if you will pardon me, Miss Pride, has *not* been normal. It is not usual to call a meeting on such an occasion."

"Evidently I have not made myself clear. I have called the meeting in order that the persons who could have effected an entry into this room, by the means I have indicated, may be given an opportunity of clearing themselves."

This pronouncement had a marked but varied effect upon her audience. Patrick Ferrier's eyebrows shot up and he glanced at Jenny who made a startled grimace. Mrs. Barrimore leant forward in her chair and looked, apparently with fear, at her husband. He, in his turn, had become purple in the face. The Mayor's habitual expression of astonishment was a caricature of itself. Dr. Maine scrutinised Miss Emily as if she were a test case for something. The Rector ran his hands through his hair and said: "Oh, but surely!"

Superintendent Coombe, with an air of abstraction, stared in front of him. He then produced his notebook and contemplated it as if he wondered where it had sprung from.

"Now, *just a minute!*" he said.

"I must add," said Miss Emily, "that Miss Jenny Williams may at once be cleared. She very kindly called for me, assisted me downstairs and to my knowledge remained in the dining-room throughout luncheon, returning to my table to perform the same kind office. Do you wish to record this?"

He opened his mouth, shut it again and actually made a note.

"It will perhaps assist the inquiry if I add that Major Barrimore did not come into the dining-room at all, that Mrs.

Barrimore left it five minutes before I did and that Mr. Patrick Ferrier was late in arriving there. They will no doubt wish to elaborate."

"By God!" Major Barrimore burst out. "I'll be damned if I do! By God, I'll—"

"No, Keith! Please!" said his wife.

"You shut up, Margaret."

"I suggest," Patrick said, "that on the whole it might be better if *you* did."

"Patrick!" said the Rector. "No, old boy."

Superintendent Coombe came to a decision.

"I'll ask you all for your attention, if you please," he said, and was successful in getting it. "I don't say this is the way I'd have dealt with the situation," he continued, "if it had been left to me. It hasn't. Miss Pride has set about the affair in her own style and has put me in the position where I haven't much choice but to take up the inquiry on her lines. I don't say it's a desirable way of going about the affair and I'd have been just as pleased if she'd have had a little chat with me first. She hasn't and that's that. I think it'll be better for all concerned if we get the whole thing settled and done with by taking routine statements from every-body. I hope you're agreeable."

Patrick said quickly: "Of course. Much the best way." He stood up. "I was late for lunch," he said, "because I was having a drink with George Pender in the bar. I went direct from the bar to the dining-room. I didn't go near the office. What about you, Mama?"

Mrs. Barrimore twisted her fingers together and looked up at her son. She answered him as if it were a matter private to them both. "Do you mean, what did I do when I left the dining-room? Yes, I see. I—I went into the hall. There was a crowd of people from the bus. Some of them asked about—oh, the usual things. One of them seemed—very unwell—and I took her into the lounge to sit down. Then I went across to the old house. And—"

Dr. Maine said: "I met Mrs. Barrimore as she came in. I was in the old house. I'd called to have a word with her about Miss Pride. To learn if she was"—he glanced at her—"if she was behaving herself," he said dryly. "I went into the old bar-parlour. Major Barrimore was there. I spoke to him for a minute or two and then had a snack lunch in the new bar. I then visited a patient who is staying in the hotel and at two-thirty I called on Miss Pride. I found her busy at the telephone summoning this meeting. At her request I have attended it."

He had spoken rapidly. Mr. Coombe said, "Just a minute if you please, Doctor," and they were all silent while he completed his notes. "Yes," he said at last. "Well, now. That leaves His Worship, doesn't it and—"

"I must say," Mr. Nankivell interrupted, "and say it I do and will, I did not anticipate, when called upon at a busy and inconvenient time, to be axed to clear myself of participation in a damn' fool childish prank. Further, I take leave to put on record that I look upon the demand made upon me as one unbecoming to the office I have the honour to hold. Having said which, I'll thank you to make a note of it, Alf Coombe. I state further that during the first part of the period in question I was in the Mayoral Chambers at the execution of my duties, from which I moved to the back office of my butchery attending to my own business which is more than can be said of persons who shall, for purposes of this discussion, remain nameless."

Mr. Coombe made a short note: "In his butchery," and turned to the Rector.

"I've been trying to think," said Mr. Carstairs. "I'm not at all good at times and places, I fear, and it's been a busy day. Let me see. O, yes. I visited the cottages this morning. Actually, the main object was to call on that wretched Mrs. Trehern. Things have been very much amiss, there. It's a sad case. And one or two other folk on the Island. I don't know when I walked back but I believe I was late for lunch. My wife, I daresay, could tell you."

"Did you come up to The Boy-and-Lobster, sir?"

"Did I? Yes, I did. As a matter of fact, Miss Pride, I intended to call on you to see if you were quite recovered, but the main entrance was crowded and I saw that luncheon had begun so—I didn't, you see."

"You went home, sir?" asked the Superintendent.

"Yes. Late."

Mr. Coombe shut his notebook. "All right," he said, "so far as it goes. Now, in the normal course of procedure these statements would be followed up and follow them up I shall, which takes time. So unless anyone has anything further to add— Yes, Miss Pride?"

"I merely observe, Superintendent, that I shall be glad to support you in your investigations. And to that end," she added, in the absence of any sign of enthusiasm, "I shall announce at once that I have arrived at my own conclusion. There is, I consider, only one individual to whom these outrages may be attributed and that person, I firmly believe, is—"

The telephone rang.

It was at Miss Emily's elbow. She said "T'ch!" and picked it up. "Yes? Are you there?" she asked.

A treble voice, audible to everybody in the room, asked: "Be that Miss Emily Pride?"

"Speaking."

"You leave us be, Miss Emily Pride, or the Lady will get you. You'll be dead as a stone, Miss Emily Pride."

"Who is that?"

The telephone clicked and began to give the dialling sound.

Patrick said: "That was a child's voice. It must have been—"

"No," said Miss Emily. "I think not. I have an acute ear for phonetics. It was an assumed accent. And it was not a child. It was the voice of Miss Elspeth Cost."

CHAPTER FOUR

Fiasco

THE PERSONS TAKING part in the Festival celebrations assembled at four o'clock on Saturday at the foot of the hill in Fisherman's Bay. There was a company of little girls wearing green cheesecloth dresses and stars in their hair, about a dozen larger girls, similarly attired, and a few small boys in green cotton smocks. In the rear of this collection came Wally Trehern, also smocked, with his hair sleeked down and a bewildered expression on his face. His hands were noticeably clean. The Mayor and City Councillors and other local dignitaries were yet to come.

Miss Cost marshalled and re-marshalled her troupe. She wore a mop cap and a hand-woven cloak of the prevailing green over a full skirt and an emerald velveteen bodice. The afternoon was sultry and her nose and eyebrows glittered. She carried a camera and a sheaf of papers clipped to a board and exhibited signs of emotional stress.

Thunderous clouds were massed in the north-west and

everybody eyed them with distrust. Not a breath of air stirred. An ominous, hot, stillness prevailed.

The enclosure was packed. An overflow of spectators had climbed the hill above the Spring and sat or lay in the blinding heat. The route from the foreshore to the Spring—"Wally's Way," in the programme—was lined with spectators. Seats in the enclosure were provided for the ailing and for the official party and other persons of importance. These included the Barrimores, Jenny, Dr. Maine and the Carstairses. The Rector, preserving his detachment, had declined any official part in the ceremony. "Though I must say," he confided to his wife, "it sounds innocuous enough, in a way, from what I've heard. I'm afraid Miss Cost's verse is really pretty dreadful, poor dear."

"Tell me the moment you see Miss Pride."

"I can't help hoping that in the event we shan't see her at all."

"I suppose that chair by Mrs. Barrimore is reserved for her."

"Let us hope she occupies it and doesn't return to her original plan. She would look *too* out of place on the ledge."

"It would put Wally off his poetry, I have no doubt," Mrs. Carstairs agreed.

"Not only that, but I understand they use it in their pageant or whatever it is."

"Then it would be very inconsiderate if she insisted."

"Mind you, Dulcie, I maintain that in principle she is right."

"Yes, dear, I'm sure you do," said Mrs. Carstairs. She gave a little sigh and may have been thinking that things had been a good deal easier over the last two years.

Patrick said to Jenny: "Did you see her before we left?"

"Yes. She's agreed not to sit on the ledge."

"How did you do it, you clever girl?"

"I told her I thought it would be unbecoming and that the children would giggle and the gentlemen look at her legs."

"Do you suppose she'll cut up rough at any stage?"

"I've no idea. Listen."

"What?"

"Wasn't that thunder?"

"I wouldn't be surprised. Look, there's Coombe coming in now. Who's that with him, I wonder. The tall chap."

"Jolly good-looking," said Jenny.

"Jolly good tailor, anyway."

"P'raps it's one of Miss Pride's smart chums. She's got masses, it appears, nearly all diplomats of the first water, she told me."

"There's the band. It must have been the big drum you heard, not thunder."

"It was thunder," said Jenny.

The band debouched from the village towards the jetty. It was a small combination entirely dominated by the drum. Behind it walked Mr. Nankivell in full regalia, supported by his Council. They embarked in the large motor launch, manned by Trehern, who was got up as a sort of wherryman. The band filled a small fleet of attendant dinghies and continued to play with determination if a trifle wildly throughout the short passage. Miss Cost could be seen darting up and down the length of her procession, taking photographs.

A union of the two elements was achieved and soon they ascended the hill. The children sang. The band attempted a diminuendo.

"Through the night of doubt and sorrow."

"Now, why *that*!" the Rector exclaimed. "You see? No, Dulcie, it's too much!"

"Look, dear. Do look. There she is."

Miss Emily had approached by the path from the hotel. She inserted her disc, entered the enclosure and advanced to her seat just before the procession arrived. Major Barrimore stood up to welcome her, looking furious.

A double gate, normally locked and only used to admit stretcher cases, was now opened. The procession marched in and disposed itself in a predestined order.

It is doubtful if any of the official party paid much attention to the Mayor's inaugural address. They were all too busy furtively keeping an eye on Miss Emily. She sat bolt upright with her hands clasped over the handle of her furled umbrella and she stared at Mr. Nankivell.

"…and so, Ladies and Gentlemen, I have great pleasure in declaring the First—the *First* Festival of Portcarrow Island Springs, O—PEN."

He sat down to a patter of applause through which Miss Cost advanced to a position near the little waterfall. Wally stood behind her. A microphone had been set up but she neglected to use it consistently. When she did speak into it, it seized upon her words and loudspeakers savagely flung them upon the heavy air. When she turned aside she changed into a voiceless puppet that opened and shut its mouth, cast up its eyes and waved its arms. The Mayor, nodding and smiling, pointed repeatedly to the microphone but Miss Cost did not observe him.

"—One Wonderful Afternoon—little Boy—so Sorrowful—who can tell?—Ancient Wisdom—Running Water—" Evidently she approached her climax but all was lost until she turned sharply and the loudspeakers bellowed "All Gone."

The words reverberated about the hillside in a very desolate fashion—"all gone—all gone—" Miss Cost was bowing and ineffably smiling. She added something that was completely inaudible and, with an arch look at her audience, turned to Wally and found he had vanished. He was extricated from the rear of the choir where he had retired to sit down on some seepage from the Spring.

Miss Cost led him forward. The back of his smock was slimy and green. Unfortunately she did not place him before the microphone but for the first time she herself directly confronted it.

"Now, Wally, *now*," roared the loudspeakers. "'*Once upon a Summer's day.*' Go *on*, dear."

At first, little of Wally's recitation was lost since he required constant prompting which Miss Cost, unwittingly, fed into the microphone. At the second stanza, however, the Mayor advanced upon her and in his turn was broadcast. "Shift over," the loudspeakers advised. "Come 'ere, you silly lad." The Mayor, quick to perceive his error, backed away.

"Oh, *dear!*" cried Miss Cost, publicly, and effected the change.

"Got it right this time!" said Major Barrimore loudly and gave a snort of laughter. Miss Cost evidently heard him. She threw him a furious glance.

Wally's recitation continued:

"*Be not froightened, sayed the Loidy...*"

"This is killing me," Jenny whispered.

"Shut up, for pity's sake. O, God!" Patrick muttered. "What now? What's he saying now?"

"Shut up."

Mrs. Carstairs turned and shook her head at them. They moaned together in agony.

Wally came to an unexpected stop and walked away.

The audience, relieved, burst into sustained applause.

Miss Emily remained immovable.

The choir, accompanied by tentative grunts from the band, began to sing. Wally, recaptured, squatted beside the waterfall, looked cheerfully about him, and pushed his hands under the stream.

"This will be the inexplicable dumb show," Patrick said.

"Look! O, look!"

From behind a boulder above the Spring emerged a large girl dressed in green cheesecloth. She was a blonde and the most had been made of her hair which was crowned by a tinsel star. From her left hand depended a long string of glittering beads, symbolic, clearly, of water. Her right hand was raised. The gesture, inappropriately, was accompanied by a really formidable roll of thunder. The sun was now overcast and the heavens were black.

Wally looked up at the newcomer, gave one of his strange cries, pointed to her and laughed uproariously.

"Thus," sang the choir, *"the Magic Spell was wroughten,
Thus the little lad was healed—"*
The Green Lady executed some weaving movements with
her left hand. A sudden clap of thunder startled her. The string
of beads fell on the ledge below. She looked helplessly after it
and continued her pantomime. The choir sang on and began a
concerted movement. They flanked the Spring and formed up
in set groups, kneeling and pointing out the green girl to the
audience. Miss Cost propelled Wally towards the ledge. It was
the dénouement.

The applause had scarcely died away when Miss Emily
rose and approached the microphone.

"Mr. Mayor," she began, "ladies and gentlemen. I wish to
protest—"

Major Barrimore had risen to his feet with an oath. At the
same moment there was a blinding flash of lightning, followed
immediately by a stentorian thunder-clap, a deluge of rain, and
a shout of uncontrollable laughter from Dr. Maine.

The stampede was immediate. Crowds poured out of the enclosure and down to the foreshore. The launch filled. There were
clamorous shouts for dinghies. The younger element ran round
the point of the bay, made for the hotel causeway and splashed
precariously across it. The Boy-and-Lobster contingent took to
the path that led directly to the hotel. It was a holocaust. Miss
Cost, wildly at large among her drenched and disorganised
troupe, was heard to scream: "It's a judgment." Unmindful, they
swept past her. She was deserted. Her velvet bodice leaked green
dye into her blouse. Green rivulets ran down her arms. Her hair
was plastered like seaweed against her face. The text of the play
fell from her hand, and lay, disregarded, in the mud.

Mrs. Barrimore held a brief exchange with Miss Emily
who had opened her umbrella and from beneath it, steadily
regarded Superintendent Coombe's late companion. She waved

her hostess aside. Mrs. Barrimore took to her heels, followed by her husband and Dr. Maine. She outdistanced them, fled the enclosure, ran like a gazelle along the path to The Boy-and-Lobster and disappeared.

Major Barrimore and Dr. Maine, who was still laughing, made after her. They were confronted at the gate by Miss Cost.

It was an ugly and grotesque encounter. She pushed her wet face towards them and her jaw trembled as if she had a rigor. She looked from one to the other. "*You*," she stuttered. "*You!* Both of you. Animals. Now wait! Now, wait and see!"

Major Barrimore said: "Look here, Elspeth," and Dr. Maine said: "My dear Miss Cost!"

She broke into uncertain laughter and mouthed at them.

"Oh, for God's sake!" Barrimore said. She whispered something and he turned on his heel and left her. He was scarlet in the face.

"Miss Cost," Maine said, "you'd better go home. You're overwrought and I'm sorry if I—"

"You *will* be sorry," she said. "All of you. Mark my words."

He hesitated for a moment. She made an uncouth and ridiculous gesture and he, too, left her.

Miss Emily was motionless under her umbrella. Miss Cost made for her, stumbling on the muddy slope. "Wicked, *wicked* woman," she said. "You will be punished."

"My poor creature—" Miss Emily began but Miss Cost screamed at her, turned aside and floundered down the path. She passed through the gates into Wally's Way and after a precipitant descent, was lost among those of her adherents who were clustered round the jetty.

Jenny and Patrick had set off after the others but, on looking back, saw Miss Emily alone in the downpour. At Jenny's suggestion they returned and she approached Miss Emily. "Miss Pride," she said. "Let's go back. Come with us. You'll be drenched."

"Thank you, dear child, I have my umbrella," said Miss Emily. She was still staring across the Spring at Superintendent

Coombe's late companion who now advanced towards her. "Please don't wait for me," she said. "I have an escort."

Jenny hesitated. "I insist," said Miss Emily impatiently. Patrick took Jenny's arm. "Come on," he said. "We're not needed." They hunched their shoulders and ran like hares.

Alleyn crossed the enclosure. "Good evening, Miss Emily," he said. "Shall we go?"

On the way to The Boy-and-Lobster he held her umbrella over her. "I am sufficiently protected by my waterproof and over-shoes," she said. "The forecast was for rain. Pray, let us share the umbrella." She took his arm. The path was now deserted.

They hardly spoke. Rain drummed down on the umbrella in a pentateuchal deluge. Earth and sea were loud with its onslaught and the hillside smelt of devouring grass and soil. Miss Emily, in her galoshes, was insecure. Alleyn closed his hand round her thin old arm and was filled with a sort of infuriated pity.

The entrance to the hotel was deserted except for the man on duty who stared curiously at them. Miss Emily drew her key from her reticule. "I prefer," she said loudly, "to retain possession. Will you come up? I have a so-called suite."

She left Alleyn in her sitting-room with injunctions to turn on the heater and dry himself while she retired to change.

He looked about him. The plastic Green Lady, still wearing its infamous legend round its neck, had been placed defiantly in a glass-fronted wall cupboard. He looked closely at it without touching it. A stack of London telephone directories stood near the instrument on the writing desk.

Miss Emily called from her bedroom. "You will find cognac and soda-water in the small cupboard. Help yourself, I beg you. And me. Cognac, *simplement*." She sounded quite gay. Alleyn poured two double brandies.

"Don't wait for me," Miss Emily shouted. "Drink at once. Remove and dry your shoes. Have you engaged the heater?"

He did everything she commanded and felt that he was putting himself at a disadvantage.

When Miss Emily reappeared, having changed her skirt, shoes and stockings, she looked both complacent and stimulated. It occurred to Alleyn that she got a sort of respectable kick out of entertaining him so dashingly in her suite. She sat in an armchair and jauntily accepted her brandy.

"First of all, you must understand that I am extremely angry with you," she said. She was almost coquettish. "Ah—ah-ah! And now you have the self-conscious air?" She shook her finger at him.

"I may look sheepish," he rejoined, "but I assure you I'm in a devil of a temper. You are outrageous, Miss Emily."

"When did you leave and how is your dear Troy?"

"At seven o'clock this morning and my dear Troy is furious."

"Ah, no!" She leaned forward and tapped his hand. "You should not have come, my friend. I am perfectly able to look after myself. It was kind but it was not necessary."

"What were you going to say to that crowd if you hadn't been cut off by a cloud-burst? No, don't tell me. I know. You must be mad, Miss Emily."

"On the contrary, I assure you. And why have you come, Roderique? As you see, I have taken no harm."

"I want to know, among other matters, the full story of that object over there. The obscene woman with the label."

Miss Emily gave him a lively account of it.

"And where, precisely, was it planted?"

"Behind one of the London telephone directories which had been placed on its edge, supported by the others."

"And you knocked the book over while you were speaking to me?"

"That is correct. Revealing the figurine."

He was silent for some time. "And you were frightened," Alleyn said at last.

"It was a shock. I may have been disconcerted. It was too childish a trick to alarm me for more than a moment."

"Do you mind if I take possession of this object?"

"Not at all."

"Has anybody but you touched it, do you know?"

"I think not. Excepting of course the culprit."

He wrapped it carefully, first in a sheet of writing-paper from the desk and then in his handkerchief. He put it in his pocket.

"Well," he said. "Let's see what we can make of all this nonsense."

He took her through the events of the last five days and found her account tallied with Superintendent Coombe's.

When she had finished he got up and stood over her.

"Now look," he said. "None of these events can be dismissed as childish. The stones might have caused a serious injury. The trip-wire almost certainly would have done so. The first threats that you got in London have been followed up. You've had two other warnings—the figurine and the telephone call. They will be followed up, too. Coombe tells me you suspect Miss Cost. Why?"

"I recognised her voice. You know my ear for the speaking voice, I think."

"Yes."

"On Monday, I interviewed her in her shop. She was in an extremity of anger. This brought on an attack of asthma and that in its turn added to her chagrin."

Alleyn asked her if she thought Miss Cost had dogged her to the steps, swarmed up the hill and thrown stones at her, asthma notwithstanding.

"No," said Miss Emily coolly. "I think that unfortunate child threw the stones. I encountered him after I had left the shop and again outside the hotel. I have no doubt he did it: possibly at his father's instigation who was incited in the first instance, I daresay, by that ass Cost. The woman is a fool and a fanatic. She is also, I think, a little mad. You saw how she comported herself after that fiasco."

"Yes, I did. All right. Now, I want your solemn promise that on no condition will you leave your rooms again this evening. You are to dine and breakfast up here. I shall call for you at ten o'clock and I shall drive you back to London or, if you prefer it, put you on the train. There are no two ways about it, Miss Emily. That is what you will do."

"I *will not* be cowed by these threats. I *will not.*"

"Then I shall be obliged to take you into protective custody and you won't much fancy that, I promise you," Alleyn said and hoped it sounded convincing.

Miss Emily's eyes filled with angry tears.

"Roderique—to me? To your old *institutrice*?"

"Yes, Miss Emily." He bent down and gave her a kiss: the first he had ever ventured upon. "To my old *institutrice*," he said. "I shall set a great strapping policewoman over you and if that doesn't answer, I shall lock you up, Miss Emily."

Miss Emily dabbed her eyes.

"Very well," she said. "I don't believe you, of course, but very well."

Alleyn put on his shoes.

"Where are you staying?" she asked.

"Coombe's giving me a bed. The pubs are full. I must go. It's seven o'clock."

"You will dine with me, perhaps?"

"I don't think—" He stopped. "On second thoughts," he said, "I should be delighted. Thank you *very* much."

"Are you going to 'taste' my wine?" she asked, ironically.

"And I might do that, too," he said.

He left her at nine.

She had settled for the eleven o'clock train from Dunlowman in the morning. He had arranged to book a seat for her and drive her to the station. He had also telephoned her *bonne-à-tout-faire*, as she called the pugnacious Cockney who, in spite of Miss Emily's newly acquired riches, served her still. He saw that the outside doors to her apartment could be locked and made certain that, on his departure, she would lock them. He bade her good night and went downstairs, wondering how big a fuss he might be making over nothing in particular.

Major Barrimore was in the office smelling very strongly of whisky, smoking a large cigar and poring uncertainly over a copy of *The Racing Supplement*. Alleyn approached him.

"Major Barrimore? Miss Pride has asked me to tell you she will be leaving at ten in the morning and would like coffee and toast in her room at eight o'clock."

"Would she, by God!" said the Major thickly and appeared to pull himself together. "Sorry," he said. "Yes, of course. I'll lay it on."

"Thank you."

Alleyn had turned away when the Major, slurring his words a little but evidently under a tight rein, said: "Afraid the lady hasn't altogether enjoyed her visit."

"No?"

"No. Afraid not. But if she's been—" he swayed very slightly and leant on the desk. "Hope she hasn't been giving us a bad chit," he said. "Dunno who I'm talking to, acourse. Have the advantage of me, there."

"I'm a police officer," Alleyn said. "Superintendent Alleyn, C.I.D."

"Good God! She's called in the Yard!"

"No. I'm an old friend of Miss Pride's. The visit was unofficial."

Major Barrimore leant across the desk with an uncertain leer. "I say," he said, "what is all this? You're no damned copper, old boy. You can't gemme t' b'lieve that. I know my drill. 'F y'ask me—more like a bloody guardee. What?"

Patrick and Jenny came into the hall from the old house.

"I think I'll just run up, first, and see how Miss Pride is," Jenny was saying.

"Must you?"

"She's all right," Major Barrimore said loudly. "She's under police protection. Ask this man. M'—I—introduce Miss Jenny

Williams and my stepson? Superintendent, or so he tells me…
Sorry, I forget your name, sir."

"Alleyn."

They murmured at each other. Patrick said to his stepfather: "I'll take the office if you'd like to knock off."

"The clerk fellah's on in ten minutes. What d'you mean?
I'm all right."

"Yes, of course."

Alleyn said to Jenny: "Miss Pride was thinking about a
bath and bed when I left her."

"She's going. In the morning," said the Major, and laughed.

"Going!" Jenny and Patrick exclaimed together. "Miss
Pride!"

"Yes," Alleyn said. "It seems a sensible move. I wonder if
you can tell me whether the causeway's negotiable and if not,
whether there'll be a ferryman on tap."

"It'll be negotiable," Patrick said, "but not very pleasant.
Jenny and I are going down. We'll row you across, sir. It won't
take ten minutes."

"That's very civil of you. Are you sure?"

"Perfectly. We'd thought of taking the boat out anyway."

"Then in that case—" Alleyn turned to Major Barrimore.
"Good night, sir."

"G'night," he said. When they had moved away he called
after Alleyn. "If you put her up to it, you've done us a damn'
good turn. Have a drink on it, won't you?"

"Thank you very much but I really must be off. Good
night."

They went out-of-doors. The sky had cleared and was alive
with stars. The air was rain-washed and fresh.

As they walked down the steps Patrick said abruptly: "I'm
afraid my stepfather was not exactly in his best form."

"No doubt he's been rather highly tried."

"No doubt," said Patrick shortly.

"You were at the Festival, weren't you?" Jenny asked.
"With Mr. Coombe?"

"I was, yes."

"You don't have to be polite about it," Patrick said. "The burning question is whether it was as funny as it was embarrassing. I can't really make up my mind."

"I suppose it depends upon how far one's sympathies were engaged."

They had reached the halfway bench. Alleyn halted for a moment and glanced up the dark slope above it.

"Yes," Jenny said. "That was where she was."

"You arrived on the scene, I think, didn't you? Miss Emily said you were a great help. What *did* happen exactly?"

Jenny told him how she had come down the steps, heard the patter of stones, Miss Emily's cry, and a high-pitched laugh. She described how she found Miss Emily with the cut on her neck. "Very much shaken," said Jenny, "but full of fight."

"A high-pitched laugh?" Alleyn repeated.

"Well, really more of a sort of squawk-like—" Jenny stopped short. "Just an odd sort of noise," she said.

"Like Wally Trehern, for instance?"

"Why do you say that?"

"He gave a sort of squawk this afternoon when that regrettable green girl appeared."

"Did he?"

"You taught him at school, didn't you?"

"How very well informed you are, Mr. Alleyn," said Patrick airily.

"Coombe happened to mention it."

"Look," Jenny said, "your visit isn't really unofficial, is it?"

"To tell you the truth," Alleyn said, "I'm damned if I know. Shall we move on?"

On the way across, Jenny said she supposed Alleyn must be worried on Miss Pride's account and he rejoined cheerfully that he was worried to hell. After all, he said, one didn't exactly relish one's favourite old girl being used as a cockshy. Patrick, involuntarily, it seemed, said that she really had rather turned herself into one, hadn't she? "Sitting on her ledge under that umbrella, you know, and admonishing the pilgrims. It made everyone feel so shy."

"*Did* she admonish them?"

"Well, I understand she said she hoped they'd enjoy a recovery but they oughtn't to build on it. They found it very off-putting."

Jenny said: "Will an effort be made to discover who's behind all these tricks?"

"That's entirely over to Superintendent Coombe."

"Matter of protocol?" Patrick suggested.

"Exactly."

The dinghy slid into deep shadow and bumped softly against the jetty. "Well," Alleyn said. "I'm very much obliged to you both. Good night."

"I can't imagine why it should be so," Jenny said, "but Miss Pride's rather turned into my favourite old girl, too."

"Isn't it extraordinary? She doesn't present any of the classic features. She is not faded or pretty, nor, as far as I've noticed, does she smell of lavender. She's by no means gentle or sweet, and doesn't exude salty common-sense. She is, without a shadow of doubt, a pig-headed, arrogant old thing." He rose and steadied himself by the jetty steps. "Do you subscribe to the Wally-gingered-up-by-Miss-Cost theory?" he asked.

"It's as good as any other," Patrick said. "I suppose."

"There's only one thing against it," Jenny said. "I don't believe Wally would ever deliberately hurt anyone. And he's a *very* bad shot."

Alleyn stepped ashore.

"I expect," said Patrick's voice quietly from the shadowed boat, "you'll be relieved to get her away."

"Yes," he said. "I shall. Good night."

As he walked down the jetty he heard the dip of Patrick's oars and the diminishing murmur of their voices.

He found Superintendent Coombe's cottage and his host waiting for him. They had a glass of beer and a talk and turned in. Alleyn thought he would telephone his wife in the morning and went fast to sleep.

He was wakened at seven by a downpour of rain. He got up, bathed and found breakfast in preparation. Mr. Coombe, a widower, did for himself.

"Bit of a storm again," he said, "but it's clearing fast. You'll have a pleasant run."

He went into his kitchen from whence, presently, the splendid smell of panfrying bacon arose. Alleyn stood at the parlour window and looked down on a deserted front, gleaming mud-flats and the exposed spine of the causeway.

"Nobody about," he said.

"It's clearing," Coombe's voice said above the sizzle of bacon. "The local people think the weather's apt to change at low tide. Nothing in it."

"It's flat out, now."

"Yes," Coombe said. "Dead water."

And by the time breakfast was over, so was the rain. Alleyn rang up his wife and said he'd be back for dinner. He put his suitcase in his car, and as it was still too early to collect Miss Emily, decided, it being low tide, to walk over the causeway up Wally's Way and thence by footpath to the hotel. He had an inclination to visit the Spring again. Coombe, who intended to fish, said he'd come as far as the jetty. Alleyn drove there and left him with the car. The return trip, with Miss Emily and her luggage, would be by water.

When he reached the Island, the bell for nine o'clock service was ringing in Mr. Carstairs's church, back on the mainland.

Wally's Way was littered with evidence of yesterday's crowds: ice-cream wrappers, cigarette cartons and an occasional bottle. He wondered whose job it was to clear up.

It was a steep pull but he took it at a fair clip and the bell was still ringing when he reached the top.

He walked towards the enclosure and looked through the netting at the Spring.

On the shelf above it, open, and lying on its side was a large black umbrella.

It was one of those moments without time that strike at body and mind together with a single blow. He looked at the welling pool below the shelf. A black shape, half-inflated, pulsed and moved with the action of the Spring. Its wet surface glittered in the sun.

The bell had stopped and a lark sang furiously overhead.

He had to get through the turnstile.

The slot machine was enclosed in a wire cage, with a padlock which was open. He had no disc.

For a second or two, he thought of using a rock, if he could find one, or hurling his weight against the netted door, but he looked at the slot mechanism and with fingers that might have been handling ice, searched his pockets. A half-crown? No. A florin? As he pushed it down, he saw a printed notice that had been tied to the netting: "Warning," it was headed, and was signed: "Emily Pride." The florin jammed. He picked up a stone, hit it home and wrenched at the handle. There was a click and he was through and running to the Spring.

She was lying face-down in the pool, only a few inches below the water, her head almost at the lip of the waterfall.

Her sparse hair, swept forward, rippled and eddied in the stream. The gash in her scalp had stopped bleeding and gaped flaccidly.

Before he had moved the body over on its back he knew whose face would be upturned towards his own. It was Elspeth Cost's.

CHAPTER FIVE

Holiday Task

WHEN HE HAD made certain, beyond all shadow of a doubt, that there was nothing to be done, he ran out of the enclosure and a few yards along the footpath. Down below, on the far side of the causeway he saw Coombe, in his shirtsleeves, with his pipe in his mouth, fishing off the end of the jetty. He looked up, saw Alleyn, waved and then straightened. Alleyn beckoned urgently and signalled that they would meet at the top of the hotel steps. Coombe, seeing him run, himself broke into a lope, back down the jetty and across the causeway. He was breathing hard when he got to the top of the steps. When Alleyn had told him, he swore incredulously.

"I'll go into the hotel and get one of those bloody discs," Alleyn said. "I had to lock the gate, of course. And I'll have to get a message to Miss Pride. I'll catch you up. Who's your div. surgeon?"

"Maine."

"Right."

There was no one in the office. He went in, tried the drawers, found the right one, and helped himself to half a dozen discs. He looked at the switchboard, plugged in the connection and lifted the receiver. He noticed with a kind of astonishment that his hand was unsteady. It seemed an eternity before Miss Emily answered.

He said: "Miss Emily? Roderick. I'm terribly sorry but there's been an accident and I'm wanted here. It's serious. Will it be a great bore if we delay your leaving? I'll come back later and explain."

"By all means," Miss Emily's voice said crisply. "I shall adjust. Don't disarrange yourself on my account!"

"You admirable woman," he said and hung up.

He had just got back on the lawful side of the desk when the hall-porter appeared, wiping his mouth. Alleyn said: "Can you get Dr. Maine quickly? There's been an accident. D'you know his number?"

The porter consulted a list and, staring at Alleyn, dialled it.

"What is it, then?" he asked. "Accident? Dearrr, dearr!"

While he waited for the call to come through, Alleyn saw that a notice, similar to the one that had been tied to the enclosure, was now displayed in the letter rack: "Warning." And signed "Emily Pride." He had started to read it when the telephone quacked. The porter established the connection and handed him the receiver.

Alleyn said: "Dr. Maine? Speaking? This is a police call. I'm ringing for Superintendent Coombe. Superintendent Alleyn. There's been a serious accident at the Spring. Can you come at once?"

"At the *Spring?*"

"Yes. You'll need an ambulance."

"What is it?"

"Asphyxia following cranial injury."

"Fatal?"

"Yes."

"I'll be there."

"Thank you."

He hung up. The porter was agog. Alleyn produced a ten-shilling note. "Look here," he said. "can you keep quiet about this? I don't want people to collect. Be a good chap, will you, and get Sergeant Pender on the telephone. Ask him to come to the Spring. Say the message is from Mr. Coombe. Will you do that? And don't talk."

He slid the note across the desk and left.

As he returned by the footpath, he saw a car drive along the foreshore to the causeway. A man with a black bag in his hand got out.

Coombe, waiting by the gate, was peering into the enclosure.

"I may have broken the slot-machine," Alleyn said. But it worked and they went through.

He had dragged the body on to the verge of the pool and masked it, as well as he could, by the open umbrella.

Coombe said: "Be damned, when I saw that brolly, if I didn't think I'd misheard you and it was the other old—Miss Pride."

"I know."

"How long ago, d'you reckon?"

"I should have thought about an hour. We'll see what the doctor thinks. He's on his way. Look at this, Coombe."

The neck was rigid. He had to raise the body by the shoulders before exposing the back of the head.

"Well, well," said Coombe. "Just fancy that, now. Knocked out, fell forward into the pool and drowned. That the story?"

"Looks like it, doesn't it? And, see here."

Alleyn lifted a fold of the dripping skirt. He exposed Miss Cost's right hand, bleached and wrinkled. It was rigidly clenched about a long string of glittering beads.

"Cor!" said Coombe.

"The place is one solid welter of footprints but I think you can pick hers: leading up to the shelf. The girl dropped the beads yesterday from above, I remember. They dangled over this ledge, half in the pool. In the stampede nobody rescued them."

"And she came back? To fetch them?"

"It's a possibility, wouldn't you think? There's her handbag on the shelf."

Coombe opened it. "Prayer-book and purse," he said.

"When's the first service?"

"Seven, I think."

"There's another at nine. She was either going to church or had been there. That puts it at somewhere before seven for the first service. Or round about eight-forty-five if she had attended it or was going to the later one. When did it stop raining? About eight-thirty, I think. If those are her prints, they've been rained into and she'd got her umbrella open. Take a look at it."

There was a ragged split in the wet cover which was old and partly perished. Alleyn displayed the inside. It was stained round the split and not with rainwater. He pointed a long finger. "That's one of her hairs," he said. "There was a piece of rock in the pool. I fished it out and left it on the ledge. It looked as if it hadn't been there long and I think you'll find it fits."

He fetched it and put it down by the body. "Any visual traces have been washed away," he said. "You'll want to keep these exhibits intact, won't you?"

"You bet I will," said Coombe.

There was a sound of footsteps and a metallic rattle. They turned and saw Dr. Maine letting himself in at the turnstile. Coombe went down to meet him.

"What's it all about?" he asked. "'Morning, Coombe."

"See for yourself, Doctor."

They joined Alleyn who was introduced. "Mr. Alleyn made the discovery," said Coombe and added: "Rather a coincidence."

Dr. Maine, looking startled, said: "Very much so."

Alleyn said: "I'm on a visit. Quite unofficial. Coombe's your man."

"I wondered if you'd been produced out of a hat," said Dr. Maine. He looked towards the Spring. The umbrella, still open, masked the upper part of the body. "Good God!" he ejaculated. "So it *has* happened after all!"

Coombe caught Alleyn's eye and said nothing. He moved quickly to the body and exposed the face. Dr. Maine stood stock-still. "*Cost!*" he said. "Old *Cost!* Never!"

"That's right, Doctor."

Dr. Maine wasted no more words. He made his examination. Miss Cost's eyes were half-open and so was her mouth. There were flecks of foam about the lips and the tongue was clenched between the teeth. Alleyn had never become completely accustomed to murder. This grotesque shell, seconds before its destruction, had been the proper and appropriate expression of a living woman. Whether here, singly, or multiplied to the monstrous litter of a battlefield, or strewn idiotically about the wake of a nuclear explosion, or dangling with a white cap over a cyanosed, tongue-protruding mask—the destruction of one human being by another was the unique offence. It was the final outrage.

Dr. Maine lowered the stiffened body on its back. He looked up at Alleyn. "Where was she?"

"Face down and half-submerged. I got her out in case there was a chance but obviously there was none."

"Any sign of rigor?"

"Yes."

"It's well on its way now," said Dr. Maine.

"There's the back of the head, Doctor," said Coombe. "There's that too."

Dr. Maine turned the body and looked closely at the head. "Where's the instrument?" he said. "Found it?"

Alleyn said: "I think so."

Dr. Maine glanced at him. "May I see it?"

Alleyn gave it to him. It was an irregular jagged piece of rock about the size of a pineapple. Dr. Maine turned it in his hands and stooped over the head. "Fits," he said.

"What's the verdict then, Doctor?" Coombe asked.

"There'll have to be a P.M. of course. On the face of it: stunned and drowned." He looked at Alleyn. "Or, as you would say: 'asphyxia following cranial injury'."

"I was attempting to fox the hotel porter."

"I see. Good idea."

"And when would it have taken place?" Coombe insisted.

"Again, you'll have to wait before you get a definite answer to that one. Not less than an hour ago, I'd have thought. Possibly much longer."

He stood up and wiped his hands on his handkerchief. "Do you know," he said, "I saw her. I saw her: it must have been about seven o'clock. Outside the church with Mrs. Carstairs. She was going in to early service. I'd got a confinement on the Island and was walking down to the foreshore. Good Lord!" said Dr. Maine. "I saw her."

"That's a help, Doctor," said Coombe. "We were wondering about church. Now, that means she couldn't have got over here until eight at the earliest, wouldn't you say?"

"I should say so. Certainly. Rather later if anything."

"And Mr. Alleyn found her at nine. I suppose you didn't notice anyone about the cottages or anything of the sort, Doctor?"

"Not a soul. It was pouring heavens-hard. Wait a moment though."

"Yes?"

He turned to Alleyn. "I've got my own launch and jetty, and there's another jetty straight opposite on the foreshore by the cottages. I took the launch across. Well, the baby being duly delivered, I returned by the same means and I do remember that when I'd started up the engine and cast off, I saw that fantastic kid—Wally Trehern—dodging about on the road up to the Spring."

"Did you watch him?" Coombe asked.

"Good lord, no. I turned the launch and had my back to the Island."

"When would that be, now, Doctor?"

"The child was born at 7:30. Soon after that."

"Yes. Well. Thanks," said Coombe, glancing rather self-consciously at Alleyn. "Now: any ideas about *how* it happened?"

"On what's before us, I'd say that if this bit of rock *is* the instrument, it struck the head from above. Wait a minute."

He climbed to the higher level above the shelf and Coombe followed him.

Alleyn was keeping a tight rein on himself. It was Coombe's case and Alleyn was a sort of accident on the scene. He thought of Patrick Ferrier's ironical remark: "Matter of protocol," and silently watched the two men as they scrambled up through bracken to the top level.

Dr. Maine said: "There are rocks lying about up here. And yes— But this is your pigeon, Coombe. You'd better take a look."

Coombe joined him.

"There's where it came from," said Maine, "behind the boulder. You can see where it was prized up."

Coombe at last said, "We'd better keep off the area, Doctor." He looked down at Alleyn: "It's clear enough."

"Any prints?"

"A real mess. People from above must have swarmed all over it when the rain came. Pity."

"Yes," Alleyn said. "Pity."

The other two men came down.

"Well," Dr. Maine said. "That's that. The ambulance should be here by now. Glad you suggested it. We'll have to get her across. How's the tide?" He went through the exit gates and along the footpath to a point from where he could see the causeway.

Alleyn said to Coombe: "I asked the porter to get on to Pender and say you'd want him. I hope that was in order."

"Thanks very much."

"I suppose you'll need a statement from me, won't you?"

Coombe scraped his jaw. "Sounds silly, doesn't it?" he said. "Well, yes, I suppose I will." He had been looking sideways at Alleyn, off and on, for some time.

"Look," he said abruptly. "There's one thing that's pretty obvious about this affair, isn't there? Here's a case where a Yard man with a top reputation is first on the scene and you might say, starts up the investigation. Look at it what way you like, it'd be pretty silly if I just said, 'Thanks, chum,' and let it go at that. Wouldn't it now? I don't mind admitting I felt it was silly, just now, with you standing by, tactful as you please and leaving it all to me."

"Absolute rot," Alleyn said. "Come off it."

"No, I mean it. And, anyway," Coombe added on a different note, "I haven't got the staff." It was a familiar plaint.

"My dear chap," Alleyn said, "I'm meant to be on what's laughingly called a holiday. Take a statement for pity's sake, and let me off. I'll remove Miss Pride and leave you with a fair field. You'll do well. 'Coombe's Big Case.'" He knew, of course, that this would be no good.

"You'll remove Miss Pride, eh?" said Coombe. "And what say Miss Pride's the key figure, still? *You* know what I'm driving at. It's sticking out a mile. Say I'm hiding up there behind that boulder. Say I hear someone directly below and take a look-see. Say I see the top of an open umbrella and a pair of female feet, which is what I've been waiting for. Who do I reckon's under that umbrella? Not Miss Elspeth Cost. Not her. O, dear me no!" said Coombe in a sort of gloomy triumph. "I say: 'That's the job,' and I bloody well let fly! But I bring down the wrong bird. I get—"

"All right, all right," Alleyn said, exasperated by the long build-up. "And you say: 'Absurd mistake. Silly old me! *I* thought you were Miss Emily Pride.'"

The upshot, as he very well knew it would be, was an understanding that Coombe would get in touch with his Chief Constable and then with the Yard.

Coombe insisted on telling Dr. Maine that he hoped Alleyn would take charge of the case. The ambulance men arrived with

Pender and for the second time in twenty-four hours, Miss Cost went in procession along Wally's Way.

Alleyn and Coombe stayed behind to look over the territory again. Coombe had a spring-tape in his pocket and they took preliminary measurements and decided to get the areas covered in case of rain. He showed Alleyn where the trip-wire had been laid: through dense bracken on the way up to the shelf. Pender had caught a glint of it in the sunshine and had been sharp enough to investigate.

They completed their arrangements. The handbag, the string of beads and the umbrella were to be dropped at the police-station by Pender who was then to return with extra help if he could get it. The piece of rock would be sent with the body to the nearest mortuary which was at Dunlowman.

When they were outside the gates, Alleyn drew Coombe's attention to the new notice, tied securely to the wire-netting.

"Did you see this?"

It had been printed by a London firm:

WARNING

Notice is given that the owner of this property wishes to disassociate herself from any claims that have been made, in any manner whatsoever, for the curative properties of the spring. She gives further notice that the present enclosure is to be removed. Any proceedings of any nature whatsoever that are designed to publicise the above claims will be discontinued. The property will be restored, as far as possible, to conditions that obtained two years ago and steps will be taken to maintain it in a decent and orderly condition.
(Signed) *Emily Pride*

"When the hell was this put up?" Coombe ejaculated. "It wasn't there yesterday. There'd have been no end of a taking-on."

"Perhaps this morning. It's been rained on. More than that. It's muddied. As if it had lain face-downwards on the ground. Look. Glove marks. No finger-prints, though."

"P'raps she dropped it."

"Perhaps," Alleyn said. "There's another on display in the hotel letter-rack. It wasn't there last night."

"Put them there herself? Miss Pride?"

"I'm afraid so."

"There you are!" Coombe said excitedly. "She came along the footpath. Somebody spotted her, streaked up Wally's Way, got in ahead and hid behind the boulder. She hung up her notice and went back to the pub. Miss Cost arrives by the other route, goes in, picks up her beads and Bob's your uncle."

"Is he, though?" Alleyn muttered, more to himself than to Coombe. "She promised me she wouldn't leave the pub. I'll have to talk to Miss Emily." He looked at Coombe. "This is going to be tricky," he said. "If your theory's the right one, and at this stage it looks healthy enough, do we assume that the stone-chucker, wire-stretcher, composite letter-writer, dumper of green lady and telephonist are one and the same person and that this person is also the murderer of Miss Cost?"

"That's what I reckon. I know you oughtn't to get stuck on a theory. I know that. But unless we find something that cuts dead across it—"

"You'll find that all right," Alleyn said. "Miss Pride, you may remember, is convinced that the ringer-up was Miss Cost."

Coombe thought this over and then said, well, all right, he knew that, but Miss Pride might be mistaken. Alleyn said Miss Pride had as sharp a perception for the human voice as was possible for the human ear. "She's an expert," he said. "If I wanted an expert witness in phonetics I'd put Miss Pride in the box."

"Well, all right, if you tell me so. So where does that get us? Does she reckon Miss Cost was behind all the attacks?"

"I think so."

"Conspiracy, like?"

"Sort of."

Coombe stared ahead of him for a moment or two. "So where does *that* get us?" he repeated.

"For my part," Alleyn said, "it gets me rather quicker than I fancy, to Wally Trehern and his papa."

Coombe said with some satisfaction that this, at any rate, made sense. If Wally had been gingered up to make the attacks, who more likely than Wally to mistake Miss Cost for Miss Pride and drop the rock on the umbrella?

"Could Wally rig a trip-wire? You said it was a workman-like job."

"His old man could," said Coombe.

"Which certainly makes sense. What about this padlocked cage over the slot-machine? Is it ever used?"

Coombe made an exasperated noise. "That was her doing." he said. "She used to make a great to-do about courting couples. Very hot, she used to get: always lodging complaints and saying we ought to do something about it. Disgusting. Desecration and all that. Well, what could I do? Put Pender on the job all day and half the night, dodging about the rocks? It couldn't be avoided and I told her so. We put this cage over to pacify her."

"Is it never locked?"

"It's supposed to be operated by the hotel at eight o'clock, morning and evening. In the summer, that is. But a lot of their customers like to stroll along to the Spring of a summer's evening. Accordingly, it is not kept up very consistently."

"We'd better get the key. I'll fix it now," Alleyn said and snapped the padlock. It was on a short length of chain: not long enough, he noticed, to admit a hand into the cage.

On the way back to the hotel they planned out the rest of the day. Coombe would ring the Yard from the station. Alleyn in the meantime would start inquiries at the hotel. They would meet in an hour's time. It was now half past ten.

They had rounded the first spur along the path and come up with an overhanging outcrop of rock, when Alleyn stopped.

"Half a minute," he said.

"What's up?"

Alleyn moved to the edge of the path and stooped. He picked something up and walked gingerly round behind the rock. "Come over here," he called. "Keep wide of those prints, though."

Coombe looked down and then followed him.

"There's a bit of shelter here," Alleyn said. "Look."

The footprints were well defined on the soft ground, and, in the lee of the outcrop, fairly dry. "Good, well-made boots," he said. "And I don't think the owner was here so very long ago. Here's where he waited and there, a little gift for the industrious officer, Coombe, is his cigar ash." He opened his hand. A scarlet paper ring lay on the palm. "Very good make," he said. "The Major smokes them. Sells them, too, no doubt, so what have you? Come on."

They continued on their way.

As soon as Alleyn went into The Boy-and-Lobster he realised that wind of the catastrophe was abroad. People stood about in groups with a covert, anxious air. The porter saw him and came forward.

"I'm very sorry, sir. It be'ant none of my doing. I kept it close as a trap. But the ambulance was seen and the stretcher party and there you are. I said I supposed it was somebody took ill at the cottages but there was Sergeant Pender, sir, and us—I mean, they—be all wondering why it's a police matter."

Alleyn said ambiguously that he understood. "It'd be a good idea," he suggested, "if you put up a notice that the Spring will be closed today."

"The Major'll have to be axed about that, sir."

"Very well. Where is he?"

"He'll be in the old house, sir. He be'ant showed up round hereabouts."

"I'll find him. Would you ring Miss Pride's rooms and say I hope to call on her within the next half-hour? Mr. Alleyn."

He went out and in again by the old pub door. There was nobody to be seen but he heard voices in what he thought was probably the ex-bar-parlour and tapped on the door. It was opened by Patrick Ferrier.

"Hallo. Good morning, sir," said Patrick and then: "Something's wrong, isn't it?"

"Yes," Alleyn said. "Very wrong. May I see your stepfather?"

"Well—yes, of course. Will you come in?"

They were all seated in the parlour—Mrs. Barrimore, Jenny Williams and the Major who looked very much the worse for wear but assumed a convincing enough air of authority, and asked Alleyn what he could do for him.

Alleyn told them in a few words what had happened. Margaret Barrimore turned white and said nothing. Jenny and Patrick exclaimed together: "*Miss Cost!* Not Miss *Cost!*"

Major Barrimore said incredulously: "Hit on the head and drowned? Hit with what?"

"A piece of rock, we think. From above."

"You mean it was an accident? Brought down by the rains, what?"

"I think not."

"Mr. Alleyn means she was murdered, Keith," said his wife. It was the first time she had spoken.

"Be damned to that!" said the Major furiously. "Murdered! Old Cost! Why?"

Patrick gave a sharp ejaculation. "Well!" his stepfather barked at him, "what's the matter with you?"

"Did you say, sir, that she was under an umbrella?"

"Yes," Alleyn said and thought: "This is going to be everybody's big inspiration."

He listened to Patrick as he presented the theory of mistaken identity.

Jenny said: "Does Miss Pride know?"

"Not yet."

"It'll be a shock for her," said Jenny. "When will you tell her?"

"As soon as I've left you." He looked round at them. "As a matter of form," he said. "I must ask you all where you were between half past seven and nine this morning. You will understand, won't you—"

"That it's purely a matter of routine," Patrick said. "Sorry. I couldn't help it. Yes, we do understand."

Mrs. Barrimore, Jenny and Patrick had got up and bathed in turn, round about eight o'clock. Mrs. Barrimore did not breakfast in the public dining-room but had toast and coffee by herself in the old kitchen which had been converted into a kitchen-living-room. Jenny had breakfasted at about nine and Patrick a few minutes later. After breakfast they had gone out-of-doors for a few minutes, surveyed the weather and decided to stay in and do a crossword together. Major Barrimore, it appeared, slept in and didn't get up until half past nine. He had two cups of coffee but no breakfast.

All these movements would have to be checked but at the moment there was more immediate business. Alleyn asked Major Barrimore to put up a notice that the Spring was closed.

He at once objected. Did Alleyn realise that there were people from all over the country—from overseas, even—who had come with the express purpose of visiting the Spring? Did he realise that it was out of the question coolly to send them about their business: some of them, he'd have Alleyn know, in damned bad shape?

Alleyn said that the Spring could probably be reopened in two days' time.

"*Two days*, my dear fellah, *two days*! You don't know what you're talking about. I've got one draft going out tonight and a new detachment coming in to-morrow. Where the hell d'you suppose I'm going to put them? Hey?"

Alleyn said it was no doubt extremely inconvenient.

"Inconvenient! It's outrageous."

"So," Alleyn suggested, "is murder."

"I've no proof of where you get your authority and I'll have you know I won't act without it. I refuse point blank," shouted the Major. "And categorically," he added as if that clenched the matter.

"The authority," Alleyn said, "is Scotland Yard and I'm very sorry, but you really can't refuse, you know. Either you decide to frame an announcement in your own words and get it out at once or I shall be obliged to issue a police notice. In any case that will be done at the Spring itself. It would be better, as I'm sure you must agree, if intending visitors were stopped here rather than at the gates."

"Of course it would," said Patrick impatiently.

"Yes, Keith. Please," said Mrs. Barrimore.

"When I want your suggestions, Margaret, I'll ask for them."

Patrick looked at his stepfather with disgust. He said to Alleyn: "With respect, sir, I suggest that my mother and Jenny leave us to settle this point."

Mrs. Barrimore at once rose.

"May we?" she asked. Jenny said: "Yes, please, may we?"

"Yes, of course," said Alleyn, and to Patrick, "Let the court be cleared of ladies, by all means, Mr. Ferrier."

Patrick gave him a look and turned pink. All the same, Alleyn thought, there was an air of authority about him. The wig was beginning to sprout and would probably become this young man rather well.

"Here. Wait a bit," said the Major. He spread his hands. "All right. *All right*," he said. "Have it your own way." He turned on his wife. "You're supposed to be good at this sort of rot, Margaret. Get out a notice and make it tactful. Say that owing to an accident in the area—no, my God, that sounds bloody awful. Owing to unforeseen circumstances—I don't know. *I* don't know. Say what you like. Talk to them. But get it *done*." Alleyn could cheerfully have knocked him down.

Mrs. Barrimore and Jenny went out.

Patrick, who had turned very white, said: "I think it will be much better if we help Mr. Alleyn as far as we're able. He wants to get on with his work, I'm sure. The facts will have to become known sooner or later. We'll do no good by adopting delaying tactics."

Major Barrimore contemplated his stepson with an unattractive smile. "Charming!" he said. "Now, I know exactly how I should behave, don't I?" He appeared to undergo a change of mood and illustrated it by executing a wide gesture and then burying his face in his hands. "I'm sorry," he said and his voice was muffled. "Give me a moment."

Patrick turned his back and walked over to the window. The Major looked up. His eyes were bloodshot and his expression dolorous. "Bad show," he said. "Apologise. Not myself. Truth of the matter is, I got a bit plastered last night and this has hit me rather hard." He stood up and made a great business of straightening his shoulders and blowing his nose. "As you were," he said bravely. "Take my orders from you. What's the drill?"

"Really, there isn't any at the moment," Alleyn said cheerfully. "If you can persuade your guests not to collect round the enclosure or use the path to it we'll be very grateful. As soon as possible we'll get the approaches cordoned off and that will settle the matter, won't it? And now, if you'll excuse me—"

He was about to go when Major Barrimore said: "Quite so. Talk to the troops, what? Well—sooner the better." He put his hand on Alleyn's arm. "Sorry, old boy," he said gruffly. "Sure you understand."

He frowned, came to attention and marched out.

"Not true," Patrick said to the window. "Just not true."

Alleyn said: "Never mind," and left him.

When he re-entered the main buildings he found Major Barrimore the centre of a group of guests who showed every sign of disgruntlement tempered with avid curiosity. He was in tremendous form. "Now, I know you're going to be perfectly splendid about this," he was saying. "It's an awful disappointment to all of us and it calls for that good old British spirit of tolerance and understanding. Take it on the chin and look as if you liked it, what? And you can take it from me——" He was still in full cry as Alleyn walked up the stairs and went to call on Miss Emily.

She was of course dressed for travel. Her luggage, as he saw through the open door, was ready. She was wearing her toque.

He told her what had happened. Miss Emily's sallow complexion whitened. She looked very fixedly at him and did not interrupt.

"Roderique," she said when he had finished. "This is my doing. I am responsible."

"Now, my dearest Miss Emily—"

"No. Please. Let me look squarely at the catastrophe. This foolish woman has been mistaken for me. There is no doubt in my mind at all. It declares itself. If I had obeyed the intention and not the mere letter of the undertaking I gave you, this would not have occurred."

"You went to the Spring this morning with your notice?"

"Yes. I had, if you recollect, promised you not to leave my apartment again last night and to breakfast in my apartment this morning. A loophole presented itself."

In spite of Miss Emily's distress there was more than a hint of low cunning in the sidelong glance she gave him. "I went out," she said. "I placed my manifesto. I returned. I took my *petit dejeuner* in my room."

"When did you go out?"

"At half past seven."

"It was raining?"

"Heavily."

"Did you meet anybody? Or see anybody?"

"I met nobody," said Miss Emily. "I *saw* that wretched child. Walter Trehern. He was on the roadway that leads from the cottages up to the Spring. It has, I believe, been called—" She closed her eyes. "Wally's Way. He was halfway up the hill."

"Did he see you?"

"He did. He uttered some sort of gibberish, gave an uncouth cry and waved his arms."

"Did he see you leave?"

"I think not. When I had affixed my manifesto and faced about, he had already disappeared. Possibly he was hiding."

"And you didn't, of course, see Miss Cost."

"No!"

"You didn't see her umbrella on your ledge above the pool? As you were tying up your notice?"

"Certainly not. I looked in that direction. It was not there."

"And that would be at about twenty to eight. It wouldn't, I think, take you more than ten minutes to walk there, from the pub?"

"No. It was five minutes to eight when I re-entered the hotel."

"Did you drop the notice, face down in the mud?"

"Certainly not. Why?"

"It's no matter. Miss Emily: please try to remember if you saw anybody at all on the village side of the causeway or indeed anywhere. Any activity round the jetty, for instance, or on the bay or in the cottages? Then, or at any time during your expedition."

"Certainly not."

"And on your return journey?"

"The rain was driving in from the direction of the village. My umbrella was therefore inclined to meet it."

"Yes. I see."

A silence fell between them. Alleyn walked over to the window. It looked down on a small garden at the back of the old pub. As he stood there, absently staring, someone came into the garden from below. It was Mrs. Barrimore. She had a shallow basket over her arm and carried a pair of secateurs. She walked over to a clump of Michaelmas daisies and began to cut them, and her movement was so uncoordinated and wild that the flowers fell to the ground. She made as if to retrieve them, dropped her secateurs and then the basket. Her hands went to her face and for a time she crouched there, quite motionless. She then rose and walked aimlessly and hurriedly about the paths, turning and returning as if the garden were a prison yard. Her fingers twisted together. They might have been encumbered with rings of which she tried fruitlessly to rid them.

"That," said Miss Emily's voice, "is a very unhappy creature."

She had joined Alleyn without attracting his notice.

"Why?" he asked. "What's the matter with her?"

"No doubt her animal of a husband ill-treats her."

"She's a beautiful woman," Alleyn said. He found himself quoting from—surely?—an inappropriate source. "'What is it she does now? Look how she rubs her hands,'" and Miss Emily replied at once: "'It is an accustomed action with her, to seem thus washing her hands.'"

"Good heavens!" Alleyn ejaculated. "What do we think we're talking about!"

Margaret Barrimore raised her head and instinctively they both drew back. Alleyn walked away from the window and then, with a glance at Miss Emily, turned back to it.

"She has controlled herself," said Miss Emily. "She is gathering her flowers. She is a woman of character, that one."

In a short time Mrs. Barrimore had filled her basket and returned to the house.

"Was she very friendly," he asked, "with Miss Cost?"

"No. I believe, on the contrary, that there was a certain animosity. On Cost's part. Not, as far as I could see, upon Mrs. Barrimore's. Cost," said Miss Emily, "was, I judged, a spiteful woman. It is a not unusual phenomenon among spinsters of Cost's years and class. I am glad to say I was not conscious, at her age, of any such emotion. My sister Fanny, in her extravagant fashion, used to say I was devoid of the mating instinct. It may have been so."

"Were you never in love, Miss Emily?"

"That," said Miss Emily, "is an entirely different matter."

"Is it?"

"In any case it is neither here nor there. What do you wish me to do, Roderique? Am I to remain in this place?" She examined him. "I think you are disturbed upon this point," she said.

Alleyn thought: "She's sharp enough to see I'm worried about her and yet she can't see why. Or can she?"

He said: "It's a difficult decision. If you go back to London I'm afraid I shall be obliged to keep in touch and bother you with questions and you may have to return. There will be an inquest, of course. I don't know if you will be called. You may be."

"With whom does the decision rest?"

"Primarily, with the police."

"With you, then?"

"Yes. It rests upon our report. Usually the witnesses called at an inquest are the persons who found the body; me, in this instance, together with the investigating officers, the pathologist and anyone who saw or spoke to the deceased shortly before the event. Or anyone else who the police believe can throw light on the circumstances. Do you think," he asked, "you can do that?"

Miss Emily looked disconcerted. It was the first time, he thought, that he had ever seen her at a loss.

"No," she said. "I think not."

"Miss Emily, do you believe that Wally Trehern came back after you had left the enclosure, saw Miss Cost under her umbrella, crept up to the boulder by a roundabout way (there's plenty of cover) and threw down the rock, thinking he threw it on you?"

"How could that be? How could he get in? The enclosure was locked."

"He may have had a disc, you know."

"What would be done to him?"

"Nothing very dreadful. He would probably be sent to an institution."

She moved about the room with an air of indecision that reminded him, disturbingly, of Mrs. Barrimore. "I can only repeat," she said at last, "what I know. I saw him. He cried out and then hid himself. That is all."

"I think we may ask you to speak of that at the inquest."

"And in the meantime?"

"In the meantime, perhaps we should compromise. There is, I'm told, a reasonably good hotel in the hills outside Dunlowman. If I can arrange for you to stay there, will you do so? The inquest may be held at Dunlowman. It would be less of a fuss for you than returning from London."

"It's inadvisable for me to remain here?"

"Very inadvisable."

"So be it," said Miss Emily. His relief was tempered by a great uneasiness. He had never known her so tractable before.

"I'll telephone the hotel," he said. "And Troy, if I may," he added with a sigh.

"Had I taken your advice and remained in London, this would not have happened."

He was hunting through the telephone book. "That," he said, "is a prime example of utterly fruitless speculation. I am surprised at you, Miss Emily." He dialled the number. The Manor Court Hotel would have a suite vacant at five o'clock the next day. There would also be a small single room. There had been cancellations. He booked the suite. "You can go over in the morning," he said, "and lunch there. It's the best we can do. Will you stay indoors today, please?"

"I have given up this room."

"I don't think there will be any difficulty."

"People are leaving?"

"I daresay some will do so."

"Oh," she said, "I am so troubled, my dear. I am so troubled."

This, more than anything else she had said, being completely out of character, moved and disturbed him. He sat her down and, because she looked unsettled and alien in her travelling toque, carefully removed it. "There," he said, "and I haven't disturbed the coiffure. Now, you look more like my favourite old girl."

"That is no way to address me," said Miss Emily. "You forget yourself." He unbuttoned her gloves and drew them off. "Should I blow in them?" he asked. "Or would that be *du dernier-bourgeois?*"

He saw with dismay that she was fighting back tears.

There was a tap at the door. Jenny Williams opened it and looked in. "Are you receiving?" she asked and then saw Alleyn. "Sorry," she said. "I'll come back later."

"Come in," Alleyn said. "She may, mayn't she, Miss Emily?"

"By all means. Come in, Jennifer."

Jenny gave Alleyn a look. He said, "We've been discussing appropriate action to be taken by Miss Emily," and told her what he had arranged.

Jenny said: "Can't the hotel take her today?" And then hurried on: "Wouldn't you like to be shot off the Island as soon as possible, Miss Pride? It's been a horrid business, hasn't it?"

"I'm afraid they've nothing until tomorrow," Alleyn said.

"Well then, wouldn't London be better, after all? It's so anti-climaxy to gird up one's loins and then ungird them. Miss Pride, if you'd at all like me to, I'd love to go with you for the train journey."

"You are extremely kind, dear child. Will you excuse me for a moment. I have left my handkerchief in my bedroom, I think."

Jenny, about to fetch it, caught Alleyn's eye and stopped short. Alleyn opened the door for Miss Emily and shut it again.

He said quickly: "What's happened? Talk?"

"She mustn't go out. Can't we get her away? Yes. Talk. Beastly, unheard-of, *filthy* talk. She mustn't know. God!" said Jenny, "how I hate *people.*"

"She's staying indoors all day."

"Has she any idea what they'll be saying?"

"I don't know. She's upset. She's gone in there to blow her nose and pull herself together. Look. Would you go with her to Dunlowman? It'll only be a few days. As a job?"

"Yes, of course. Job be blowed."

"Well, as her guest. She wouldn't hear of anything else."

"All right. If she wants me. She might easily not."

"Go out on a pretence message for me and come back in five minutes. I'll fix it."

"O.K."

"You're a darling, Miss Williams."

Jenny pulled a grimace and went out.

When Miss Emily returned she was in complete control of herself. Alleyn said Jenny had gone down to leave a note for him at the office. He said he'd had an idea. Jenny, he understood from Miss Emily, herself was hard up and had to take holiday jobs to enable her to stay in England. Why not offer her one as companion for as long as the stay in Dunlowman lasted?

"She would not wish it. She is the guest of the Barrimores and the young man is greatly attached."

"I think she feels she'd like to get away," Alleyn lied. "She said as much to me."

"In that case," Miss Emily hesitated. "In that case I—I shall make the suggestion. Tactfully, of course. I confess it—it would be a comfort." And she added firmly: "I am feeling old."

It was the most devastating remark he had ever heard from Miss Emily.

CHAPTER SIX

Green Lady

WHEN HE ARRIVED downstairs it was to find Major Barrimore and the office clerk dealing with a group of disgruntled visitors who were relinquishing their rooms. The Major appeared to hang on to his professional aplomb with some difficulty. Alleyn waited and had time to read a notice that was prominently displayed and announced the temporary closing of the Spring owing to unforeseen circumstances.

Major Barrimore made his final bow, stared balefully after the last guest and saw Alleyn. He spread his hands. "My God," he said.

"I'm very sorry."

"Bloody people!" said the Major in unconscious agreement with Jenny. "God, how I hate bloody people."

"I'm sure you do."

"They'll all go! The lot! They'll cackle away among themselves and want their money back and change their minds and jibber and jabber and in the bloody upshot, they'll be off. The whole bloody boiling of them. And the next thing: a new draft! Waltzing in and waltzing out again. What the—" His language grew more fanciful; he sweated extremely. A lady with a cross face swept out of the lounge and up the stairs. He bowed to her distractedly. "That's right, madam," he whispered after her. "That's the drill. Talk to your husband and pack your bags and take your chronic eczema to hell out of it." He smiled dreadfully at Alleyn. "And what can I do for *you*?" he demanded.

"I hardly dare ask you for a room."

"You can have the whole pub. Bring the whole Yard."

Alleyn offered what words of comfort he could muster. Major Barrimore received them with a moody sneer but presently became calmer. "I'm not blaming you," he said. "You're doing your duty. Fine service, the police. Always said so. Thought of it myself when I left my regiment. Took on this damned poodlefaking instead. Well, there you are."

He booked Alleyn in and even accepted, with gloomy resignation, the news that Miss Emily would like to delay her departure for another night.

As Alleyn was about to go he said: "Could you sell me a good cigar? I've left mine behind and I can't make do with a pipe."

"Certainly. What do you smoke?"

"Las Casas, if you have them."

"No can do. At least—well, as a matter of fact, I do get them in for myself, old boy. I'm a bit short. Look here—let you have three, if you like. Show there's no ill-feeling. But not a word to the troops. If you want more, these things are smokable."

Alleyn said: "Very nice of you but I'm not going to cut you short. Let me have one Las Casas and I'll take a box of these others."

He bought the cigars.

The Major had moved to the flap end of the counter. Alleyn dropped his change and picked it up. The boots, he thought, looked very much as if they'd fit. They were wet round the welts and flecked with mud.

He took his leave of the Major.

When he got outside the hotel he compared the cigar band with the one he had picked up and found them to be identical.

Coombe was waiting for him. Alleyn said: "We'd better get the path cordoned off as soon as possible. Where's Pender?"

"At the Spring. Your chaps are on their way. Just made the one good train. They should be here by five. I've laid on cars at Dunlowman. And I've raised another couple of men. They're to report here. What's the idea, cordoning the path?"

"It's that outcrop," Alleyn said and told him about the Major's cigars. "Of course," he said, "there may be a guest who smokes his own Las Casas and who went out in a downpour at the crack of dawn to hide behind a rock, but it doesn't seem likely. We may have to take casts and get hold of his boots."

"The Major! I *see*!"

"It may well turn out to be just one of those damn' fool things. But *he* said he got up late."

"It'd fit. In a way, it'd fit."

"At this stage," Alleyn said. "Nothing fits. We collect. That's all."

"Well, I know that," Coombe said quickly. He had just been warned against the axiomatic sin of forming a theory too soon. "Here are these chaps now," he said.

Two policemen were walking over the causeway.

Alleyn said: "Look, Coombe. I think our next step had better be the boy. Dr. Maine saw him and so did Miss Pride. Could you set your men to patrol the path and then join me at Trehern's cottage?"

"There may be a mob of visitors there. It's a big attraction."

"Hell! Hold on. Wait a bit, would you?"

Alleyn had seen Jenny Williams coming out of the old pub. She wore an orange-coloured bathing dress and a short white coat and looked as if she had had twice her fair share of sunshine.

He joined her. "It's all fixed with Miss Emily," she said, "I'm a lady's companion as from tomorrow morning. In the meantime, Patrick and I are thinking of a bathe."

"I don't know what we'd have done without you. And loath as I am to put anything between you and the English Channel, I have got another favour to ask."

"Now, what is all this?"

"You know young Trehern, don't you? You taught him? Do you get on well with him?"

"He didn't remember me at first. I think he does now. They've done their best to turn him into a horror but—yes—I can't help having a—I suppose it's a sort of compassion," said Jenny.

"I expect it is," Alleyn agreed. He told her he was going to see Wally and that he'd heard she understood the boy and got more response from him than most people. Would she come down to the cottage and help with the interview?

Jenny looked very straight at him and said: "Not if it means you want me to get Wally to say something that may harm him."

Alleyn said: "I don't know what he will say. I don't in the least know whether he is in any way involved in Miss Cost's death. Suppose he was. Suppose he killed her, believing her to be Miss Emily. Would you want him to be left alone to attack the next old lady who happened to annoy him? Think."

She asked him, as Miss Emily had asked him, what would be done with Wally if he was found to be guilty. He gave her the same answer: nothing very dreadful. Wally might be sent to an appropriate institution. It would be a matter for authorised psychiatrists. "And they do have successes in these days, you know. On the other hand, Wally may have nothing whatever to do with the case. But I must find out. Murder," Alleyn said abruptly, "is always abominable. It's hideous and outlandish. Even when the impulse is understandable and the motive overpowering, it is still a terrible, unique offence. As the law stands, its method of dealing with homicide is, as I think, open to the gravest criticism. But for all that, the destruction of a human being remains what it is: the last outrage."

He was to wonder after the case had ended, why on earth he had spoken as he did.

Jenny stared out, looking at nothing. "You must be an unusual kind of cop," she said. And then: "O.K. I'll tell Patrick and put on a skirt. I won't be long."

The extra constables had arrived and were being briefed by Coombe. They were to patrol the path and stop people climbing about the hills above the enclosure. One of them would be stationed near the outcrop.

Jenny reappeared wearing a white skirt over her bathing dress.

"Patrick," she said, "is in a slight sulk. I asked him to pick me up at the cottage."

"My fault, of course. I'm sorry."

"He'll get over it," she said cheerfully.

They went down the hotel steps. Jenny moved ahead. She walked very quickly past Miss Cost's shop, not looking at it. A group of visitors stared in at the window. The door was open and there were customers inside.

Coombe said: "The girl that helps is carrying on."

"Yes. All right. Has she been told not to destroy anything—papers—rubbish—anything?"

"Well, yes. I mean, I said: just serve the customers and attend to the telephone calls. It's a sub-station for the Island. One of the last in the country."

"I think the shop would be better shut, Coombe. We can't assume anything at this stage. We'll have to go through her papers. I suppose the calls can't be operated through the central station?"

"Not a chance."

"Who is this assistant?"

"Cissy Pollock. She was that green girl affair in the show. Pretty dim type, is Cissy."

"Friendly with Miss Cost?"

"Thick as thieves, both being hell-bent on the Festival."

"Look. Could you wait until the shop clears and then lock up? We'll have to put somebody on the board or simply tell the subscribers that the Island service is out of order."

"The Major'll go mad. Couldn't we shut the shop and leave Cissy on the switchboard?"

"I honestly don't think we should. It's probably a completely barren precaution but at this stage—"

"'We must not'," Coombe said, "'allow ourselves to form a hard-and-fast theory to the prejudice of routine investigation.' I know. But I wouldn't mind taking a bet on it that Miss Cost's got nothing to do with this case."

"Except insofar as she happens to be the body?"

"You know what I mean. All right: she fixed the earlier jobs. All right: she may have got at that kid and set him on to Miss Pride. In a way, you might say she organised her own murder."

"Yes," Alleyn said. "You might indeed. It may well be that she did." He glanced at his colleague. "Look," he said. "Pender will be coming back this way anytime now, won't he? I suggest you put him in the shop just to see Miss Cissy Thing doesn't exceed her duty. He can keep observation in the background and leave you free to lend a hand in developments at Wally's joint or whatever it's called. I'll be damned glad of your company."

"All right," Coombe said. "If you say so."

This, Alleyn thought, "is going to be tricky."

"Come on," he said and put his hand on Coombe's shoulder. "It's a hell of a bind but, as the gallant Major would say, it *is* the drill."

"That's right," said Superintendent Coombe. "I know that. See you later, then."

Alleyn left him at the shop.

Jenny was waiting down by the seafront. They turned left, walked round the arm of the bay, and arrived at the group of fishermen's dwellings. Boats pulled up on the foreshore, a ramshackle jetty and the cottages themselves, tucked into the hillside, all fell, predictably, into a conventional arrangement.

"In a moment," said Jenny, "you will be confronted by Wally's Cottage, but *not* as I remember it. It used to be squalid and dirty and it stank to high heaven. Mrs. Trehern is far gone in gin and Trehern, as you may know, is unspeakable. But somehow or another the exhibit has been evolved: very largely through the efforts of Miss Cost, egged on—well—"

"By whom? By Major Barrimore?"

"Not entirely," Jenny said quickly. "By the Mayor, who is called Mr. Nankivell, and his councillors and anybody in Portcarrow who is meant to be civic-minded. And principally, I'm afraid, by Mrs. Fanny Winterbottom and her financial advisors. Or so Patrick says. So, of course, does your Miss Emily. It's all kept up by the estate. There's a guild or something that looks after the garden and supervises the interior. Miss Emily calls the whole thing 'complètement en toc.' There you are," said Jenny as they came face-to-face with their destination. "That's Wally's Cottage, that is."

It was, indeed, dauntingly pretty. Hollyhocks, daisies, foxgloves and antirrhinums flanked a cobbled path: honeysuckle framed the door. Fishing-nets of astonishing cleanliness festooned the fence. Beside the gate, in gothic lettering, hung a legend: "Wally's Cottage. Admission 1/-. West-country Cream-Teas, Ices."

"There's an annex at the back," explained Jenny. "The teas are run by a neighbour, Mrs. Trehern not being up to it. The Golden Record's in the parlour with other exhibits."

"The Golden Record?"

"Of cures," said Jenny shortly.

"Will Wally be on tap?"

"I should think so. And his papa, unless he's ferrying. There are not nearly as many visitors as I'd expected. O!" exclaimed Jenny stopping short. "I suppose—will that be because of what's happened? Yes, of course it will."

"We'll go in," Alleyn said, producing the entrance money.

Trehern was at the receipt of custom.

He leered ingratiatingly at Jenny and gave Alleyn a glance in which truculence, subservience and fear were unattractively mingled. Wally stood behind his father. When Alleyn looked at him he grinned and held out his hands.

Jenny said: "Good morning, Mr. Trehern. I've brought Mr. Alleyn to have a look round. Hallo, Wally."

Wally moved towards her. "You come and see me," he said. "You come to school. One day soon." He took her hand and nodded at her.

"Look at that, now!" Trehern ejaculated. "You was always the favourite, miss. Nobody to touch Miss Williams for our poor little chap, is there, then, Wal?"

There were three visitors in the parlour. They moved from one exhibit to another, listened, and looked furtively at Jenny.

Alleyn asked Wally if he ever went fishing. He shook his head contemptuously and, with that repetitive, so obviously conditioned, gesture, again exhibited his hands. A trained animal, Alleyn thought with distaste. He moved away and opened the Golden Record which was everything that might be expected of it: like a visitors' book at a restaurant in which satisfied clients are invited to record their approval. He noted the dates where cures were said to have been effected and moved on.

The tourists left with an air of having had their money's-worth by a narrow margin.

Alleyn said: "Mr. Trehern, I am a police officer and have been asked to take charge of investigations into the death of Miss Elspeth Cost. I'd like to have a few words with Wally, if I may. Nothing to upset him. We just wondered if he could help us."

Trehern opened and shut his hands as if he felt for some object to hold on by. "I don't rightly know about that," he said. "My little lad be'ant like other little lads, mister. He'm powerful easy put out. Lives in a world of his own, and not to be looked to if it's straight-out facts that's required. No hand at facts, be you, Wal? Tell you the truth, I doubt he's took in this terrible business of Miss Cost."

"She'm dead," Wally shouted. "She'm stoned dead." And he gave one of his odd cries. Trehern looked very put out.

"Poor Miss Cost," Jenny said gently.

"Poor Miss Cost," Wally repeated cheerfully. Struck by some association of ideas, he suddenly recited: *"Be not froightened, sayed the loidy. Ended now is all your woe,"* and stopped as incontinently as he had begun.

Alleyn said: "Ah! That's your piece you said yesterday, isn't it?" He clapped Wally on the shoulders. "Hallo, young fellow, you've been out in the rain! You're as wet as a shag. That's the way to get rheumatism."

Trehern glowered upon his son. "Where you been?" he asked.

"Nowheres."

"You been mucking round they boats. Can't keep him away from they boats," he said ingratiatingly. "Real fisherman's lad, our Wal. Be'ant you, Wal?"

"I dunno," Wally said nervously.

"Come and show me these things," Alleyn suggested. Wally at once began to escort him round the room. It was difficult to determine how far below normal he was. He had something to say about each regrettable exhibit and what he said was always, however uncouth, applicable. Even if it was parrot-talk, Alleyn thought, it at least proved that Wally could connect the appropriate remark with the appointed object.

Jenny stayed for a minute or two, talking to Trehern who presently said something of which Alleyn only caught the tone of the voice. This was unmistakable. He turned quickly, saw that she was disconcerted and angry and called out: "How do you feel about tea and a bun? Wally, do you like icecream?"

Wally at once took Jenny's hand and began to drag her to a door marked "Teas" at the end of the room.

There was nobody else in the tea-room. An elderly woman, whom Jenny addressed by name, took their order.

"Was he being offensive, that type in there?" Alleyn asked in French.

"Yes."

"I'm sorry."

"It doesn't matter in the least," Jenny said. "What sort of tea do you like? Strong?"

"Weak and no milk." Alleyn contemplated Wally whose face was already daubed with icecream. He ate with passionate, almost trembling, concentration.

"It was raining this morning, wasn't it, Wally?"

He nodded slightly.

"Were you out in the rain?"

Wally laughed and blew icecream across the table.

"Wally, don't," Jenny said. "Eat it properly, old boy. You were out in the rain, weren't you? Your shoes are muddy."

"So I wur, then. I don't mind the rain, do I?"

"No," Jenny said and added rather sadly: "You're a big boy now."

"I don't suppose," Alleyn suggested, "there was anybody else out in that storm, was there? I bet there wasn't."

"Was there, Wally? Out in the rain?"

"There wur! *There wur!*" he shouted and banged the table.

"All right. All right. Who was it?"

Wally thrust his tongue into the cornet. "There wur," he said.

"This is heavy work," Alleyn observed mildly.

Jenny asked the same question and Wally at once said: "I seen 'er. I seen the old b... *Yah!*"

"Who do you mean? Who did you see?"

He flourished his right arm: the gesture was as uncoordinated and wild as a puppet's, but it was not to be mistaken. He made as if to throw something. Jenny caught back an exclamation.

"Who did you see? Was it—" Jenny looked at Alleyn who nodded. "Was it Miss Pride?"

Pridey-Pridey bang on the bell
Smash and bash 'er and send 'er to hell."

"*Wally!* who taught you that?"

"The kids," he said promptly, and began again: "*Pridey-Pridey*—"

"Stop. Don't do that, Wally. Be quiet." She said to Alleyn: "It's true, I heard them, yesterday evening."

Wally pushed the last of the cornet into his mouth. "I want another," he said indistinctly.

Coombe had come in from the parlour. Wally's back was towards him. Alleyn gave a warning signal and Coombe stayed where he was. Trehern loomed up behind him, smirking and curious. Coombe turned and jerked his thumb. Trehern hesitated and Coombe shut the door in his face.

"More," said Wally.

"You may have another," Alleyn said, before Jenny could protest. "Tell me what happened when you were out in the rain this morning."

He lowered his head and glowered. "Another one. More," he said.

"Where was Miss Pride?"

"Up along."

"By the gate?"

"By the gate," he repeated like an echo.

"Did you see her go away?"

"She come back."

Jenny's hand went to her lips.

Alleyn said: "Did Miss Pride come back?"

He nodded.

"Along the path? When?"

"She came back," Wally shouted irritably. "Back!"

"A long time afterwards?"

"Long time."

"And went into the Spring? She went through the gate and into the Spring? Is that right?"

"It's *my* Spring. She be'ant allowed up to my Spring." He again made his wild throwing gesture. " Get out!" he bawled.

"Did you throw a rock at Miss Pride? Like that?"

Wally turned his head from side to side. "You dunno what I done," he said. "I ain't telling."

"Tell Miss Williams."

"No, I won't, then."

"Did you throw stones, Wally?" Jenny asked. "One evening? Did you?"

He looked doubtfully at her and then said: "Where's my dad?"

"In there. Wally, tell me."

He leant his smeared face towards her and she stooped her head. Alleyn heard him whisper: "It's a secret."

"What is?"

"They stones. Like my dad said."

"Is the rock a secret, too?"

He pulled back from her. "I dunno nothing about no rock," he said vacantly. "I want another."

"Was Miss Cost at the Spring?" Alleyn asked.

Wally scowled at him.

"Wally," Jenny said, taking his hand, "did you see Miss Cost? In the rain? This morning? Was Miss Cost at the Spring?" "At the fustyvell."

"Yes, at the Festival. Was she at the Spring this morning too? In the rain?"

"This is getting positively fugal," Alleyn muttered.

"This morning," Jenny repeated.

"Not this morning. At the fustyvell," said Wally. "I want another one."

"In a minute," Alleyn said. "Soon. Did you see a man this morning in a motor-boat?" And, by a sort of compulsion, he added, "In the rain?"

"My dad's got the biggest launch."

"Not your dad's launch. Another man in another launch. Dr. Maine. Do you know Dr. Maine?"

"Doctor," said Wally vacantly.

"Yes. Did you see him?"

"I dunno."

Alleyn said to Jenny: "Maine noticed him at about half past seven." He waited for a moment and then pressed on: "Wally: where were you when you saw the lady at the Spring? Where were you?"

Wally pushed his forefinger round and round the table, leaving a greasy trail on the plastic surface. He did this with exaggerated violence and apparently no interest.

"You couldn't get in, could you?" Alleyn suggested. "You couldn't get through the gates."

With his left hand, Wally groped under his smock. He produced a number of entrance discs, let them fall on the table and shoved them about with violent jabs from his forefinger. They clattered to the floor.

"Did you go into the Spring this morning?"

He began to make a high whimpering sound.

"It's no good," Jenny said. "When he starts that it's no good. He'll get violent. He may have an attack. Really, you mustn't. *Really*. I promise, you mustn't."

"Very well," Alleyn said. "I'll get him his icecream."

"Never mind, Wally, it's all right," Jenny said. "It's all right now. Isn't it?"

He looked at her doubtfully and then, with that too familiar gesture, reached his hands out towards her.

"Oh, don't!" Jenny whispered. "Oh, Wally, *don't* show me your hands."

When Wally had absorbed his second icecream they left the tea-room by a door that, as it turned out, led into the back garden.

Coombe said, "We've come the wrong way," but Alleyn was looking at a display of greyish undergarments hung out to dry. A woman of unkempt appearance was in the yard. She stared at them with bleared disfavour.

"Private," she said and pointed to a dividing fence. "You'm trespassing."

"I'm sorry, Mrs. Trehern," Jenny said. " We made a mistake."
Trehern had come out through a back door. "Get in,
woman," he said. "Get in." He took his wife by her arm and
shoved her back into the house. "There's the gate," he said to
Alleyn. "Over yon."

Alleyn had wandered to the clothes-line. A surplus length
dangled from the pole. It had been recently cut.

"I wonder," he said, "if you could spare me a yard of this.
The bumper-bar on my car's loose."

"Be'ant none to spare. Us needs it. Rotten anyways and no
good to you. There's the gate."

"Thank you," Alleyn said and they went out.

"Was it the same as the trip-wire?" he asked Coombe.

"Certainly was, but I reckon they all use it."

"It's old but it's been newly cut. Have you kept the
trip-wire?"

"Yes."

"How was it fastened?"

"With iron pegs. They use them when they dry out their
nets."

"Well, let's move on, shall we?"

Patrick was sitting in a dinghy alongside the jetty, looking
aloof and disinterested. Wally made up to a new pair of
sightseers.

"That was very nice of you," Alleyn said to Jenny. "And I'm
more than obliged."

"I hated it. Mr. Alleyn, he really isn't responsible. You can
see what he's like."

"Do you think he threw the stones at Miss Emily the other
night?"

She said, very unhappily: "Yes."

"So do I."

"But nothing else. I'm sure: nothing more than that."

"You may be right. I'd be very grateful, by the way, if you'd
keep the whole affair under your hat. Will you do that?"

"Yes," she said slowly. "All right. Yes, of course, if you say so."

"Thank you *very* much. One other thing. Have you any idea who the Green Lady could have been?"

Jenny looked startled. "No, I haven't. Somehow or another I've sort of forgotten to wonder. She may not have been real at all."

"What did he say about her?"

"Only that she was very pretty and her hair shone in the sun. And that she said his warts would be all gone."

"Nothing else?"

"No—nothing."

"Has he got that sort of imagination—to invent her?"

Jenny said slowly: "I don't think he has."

"I don't think so either." ·

"Not only that," Jenny said. "He's an extraordinarily truthful little boy. He never tells lies—never."

"That's an extremely valuable piece of information," Alleyn said. "Now go and placate your young man."

"I'll be blowed if I do. He can jolly well come off it," she rejoined but Alleyn thought she was not altogether displeased with Patrick. He watched her climb down into the dinghy. It ducked and bobbed towards the far point of the bay. She looked up and waved to him. Her tawny hair shone in the bright sunshine.

"That's a pleasing young lady," said Coombe. "What did you make of the lad?"

"We're not much further on, are we?"

"Aren't we, though? He as good as said he threw the stones that evening and what's more he has good as let on his dad had told him to keep his mouth shut."

"Yes. Yes, it looked like that, didn't it?"

"Well, then?"

"He wouldn't say anything about the rock. He says he saw Miss Pride leave and return. The figure that returned may have been Miss Cost."

"Ah!" said Coombe with satisfaction.

"Dr. Maine, you remember, noticed Wally dodging about

the road up to the Spring soon after half past seven. Miss Pride saw him at much the same time. Miss Pride got back to the pub at five to eight. She didn't encounter Miss Cost. Say the seven o'clock service ended about ten to eight—we'll have to find out about that; it would mean that Miss Cost would get to the causeway—when?"

"About eight."

"Just after Miss Pride had gone indoors. And to the Spring?"

"Say a quarter past."

"And I found her body at ten past nine."

Coombe said: "The kid would have had time between seven-thirty and eight-fifteen, to let himself into the enclosure and take cover behind that boulder. Before she came."

"Why should he do that? He thought Miss Pride had gone. He saw her go. Why should he anticipate her return?"

"Just one of his silly notions."

"Yes," Alleyn said. "One of his silly notions. Put that boy in the witness-box and we'd look as silly as he does. If he's at the end of this case, Coombe, we'll only get a conviction on factual evidence, not on anything the poor little devil says. Unmistakable prints of his boots behind the boulder, for instance."

"You saw the ground. A mess." Coombe reddened. "I suppose I slipped up there. We were *on* the place before I thought."

"It's so easy," Alleyn said, saving his face for him. "Happens to the best of us."

"It was all churned up, wasn't it? Almost as if—?"

"Yes?"

"Now I come to think of it, almost as if, before the doctor and I went up, someone had kind of scuffled it."

"Yes. Behind the boulder and the trace of the rock. There was a flat bit of stone, did you notice, lying near the bank. Muddy edge. It might have been used to obliterate prints."

"I suppose," Coombe said, "in a quiet type of division like this, you get a bit rusty. I could kick myself. At my time of life!"

"It may not amount to much. After all, we can isolate your prints and Dr. Maine's from the rest."

"Well, yes. Yes, you can do that, all right. But still!"

Alleyn looked at his watch. It was just on noon. He suggested that they return to the mainland and call on the rectory. The tide was coming in and they crossed the channel by dinghy. There was Alleyn's car by the jetty with his luggage in it. If things had gone according to plan, he would have been halfway to Troy by now.

They left it where it stood. The rectory was a five-minutes' walk along the front. It stood between a small and charming Norman church and Dr. Maine's Convalescent Home: a pleasant late-Georgian house with the look, common to parsonages, of being exposed to more than its fair share of hard usage.

"It was a poorish parish, this," Coombe said, "but with the turn things have taken over the last two years, it's in better shape. The stipend's gone up for one thing. A lot of people that reckon they've benefited by the Spring make donations. It'd surprise you to know the amounts that are put into the restoration-fund boxes. I'm people's warden," he added, "should have been there myself at ten-thirty for the family service. The Rector'll be back home by now. It's his busy day, of course."

They found Mrs. Carstairs briskly weeding. She wore a green linen dress and her hair, faded yellow, made an energetic sort of halo round her head. Her church-going hat, plastic raincoat, gloves and prayer-book were scattered in a surrealistic arrangement along the border. When Alleyn was introduced she shook hands briskly and said she supposed he'd come about this dreadful business and wanted to see her husband who was, of course, appalled.

"He's in the study," she said to Coombe. "Those accounts from the dry-rot people are *all* wrong again, Mr. Coombe, and the Mayor suggests a combined memorial service but we don't *quite* think—however."

"I'd really like a word with *you*, if I may," Alleyn said.

"We're trying to trace Miss Cost's movements early this morning."

"Oh, *dear*! Yes. Well, of *course*."

She confirmed Dr. Maine's account. Miss Cost had attended the first celebration at seven o'clock and they had met at the gate. "She was in a great fuss, poor thing, because of my necklace."

"Your necklace?"

"Yes. It's really rather a nice old one. Pinchbeck and paste but long and quite good. I lent with reluctance but she was so keen to have it because of the glitter and then, of course, what must her great Cissy do but drop it at the first thunder-clap and in the stampede, nobody remembered. I said we'd retrieve it after church or why not let Cissy go? But no, she made a great to-do, *poor* Miss Cost (when one *thinks*) and insisted that she would go herself. She was rather an *on-goer*: conversationally, if you know what I mean: on and on and I wanted to go into church and say my prayers and it was pouring. So then she saw Dr. Maine and she was curious to know if it was Mrs. Trethaway's twins, though of course in the event it *wasn't* twins (that was all nonsense), so I'm afraid I left her to tackle him as she clearly died to do. And after church I saw her streak off through the rain before anyone could offer. Isn't it *dreadful*?" Mrs. Carstairs asked energetically. "Well, isn't it? Adrian! Can you spare a moment, dear?"

"Coming."

The Rector, wearing his cassock, emerged through French windows. He said how extraordinary it was that Alleyn should have been at Portcarrow, added that they were lucky to have him and then became doubtful and solemn. "One finds it hard to believe," he said. "One is appalled."

Alleyn asked him when the first service ended and he said at about a quarter to eight. "I'd expected a large congregation. There are so many visitors. But the downpour, no doubt, kept a lot of folk away and there were only six communicants. The nine o'clock was crowded."

Alleyn wondered absently why clergymen were so prone to

call people "folk" and asked Mr. Carstairs if he knew Miss Cost very well. He seemed disturbed and said: well, yes, insofar as she was a member of his congregation. He glanced at his wife and added: "Our friendship with Miss Cost was perhaps rather limited by our views on the Spring. I could not sympathise or, indeed, approve of her, as I thought, rather extravagant claims. I thought them woolly," said the Rector. "Woolly and vulgar." He expounded, carefully, his own attitude which, in its anxious compromise, declared, Alleyn thought, its orthodoxy.

"And you saw her," he asked, "after the service?"

They said simultaneously that they did.

"I'm one of those parsons who come out to the porch and see folk off," the Rector explained. "But Miss Cost was on her way when I got there. Going down the path. Something about my wife's necklace. Wasn't it, Dulcie?"

"Yes, dear. I told Mr. Alleyn."

Coombe said: "The necklace has been recovered and will be returned in due course, Mrs. Carstairs."

"Oh, dear!" she said. "Will it? I—I don't think—"

"Never mind, dear," said her husband.

Alleyn asked if anybody from the Island had been at the first service. Nobody, it appeared. There were several at the nine o'clock.

"The Barrimores, for instance?"

No, not the Barrimores.

There was a silence through which the non-attendance of the Barrimores was somehow established as a normal state-of-affairs.

"Although," Mrs. Carstairs said, in extenuation of a criticism that no one had voiced, "Margaret used to come *quite* regularly at one time, Adrian. Before Wally's Warts, you remember?"

"Not that there's any connection, Dulcie."

"Of course not, dear. And Patrick and *nice* Jenny Williams have been to evensong, we must remember."

"So we must," her husband agreed.

"Poor things. They'll all be terribly upset no doubt," Mrs. Carstairs said to Alleyn. "Such a shock for everyone."

Alleyn said carefully: "Appalling. And apart from everything else a great worry for Barrimore, one imagines. After all, it won't do his business any good, this sort of catastrophe."

They looked uncomfortable and faintly shocked. "Well—" they both said and stopped short.

"At least," Alleyn said casually, "I suppose The Boy-and-Lobster *is* his affair, isn't it?"

"It's the property of the estate," Coombe said. "Miss Pride's the landlord. But I have heard they put everything they'd got into it."

"*She* did," Mrs. Carstairs said firmly. "It was Margaret Barrimore's money, wasn't it, Adrian?"

"My dear, I don't know. In any case—"

"Yes, dear. Of course," said Mrs. Carstairs, turning pink. She glanced distractedly at the knees of her linen dress. "Oh, look!" she said. "Now, I shall have to change. It was that henbane that did it. What a disgrace I am. Sunday and everything."

"You melt into your background, my dear," the Rector observed. "Like a wood-nymph," he added, with an air of recklessness.

"Adrian, you are awful," said Mrs. Carstairs automatically. It was clear that he was in love with her.

Alleyn said: "So there would be a gap of about an hour and a quarter between the first and second services?"

"This morning, yes," said the Rector. "Because of the rain, you see, and the small attendance at seven."

"How do you manage?" Alleyn asked Mrs. Carstairs. "Breakfast must be quite a problem."

"Oh, there's usually time to boil an egg before nine. This morning, as you see, we had over an hour. At least," she corrected herself. "*You* didn't, did you, dear? Adrian had to make a visit: poor old Mr. Thomas," she said to Coombe. "Going, I'm afraid."

"So you were alone after all. When did you hear of the tragedy, Mrs. Carstairs?"

"Before matins. Half past ten. Several people had seen the—well, the ambulance and the stretcher, you know. And Adrian met Sergeant Pender and—and there it was."

"Is it true?" the Rector asked abruptly. "Was it—deliberate? Pender said—I mean?"

"I'm afraid so."

"How very dreadful," he said. "How appallingly dreadful."

"I know," Alleyn agreed. "A woman, it appears, with no enemies. It's incomprehensible."

Coombe cleared his throat. The Carstairses glanced at each other quickly and as quickly looked away.

"Unless, I suppose," Alleyn said, "you count Miss Pride?"

"There, I'm afraid," the Rector said, and Alleyn wondered if he'd caught an overtone of relief, "there, it was all on Miss Cost's side, poor soul."

"You might say," his wife added, "that Miss Pride had the whip-hand."

"Dulcie!"

"Well, Adrian, you know what I mean."

"It's quite beside the point," said the Rector with authority.

A telephone rang in the house. He excused himself and went indoors.

"There was nothing, I suppose, in her day-to-day life to make people dislike her," Alleyn said. "She seems, as far as I can make out, to have been a perfectly harmless obsessive."

Mrs. Carstairs began to pick up her scattered belongings, rather as if she was giving herself time to consider. When she straightened up, with her arms full, she was quite red in the face.

"She wasn't always perfectly kind," she said.

"Ah! Which of us is?"

"Yes, I know. You're quite right. Of course," she agreed in a hurry.

"Did she make mischief?" he asked lightly.

"She tried. My husband— Naturally, we paid no attention. My husband feels very strongly about that sort of thing. He calls it a cardinal sin. He preaches *very* strongly against. *Always*." Mrs. Carstairs looked squarely at Alleyn. "I'm offending, myself, to tell you this. I can't think what came over me. You must have a—have a talent for catching people off guard."

He said wryly: "You make my job sound very unappetising. Mrs. Carstairs, I won't bother you much longer. One more question and we're off. Have you any idea who played those ugly tricks on Miss Pride? If you have, I do hope you will tell me."

She seemed, he thought, to be relieved. She said at once: "I've always considered she was behind them. Miss Cost."

"Behind them? You thought she encouraged someone else to take the active part?"

"Yes."

"Wally Trehern?"

"Perhaps."

"And was that what you were thinking of when you said Miss Cost was not always kind?"

"Oh, no!" she ejaculated and stopped short. "Please don't ask me any more questions, Mr. Alleyn. I shall not answer them, if you do."

"Very well," he said. He thanked her and went away, followed, uncomfortably, by Coombe.

They lunched at the village pub. The whole place was alive with trippers. The sun glared down, the air was degraded by transistors and the ground by litter. Groups of sightseers in holiday garments crowded the foreshore, eating, drinking and pointing out the Island to each other. The tide was full. The hotel launch and a number of dinghies plied to and fro and their occupants stared up at the enclosure. It was obvious that the murder of Miss Cost was now common knowledge.

The enclosure itself was not fully visible from the village, being masked by an arm of Fisherman's Bay, but two constables could be seen on the upper pathway. Visitors returning from the Island told each other and anybody that cared to listen, that you couldn't get anywhere near the Spring. "There's nothing to see," they said. "The coppers have got it locked up. You wouldn't know."

When they had eaten a flaccid lunch they called on the nearest J.P. and picked up a search-warrant for Wally's Cottage. They went on to the station where Alleyn collected a short piece of the trip-wire. It was agreed that he would return to The Boy-and-Lobster. Coombe was to remain at the station, relieving his one spare constable, until the Yard men arrived. He would then telephone Alleyn at The Boy-and-Lobster. Pender would remain on duty at Miss Cost's shop.

Coombe said: "It's an unusual business, this. You finding the body and then this gap before your chaps come in."

"I hope you'll still be on tap, but I do realise it's taking more time than you can spare."

"Well, you know how it is." He waited for a moment and then said: "I appreciate your reluctance to form a theory too soon. I mean, it's what we all know. You can't. But as I'm pulling out I can't help saying it looks a sure thing to me. Here's this dopey kid as good as letting on he pitched in with the stones. There's more than a hint that his old man was behind it and a damn' good indication that he set the trip-wire. The kid says Miss Pride came back and there's every likelihood he mistook Miss Cost for her. I reckon he'd let himself into the enclosure and was up by the boulder. He looked down and saw the umbrella below and let fly at it. I mean, well, it hangs together, doesn't it?"

"Who do you think planted the figurine in Miss Pride's sitting-room and sent her the anonymous message and rang her up?"

"Well, *she* reckons Miss Cost."

"So Miss Cost's death was the end product of the whole series? Laid on, you might say, by herself?"

"In a sense. Yes."

"Has it struck you at all," Alleyn asked, "that there's one

feature of the whole story about which nobody seems to show the slightest curiosity?"

"I can't say it has."

Alleyn took from his pocket the figurine that he had wrapped in paper and in his handkerchief. He opened it up and, holding it very gingerly, stood it on Coombe's desk. The single word, "Death," gummed to a sheet of paper, was still fixed in position.

"Nobody," Alleyn said, "as far as I can gather, has ever asked themselves who was the original Green Lady."

"That piece of paper," Alleyn said, "is not the kind used for the original messages. It's the same make as this other piece which is a bit of The Boy-and-Lobster letter paper. The word 'Death' is not in a type that is used in your local rag. I can't be sure but I think it's from a London sporting paper called *The Racing Supplement*. The printer's ink, as you see, is a bluish black and the type's distinctive. Was Miss Cost a racing fan?"

"Her?" Coombe said. "Don't be funny."

"The Major is. He takes *The Racing Supplement*."

"Does he, by gum!"

"Yes. Have you got a dabs-kit handy?"

"Nothing very flash, but, yes, we've got the doings."

Alleyn produced his box of cigars. He opened this up. "There ought to be good impressions inside the lid. Bailey can give it the full works, if necessary, but we'll take a fly at it, shall we?"

Coombe got out his insufflator and a lens. They developed a good set of prints on the lid and turned to the paper impaled over the figurine's head.

After a minute or two Alleyn gave a satisfied grunt.

"Fair enough," he said. "The index and thumb prints are as good as you'd ask. I think I'll call on the gallant Major."

He left Coombe still poring lovingly over the exhibits,

walked down to his car, collected his suitcases and crossed by the hotel launch to the Island. Trehern was in charge. His manner unattractively combined truculence with servility.

It was now two o'clock.

The Major, it presently transpired, was in the habit of taking a siesta.

"He got used to it in India," Mrs. Barrimore said. "People do."

Alleyn had run into her at the door of the old pub. She was perfectly composed and remote in her manner: a beautiful woman who could not, he thought, ever be completely unaware of the effect she made. It was inescapable. She must, over and over again, have seen it reflected in the eyes of men who looked at, and at once recognised, her. She was immensely attractive.

He said: "Perhaps, in the meantime, I may have a word with you?"

"Very well. In the parlour, if you like. The children are out, just now."

"The children?"

"Jenny and Patrick. I should have said 'the young,' I expect. Will you come in?"

He could hardly recognise the woman he had seen in her garden, veering this way and that like a rudderless ship and unable to control her hands. She sat perfectly still and allowed him to look at her while she kept her own gaze on her quietly interlaced fingers.

He supposed she must have had a hand in the transformation of the old bar-parlour into a private living-room; if so she could have taken little interest in the process. Apart from the introduction of a few unexceptionable easy-chairs, one or two photographs, a non-committal assembly of books and a vase of the flowers she had so mishandled in the garden, it must be much as it was two years ago: an impersonal room.

Alleyn began by following the beaten paths of routine investigation. He tried to establish some corroboration of her alibi, though he did not give it this name, for the period covered by Miss Emily's visit to the enclosure up to the probable time of Miss Cost's death. There was none to be had. Nobody had visited the kitchen-dining-room while she drank her coffee and ate her toast. The servants were all busy in the main building. Jenny and Patrick had breakfasted in the public dining-room, her husband was presumably asleep. Alleyn gathered that they occupied separate rooms. She had no idea how long this solitary meal had lasted. When it was over she had attended to one or two jobs, interviewed the kitchen staff and then gone up to her room and changed from a housecoat to a day dress. When she came downstairs again she had found the young people in the parlour. Alleyn had arrived soon afterwards.

"And for the rest of the morning," he asked casually, "did you go out at all?"

"No farther than the garden," she said after a fractional pause. "I went into the garden for a time."

"To cut flowers?" he suggested, looking at those in the room.

She lifted her eyes to his for a moment. "Yes," she said, "to cut flowers. I do the flowers on Sunday as a rule—it takes quite a time. Jenny helped me," she added as an afterthought.

"In the garden?"

Again the brief look at him, this time perhaps, fractionally less controlled. "No. Not in the garden. In the house. Afterwards."

"So you were alone in the garden?"

She said quickly with the slight hesitation he had noticed before in her speech: "Yes. Alone. Why d-do you keep on about the garden? What interest can it have for you? It was after—afterwards. Long afterwards."

"Yes, of course. Did the news distress you very much, Mrs. Barrimore?"

The full, unbridled mouth, so much at variance with the rest of her face, moved as if to speak, but, as in a badly synchro-

nised sound film, her voice failed. Then she said: "Naturally.
It's a terrible thing to have happened, isn't it?"

"You were fond of Miss Cost?"

Something in her look reminded him, fantastically, of the
strange veiling of a bird's eyes. Hers were heavy-lidded and
she had closed them for a second. "Not particularly," she said.
"We had nothing—" She stopped, unaccountably.

"Nothing in common?"

She nodded. Her hands moved but she looked at them
and refolded them in her lap.

"Had she made enemies?"

"I don't know of any," she said at once as if she had anticipated the question. "I know very little about her."

Alleyn asked her if she subscribed to the theory of
mistaken identity and she said that she did. She was emphatic
about this and seemed relieved when he spoke of it. She was,
she said, forced to think that it might have been Wally.

"Excited, originally, by Miss Cost herself?"

"I think it's possible. She was— It doesn't matter."

"Inclined to be vindictive?"

She didn't answer.

"I'm afraid," Alleyn said, "that in these cases one can't
always avoid speaking ill of the dead. I did rather gather from
something in Mrs. Carstairs's manner—"

"Dulcie Carstairs!" she exclaimed, spontaneously and
with animation. "She never says anything unkind about
anybody."

"I'm sure she doesn't. It was just that—well, I thought she
was rather desperately determined not to do so in this case."

She gave him a faint smile. It transfigured her face.

"Dear Dulcie," she murmured.

"She and the Rector are horrified, of course. They struck
me as being such a completely unworldly pair, those two."

"Did they? You were right. They are."

"I mean—not only about Miss Cost but about the whole
business of the Spring being more or less discredited by the

present owner. The events of the last two years must have made a great difference to them, I suppose."

"Yes," she said. "Enormous."

"Were they very hard up before?"

"Oh, yes. It was a dreadfully poor parish. The stipend was the least that's given, I believe, and they'd no private means. We were all so sorry about it. Their clothes! She's nice looking but she needs careful dressing," said Mrs. Barrimore with all the unconscious arrogance of a woman who would look lovely in a sack. "Of course everyone did what they could. I don't think she ever bought anything for herself."

"She looked quite nice this morning, I thought."

"Did she?" For the first time, Margaret Barrimore spoke as if there was some kind of rapprochement between them. "I thought men never noticed women's clothes," she said.

"Do you bet me I can't tell you what you wore yesterday at the Spring?"

"Well?"

"A white linen dress with a square neck and a leather belt. Brown Italian shoes with large buckles. Brown suede gloves. A wide string-coloured straw hat with a brown velvet ribbon. A brown leather bag. No jewellery."

"You win," said Mrs. Barrimore. "You don't look like the sort of man who notices but I suppose it's part of your training and I shouldn't feel flattered. Or should I?"

"I would like you to feel flattered. And now I'm going to ruin my success by telling you that Mrs. Carstairs, too, wore a linen dress, this morning." He described it. She listened to this talk about clothes as if it was a serious matter.

"White?" she asked.

"No. Green."

"Oh, yes. That one."

"Was it originally yours?"

"If it's the one I think it is, yes."

"When did you give it to her?"

"I don't in the least remember."

"Well—as long as two years ago?"

"Really, I've no idea."

"Try."

"But I *don't* remember. One doesn't remember. I've given her odd things from time to time. You make me feel as if I'm parading—as if I'm making a lot of it. As if it was charity. Or patronage. It was nothing. Women do those sorts of things."

"I wouldn't press it if I didn't think it might be relevant."

"How can it be of the slightest interest?"

"A green dress? If she had it two years ago? Think."

She was on her feet with a quick controlled movement.

"But that's nonsense! You mean—Wally?"

"Yes. I do. The Green Lady."

"But—most people have always thought he imagined her. And even if he didn't—there are lots of green dresses in the summertime."

"Of course. What I'm trying to find out is whether this was one of them. Is there nothing that would call to mind when you gave it to her?"

She waited for a moment, looking down at her hands.

"Nothing. It was over a year ago, I'm sure." She turned aside. "Even if I could remember, which I can't, I don't think I would want to tell you. It can't have any bearing on this ghastly business—how could it?—and suppose you're right, it's private to Dulcie Carstairs."

"Perhaps she'd remember."

"I don't believe it. I don't for a moment believe she would think of playing a—a fantastic trick like that. It's not like her. She was never the Green Lady."

"I haven't suggested she was, you know." Alleyn walked over to her. She lifted her head and looked at him. Her face was ashen.

"Come," he said, "don't let us fence any more. You were the Green Lady, weren't you?"

CHAPTER SEVEN

The Yard

HE WONDERED IF she would deny it and what he could say if she did. Very little. His assumption had been based largely on a hunch and he liked to tell himself that he didn't believe in hunches. He knew that she was deeply shocked. Her white face and the movement of her hands gave her away completely but she was, as Miss Emily had remarked, a woman of character.

She said: "I have been very stupid. You may, I suppose, congratulate yourself. What gave you the idea?"

"I happened to notice your expression when that monstrous girl walked out from behind the boulder. You looked angry. But, more than that, I've been told Wally sticks to it that his Green Lady was tall and very beautiful. Naturally, I thought of you."

A door slammed upstairs. Someone, a man, cleared his throat raucously.

She twisted her hands into his. Her face was a mask of

terror. "Mr. Alleyn, promise me, for God's sake, promise me you won't speak about this to my husband. It won't help you to discuss it with him. I swear it won't. You don't know what would happen if you did."

"Does he not know?"

She tried to speak but only looked at him in terror.

"He *does* know?"

"It makes no difference. He would be—he would be angry. That you knew."

"Why should he mind so much? You said what you said, I expect, impulsively. And it worked. Next morning the boy's hands were clean. You couldn't undo your little miracle."

"No, no, no, you don't understand. It's not that. It's—O God, he's coming down. O God, how can I make you? What shall I do! Please, please."

"If it's possible I shall say nothing." He held her hands firmly for a moment until they stopped writhing in his. "Don't be frightened," he said and let her go. "He'd better not see you like this. Where does that door lead to? The kitchen?" He opened it. "There you are. Quickly."

In a moment she was gone.

Major Barrimore came heavily downstairs. He yawned, crossed the little hall and went into the old private bar. The slide between it and the parlour was still there. Alleyn heard the clink of glass. A mid-afternoon drinker, he thought and wondered if the habit was long-established. He picked up his suitcase, went quietly into the hall and out at the front door. He then noisily returned.

"Anyone at home?" he called.

After an interval, the door of the private opened and Barrimore came out, dabbing at his mouth with a freshly laundered handkerchief and an unsteady hand. He was, as usual, impeccably turned out. His face was puffy and empurpled and his manner sombre.

"Hallo," he said. "You."

"I'm on my way to sign in," Alleyn said cheerfully. "Can

you spare me a few minutes? Routine, as usual. One's never done with it."

Barrimore stared dully at him and then opened the door of the parlour. "In here," he said.

Margaret Barrimore had left the faintest recollection of her scent behind her but this was soon lost in the Major's blended aura of Scotch-cigar-and-hair-lotion.

"Well," he said. "What's it, this time? Made any arrests?"

"Not yet."

"Everybody nattering about the boy, I s'pose. You'd think they'd all got their knife into the poor kid."

"You don't agree?"

"I don't. He's too damn' simple, f'one thing. No harm in him, f'r' nother. You get to know 'bout chaps' character in a regiment. Always pick the bad 'uns. He's not."

"Have you any theories yourself?"

The Major predictably said, "No names, no pack drill."

"Quite. But I'd be glad of your opinion."

"You wouldn't, old boy. You'd hate it."

Now, Alleyn thought, "this is it. I know what this is going to be." "I?" he said, "why?"

"Heard what they're saying in the village?"

"No. What are they saying?"

"I don't necessarily agree, you know. Still, they hated each other's guts, those two. Face it."

"Which two?"

"The females. Beg pardon: the ladies. Miss P. and Miss C. And she was *there*, old boy. Can't get away from it. She was on the spot. Hanging up her bloody notice."

"*How do you know?*" Alleyn said and was delighted to speak savagely.

"Here! Steady! Steady, the Buffs!"

"The path has been closed. No one has been allowed near the enclosure. How do you know Miss Pride was there? How do you know she hung up her notice?"

"By God, sir—"

"I'll tell you. You were there yourself."

The blood had run into patches in the Major's jowls. "You must be mad," he said.

"You were on the path. You took shelter behind an outcrop of stone by the last bend. After Miss Pride had left and returned to the hotel, you came out and went to the enclosure."

He was taking chances again, but, looking at that outfaced blinking man, he knew he was justified.

"You read the notice, lost your temper and threw it into the mud. The important thing is that you were there. If you want to deny it you are, of course, at perfect liberty to do so."

Barrimore drew his brows together and went through a parody of brushing his moustache. He then said: "Mind if I get a drink?"

"You'd better not, but I can't stop you."

"You're perfectly right," said the Major. He went out. Alleyn heard him go into the private and pushed back the slide. The Major was pouring himself a Scotch. He saw Alleyn and said: "Can I persuade you? No. S'pose not. Not the drill."

"Come back," Alleyn said.

He swallowed his whisky neat and returned.

"Better," he said. "Needed it." He sat down. "There's a reasonable explanation," he said.

"Good. Let's have it."

"I followed her."

"Who? Miss Pride?"

"That's right. Now, look at it this way. I wake. Boiled owl. Want a drink of water. Very well. I get up. Raining cassandogs. All v'y fine. Look outer th' window. Cassandogs. And there *she* is with her bloody great brolly, falling herself in, down below. Left wheel and into the path. What's a man going to do? Coupler aspirins and into some togs. Trench coat. Hat. Boots. See what I mean? You can't trust her an inch. Where was I?"

"Following Miss Pride along the path to the enclosure."

"Certainly. She'd gained on me. All right. Strategy of

indirect approach. Keep under cover. Which I did. Just like you said, old boy. Perfectly correct. Don't fire till you see the whites of their eyes." He leered at Alleyn.

"Do you mean that you confronted her?"

"Me! No, thank you!"

"You mean you kept under cover until she'd gone past you on her way back to the hotel."

"What I said. Or did I?"

"Then you went to the enclosure?"

"Nasherally."

"You read the notice and threw it aside?"

"'Course."

"And then? What did you do?"

"Came back."

"Did you see Wally Trehern?"

The Major stared. "I did not."

"Did you meet anyone?"

A vein started out on Barrimore's forehead. Suddenly, he looked venomous.

"Not a soul," he said loudly.

"Did you see anyone?"

"No?"

"You met Miss Cost. You must have done so. She was on the path a few minutes after Miss Pride got back. You either met her at the enclosure itself or on the path. Which was it?"

"I didn't see her. I didn't meet her."

"Will you sign a statement to that effect?"

"I'll be damned if I do." Whether through shock or by an astonishing effort of will, he had apparently got himself under control. "I'll see you in hell first," he said.

"And that's your last word?"

"Not quite." He got up and confronted Alleyn, staring into his face. "If there's any more of this," he said, "I'll ring up the Yard and tell your O.C. you're a prejudiced and therefore an untrustworthy officer. I'll have you court-martialled, by God! Or whatever they do in your show."

"I really think you'd better not," Alleyn said mildly.

"No? I'll tell them what's no more than the case: You're suppressing evidence against an old woman who seems to be a very particular friend. No accounting for taste."

"Major Barrimore," Alleyn said. "You will not persuade me to knock your tongue down your throat but you'd do yourself less harm if you bit it off."

"I know what I'm talking about. You can't get away from it. Ever since she came here she's had her knife into poor old Cost. Accusing her of writing letters. Chucking stones. Telephone messages. Planting ornaments."

"Yes," Alleyn said. "Miss Pride was wrong there, wasn't she? Miss Cost didn't put the Green Lady in Miss Pride's room. You did."

Barrimore's jaw dropped.

"Well," Alleyn said. "Do you deny it? I shouldn't if I were you. It's smothered in your fingerprints and so's the paper round its neck."

"You're lying. You're bluffing."

"If you prefer to think so. There's been a conspiracy between you, against Miss Pride, hasn't there? You and Miss Cost, with the Treherns in the background? You were trying to scare her off. Miss Cost started it with threatening messages pieced together from the local paper. You liked the idea and carried on with the word 'Death' cut out of your *Racing Supplement* and stuck round the neck of the image. You didn't have to ask Miss Cost for one. They're for sale in your pub."

"Get to hell out of here. *Get out.*"

Alleyn picked up his suitcase. "That's all for the present. I shall ask you to repeat this conversation before a witness. In the meantime, I suggest that you keep off the whisky and think about the amount of damage you've done to yourself. If you change your mind about any of your statements I'm prepared to listen to you. You will see to it, if you please, that Miss Pride is treated with perfect civility during the few hours she is most unfortunately obliged to remain here as your guest."

He had got as far as the door when the Major said: "Hold on. Wait a bit."

"Well?"

"Daresay I went too far. Not myself. Fellah shouldn't lose his temper, should he? What!"

"On the contrary," said Alleyn, "the exhibition was remarkably instructive." And went out.

"And after all that," he thought, "I suppose I should grandly cancel my room and throw myself on Coombe's hospitality again. I won't though. It's too damned easy and it's probably exactly what Barrimore hopes I'll do."

He collected his key at the office and went up to his room. It was now a quarter past three. Miss Emily would still be having her siesta. In an hour and forty-five minutes, Detective-Inspector Fox, Detective-Sergeant Bailey and Detective-Sergeant Thompson would arrive. Curtis, the pathologist, would be driving to Dunlowman under his own steam. Coombe had arranged for Dr. Maine to meet him there. The nearest mortuary was at Dunlowman. Alleyn would be damned glad to see them all.

He unpacked his suitcase and began to write his notes on hotel paper. It was the first time he'd ever embarked on a case without his regulation kit and he felt uncomfortable and amateurish. He began to wonder if, after all, he should hand over to Fox or somebody else. Triumph for the gallant Major, he thought.

For a minute or two he indulged in what he knew to be fantasy. Was it, in the smallest degree, remotely possible that Miss Emily, inflamed by Miss Cost's activities, could have seen her approaching, bolted into the enclosure, hidden behind the boulder and under a sudden access of exasperation, hurled a rock at Miss Cost's umbrella? It was not. But supposing for a moment that it was? What would Miss Emily then have done? Watched

Miss Cost as she drowned in the pool; as her hair streamed out over the fall; as her dress inflated and deflated in the eddying stream? Taken another bit of rock, and scraped out her own footprints and walked back to The Boy-and-Lobster? And, where, all that time, was the Major? What became of his admission that he tore down the notice and threw it away? Suppose there was an arrest and a trial and defending counsel used Miss Emily as a counterblast? Could her innocence be established? Only, as things stood, by the careful presentation of the Major's evidence and the Major thought, or pretended to think, she was guilty. And, in any case, the Major was a chronic alcoholic.

He got up and moved restlessly about the room. A silly, innocuous print of anemones in a mug had been hung above the bed. He could have wrenched it down and chucked it, with as much fury as had presumably inspired the Major, into the wastepaper basket.

There must have been an encounter between Barrimore and Miss Cost. He had seen Emily pass and repass, had come out of concealment and gone to the enclosure. By that time Miss Cost was approaching. Why, when he saw her, should he again take cover, and where? No, they must have met. What, then, did they say to each other in the pouring rain? Did she tell him she was going to retrieve the necklace? Or did he, having seen her approaching, let himself into the enclosure and hide behind the boulder? But why? And where, all this time, was Wally? Dr. Maine and Miss Emily had both seen him, soon after half past seven. He had shouted at Miss Emily and then ducked out of sight. The whole damned case seemed to be littered with people that continually dodged in and out of concealment. What about Trehern? Out and about in the landscape with the rest of them? Inciting his son to throw rocks at a supposed Miss Emily? Dr. Maine had not noticed him but that proved nothing.

Next, and he faced this conundrum with distaste, what about Mrs. Barrimore, alias the Green Lady? Did she fit in anywhere or had he merely stumbled down an odd, irrelevant byway? But why was she so frightened at the thought of her husband being told of her masquerade? The Green Lady episode had brought Barrimore nothing but material gain. Wouldn't he simply have ordered her to shut up about it and if anything, relished the whole story? She had seemed to suggest that the fact of Alleyn himself being aware of it would be the infuriating factor. And why had she been so distressed when she was alone in the garden? At that stage there was no question of her identity with the Green Lady being discovered.

Finally, of course, was Miss Cost murdered, as it were, in her own person, or because she was mistaken for Miss Emily?

The answer to that one must depend largely upon motive and motive is one of the secondary elements in police investigation. The old tag jog-trotted through his mind. "*Quis? Quid? Ubi? Quibus auxilis? Cur? Quomodo? Quando?*" Which might be rendered: "Who did the deed? What was it? Where was it done? With what? Why was it done? And how done? When was it done?" The lot!

He completed his notes and read them through. The times were pretty well established. The weapon. The method. The state of the body. The place—no measurements yet, beyond the rough ones he and Coombe had made on the spot. Bailey would attend to all that. The place? He had described it in detail. The boulder?—between the boulder and the hill behind it was a little depression, screened by bracken and soft with grass. A "good spot for courting couples," as Coombe had remarked, "when it wasn't raining." The ledge—

He was still poring over his notes when the telephone rang. Mr. Nankivell, the Mayor of Portcarrow, would like to see him.

"Ask him to come up," Alleyn said and put his notes in the drawer of the desk.

Mr. Nankivell was in a fine taking-on. His manner suggested a bothering confusion of civic dignity, awareness of Alleyn's reputation and furtive curiosity. There was another element, too. As the interview developed, so did his air of being someone who has information to impart and can't quite make up his mind to divulge it. Mr. Nankivell, for all his *opéra bouffe* façade, struck Alleyn as being a pretty shrewd fellow.

"This horrible affair," he said, "has taken place at a very regrettable juncture, Superintendent Alleyn. This, sir, is the height of our season. Portcarrow is in the public eye. It has become a desirable resort. We'll have the Press down upon us and the type of information they'll put out will not conduce to the general benefit of our community. A lot of damaging clap-trap is what we may expect from those chaps and we may as well face up to it."

"When does the local paper come out?"

"Tuesday," said the Mayor gloomily. "But they've got their system. Thick as thieves with London—agents, as you might say. They'll have handed it on."

"Yes," Alleyn said. "I expect they will."

"Well, there now!" Mr. Nankivell said, waving his arm. "There yarr! A terrible misfortunate thing to overtake us."

Alleyn said: "Have you formed any opinion yourself, Mr. Mayor?"

"So I have, then. Dozens. And each more objectionable than the last. The stuff that's being circulated already by parties that ought to know better! Now, I understand, sir, and I hope you'll overlook my mentioning it, that Miss Pride is personally known to you."

With a sick feeling of weariness Alleyn said, "Yes. She's an old friend." And before Mr. Nankivell could go any further he added: "I'm aware of the sort of thing that is being said about Miss Pride. I can assure you that, as the case has developed, it is clearly impossible that she could have been involved."

"Is that so? Is that the case?" said Mr. Nankivell. "Glad to hear it, I'm sure." He did not seem profoundly relieved, however. "And then," he said, "there's another view. There's a notion that the one lady was took for the other! Now, there's a very upsetting kind of a fancy to get hold of. When you think of the feeling there's been and them that's subscribed to it."

"Yourself among them?" Alleyn said lightly. "Ridiculous, when you put it like that, isn't it?"

"I should danged well hope it is ridiculous," he said violently and at once produced his own alibi. "Little though I ever thought to be put in the way of making such a demeaning statement," he added angrily. "However. Being a Sunday, Mrs. Nankivell and I did not raise up until nine o'clock and was brought our cup of tea at eight by the girl that does for us. The first I hear of this ghastly affair is at ten-thirty when Mrs. Nankivell and I attended chapel and then it was no more than a lot of chatter about an accident and George Pender, looking very big, by all accounts, and saying he'd nothing to add to the information. When we come out it's all over the village. I should of been informed at the outset but I wasn't. Very bad."

Alleyn did his best to calm him.

"I'm very grateful to you for calling," he said. "I was going to ring up and ask if you could spare me a moment this afternoon but I wouldn't have dreamt of suggesting you took the trouble to come over. I really must apologise."

"No need, I'm sure," said Mr. Nankivell, mollified.

"Now, I wonder, if, in confidence, Mr. Mayor, you can help me at all. You see, I know nothing about Miss Cost and it's always a great help to get some sort of background. For instance, what was she like? She was, I take it, about forty to forty-five years old and, of course, unmarried. Can you add anything to that? A man in your position is usually a very sound judge of character, I've always found."

"Ah!" said the Mayor, smoothing the back of his head. "It's an advantage, of course. Something that grows on you with experience, you might say."

"Exactly. Handling people and getting to know them. Now, between two mere males, how would you sum up Miss Elspeth Cost?"

Mr. Nankivell raised his brows and stared upon vacancy. A slow, knowing smile developed. He wiped it away with his fingers but it crept back.

"A proper old maiden, to be sure," he said.

"Really?"

"Not that she was what you'd call ancient: forty-five, as you rightly judged and a tricksy time of life for females, which is a well-established phenomenon, I believe."

"Yes, indeed. You don't know," Alleyn said cautiously, "what may turn up."

"God's truth, if you never utter another word," said Mr. Nankivell with surprising fervour. He eased back in his chair, caught Alleyn's eye and chuckled. "The trouble I've had along of that lady's crankiness," he confided, "you'd never credit."

Alleyn said "Tch!"

"Ah! With some it takes the form of religious activities. Others go all out for dumb animals. Mrs. Nankivell herself, although a very level-headed lady, worked it off in cats which have in the course of nature simmered down to two. Neuters, both. But with Miss Cost, not to put too fine a point on it, with Miss Cost, it was a matter of her female urges."

"Sex?"

"She spotted it everywhere," Mr. Nankivell exclaimed. "Up hill and down dell, particularly the latter. Did I know what went on in the bay of an evening? Was I aware of the opportunities afforded by open dinghies? Didn't we ought to install more lights along the front? And when it came to the hills round about the Spring she was a tiger. Alf Coombe got it. The Rector got it, the doctor got it and I came in for it, hot and strong, continuous. She was a masterpiece."

Alleyn ventured a sympathetic laugh.

"You may say so, but beyond a joke nevertheless. And that's not the whole story. The truth of the matter is, and I tell you this, sir, in the strictest confidence, the silly female was—dear me, how can I put it?—she was chewed up by the very fury she come down so hard upon. Now, that's a fact and well-known to all and sundry. She was a manhunter, was poor Elspeth Cost. In her quiet, mousy sort of fashion, she raged to and fro seeking whom she might devour. Which was not many."

"Any success?"

The Mayor, to Alleyn's infinite regret, pulled himself up. "Well, now," he said. "That'd be talking. That'd be exceeding, sir."

"I can assure you that if it has no bearing on the case, I shall forget it. I'm sure, Mr. Mayor, you would prefer me to discuss these, quite possibly irrelevant matters with you, rather than make widespread inquiries through the village. We both know, don't we, that local gossip can be disastrously unreliable?"

Mr. Nankivell thought this over. "True as fate," he said at last. "Though I'm in no position myself to speak as to facts and don't fancy giving an impression that may mislead you. I don't fancy that, at all."

This seemed to Alleyn to be an honest scruple and he said warmly: "I think I can promise you that I shan't jump to conclusions."

The Mayor looked at him. "Very good," he said. He appeared to be struck with a sudden thought. "I can tell you this much," he continued with a short laugh. "The Rector handled her with ease, being well-versed in middle-aged maidens. And she had no luck with me and the doctor. Hot after him, she was, and drawing attention and scorn upon herself right and left. But we kept her at bay, poor wretch, and in the end she whipped round against us with as mighty a fury as she'd let loose on the pursuit. Very spiteful. Same with the Major."

"What!" Alleyn ejaculated. "Major Barrimore!"

Mr. Nankivell looked extremely embarrassed. "That remark," he said, "slipped out. All gossip, I daresay, and better forgotten, the whole lot of it. Put about by the Ladies' Guild upon which Mrs. Nankivell sits, *ex officio*, and, as she herself remarked, not to be depended upon."

"But what is it that the Ladies' Guild alleges? That Miss Cost set her bonnet at Major Barrimore and he repelled her advances?"

"Not azackly," said the Mayor. His manner strangely suggested a proper reticence undermined by an urge to communicate something that would startle his hearer.

"Come on, Mr. Mayor," Alleyn said. "Let's have it, whatever it is. Otherwise you'll get me jumping to a most improper conclusion."

"Go on, then," invited Mr. Nankivell, with hardihood, "Jump!"

"You're not going to tell me that Miss Cost is supposed to have had an affair with Major Barrimore?"

"Aren't I? I am, then. And a proper, high-powered, blazing set—to at that. While it lasted," said Mr. Nankivell.

Having taken his final hurdle, Mr. Nankivell galloped freely down the straight. The informant, it appeared, was Miss Cissy Pollock, yesterday's Green Lady and Miss Cost's assistant and confidante. To her, Miss Cost was supposed to have opened her heart. Miss Pollock, in her turn, had retailed the story, under a vow of strictest secrecy, to the girlfriend of her bosom whose mother, a close associate of Mrs. Nankivell, was an unbridled gossip. You might as well, the Mayor said, have handed the whole lot over to the Town Crier and have done with it. The affair was reputed to have been of short duration and to have taken place at the time of Miss Cost's first visit to the Island. There was dark talk of an equivocal nature about visits paid by Major Barrimore, to an unspecified rival in Dunlowman. He was, Mr. Nankivell remarked, a full-blooded man.

With the memory of Miss Cost's face, as Alleyn had seen it that morning made hideous by death, this unlovely story took on a grotesque and appalling character. Mr. Nankivell himself seemed to sense something of this reaction—he became uneasy and Alleyn had to assure him, all over again, that it was most unlikely that the matter would turn out to be relevant and that supposing it was, Mr. Nankivell's name would not appear as everything he had said came under the heading of hearsay and would be inadmissible as evidence. This comforted him and he took his leave with the air of a man who, however distasteful the task, has done his duty.

When he had gone, Alleyn got his notes out again and added a fairly lengthy paragraph. He then lit his pipe and walked over to the window.

It looked down on the causeway, the landing jetty and the roof of Miss Cost's shop. Across the channel, in the village, trippers still dappled the foreshore. There were several boats out in the calm waters and among them, pulling towards the Island, he saw Patrick's dinghy with Jenny Williams in the stern. She sat bolt upright and seemed to be looking anywhere but at her companion. He was rowing with exaggerated vigour, head down and shoulders hunched. Even at that distance, he looked as if he was in a temper. As they approached the jetty, Jenny turned towards him and evidently spoke. He lifted his head, seemed to stare at her and then back-paddled into a clear patch of water and half-shipped his oars. The tide was going out and carried them very slowly towards the point of Fisherman's Bay. They were talking now. Jenny made a quick repressed gesture and shook her head.

"Lovers' quarrel," Alleyn thought. "Damned awkward in a boat. He won't get anywhere, I daresay."

"You won't get anywhere," Jenny was saying in a grand voice, "by sulking."

"I am *not* sulking."

"Then you're giving a superb imitation of it. As the day's been such a failure why don't we pull in and bring it to an inglorious conclusion?"

"All right," he said but made no effort to do so.

"Patrick."

"What?"

"Couldn't you just mention what's upset your applecart? It'd be better than huffing and puffing behind a thundercloud."

"You're not so marvellously forthcoming yourself."

"Well, what am I meant to do? Crash down on my knees in the bilge water and apologise for I don't know what?"

"You do know what."

"Oh, Lord!" Jenny pushed her fingers through her dazzling hair, looked at him and began to giggle. "Isn't this *silly?*" she said.

The shadow of a grin lurked about Patrick's mouth and was suppressed. "Extremely silly," he said. "I apologise for being a figure of fun."

"Look," Jenny said. "Which is it? Me going off with Mr. Alleyn to see Wally? Me being late for our date? Or me going to Dunlowman with Miss Emily tomorrow? Or the lot? Come on."

"You're at perfect liberty to take stewed tea and filthy cream buns with anybody you like for as long as you like. It was evidently all very private and confidential and far be me from it—I mean it from me—to muscle in where I'm not wanted."

"But I *told* you. He asked me not to talk about it."

Patrick inclined, huffily. "So I understand," he said.

"Patrick! I'm sorry, but I do find that I respect Mr. Alleyn. I'm *anti* a lot of things that I suppose you might say he seems to stand for, although I'm not so sure, even, of that. He strikes me as being—well—far from reactionary," said young Jenny.

"I'm sure he's a paragon of enlightenment."

She wondered how it would go if she said: "Let's face it, you're jealous," and very wisely decided against any such gambit. She looked at Patrick: at his shock of black hair, at his arms and the split in his open shirt where the sunburn stopped and at his intelligent, pig-headed face. She thought: "He's a stranger and yet he's so very familiar." She leant forward and put her hand on his bony knee.

"Don't be unhappy," she said. "What is it?"

"Good God!" he said. "Can you put it out of your mind so easily! It's Miss Cost, with her skull cracked. It's Miss Cost, face down in our wonderful Spring. It's your pin-up detective, inching his way into our lives. Do you suppose I enjoy the prospect of—" He stopped short. "I happen," he said, "to be rather attached to my mother."

Jenny said quickly: "Patrick—yes, of course you are. But—"

"You must know damned well what I mean."

"All right. But surely it's beside the point. Mr. Alleyn can't think—"

"Can't he?" His eyes slid away from her. "She was a poisonous woman," he said.

A silence fell between them and suddenly Jenny shivered: unexpectedly as if some invisible hand had shaken her.

"What's the matter?" he said irritably. "Are you cold?"

He looked at her miserably and doubtfully.

Jenny thought: "I don't know him. I'm lost." And at once was caught up in a wave of compassion.

"Don't let's go on snarling," she said. "Let's go home and sort ourselves out. It's clouded over and I'm getting rather cold."

He said: "I don't blame you for wanting to get away from this mess. What a party to have let you in for! It's better you should go to Dunlowman."

"Now *that*," said Jenny, "is really unfair and you know it, darling."

He glowered at her. "You don't say that as a rule. Everyone says 'darling' but you don't."

"That's right. I'm saying it now for a change. Darling."

He covered her hand with his. "I'm sorry," he said. "I am really sorry. Darling Jenny."

From his bedroom window Alleyn watched and thought: "He'll lose his oar."

It slipped through the rowlock. Patrick became active with the other oar. The dinghy bobbed and turned about. They both reached dangerously overboard. Through the open window Alleyn faintly caught the sound of their laughter.

"That's done the trick," he thought. The telephone rang and he answered it.

"Fox here, sir," said a familiar placid voice. "Speaking from Portcarrow station."

"You sound like the breath of spring."

"I didn't quite catch what you said."

"It doesn't matter. Have you brought my homicide kit?"

"Yes."

"Then come, Birdie, come."

Mr. Fox replaced the receiver and said to Superintendent Coombe and the Yard party: "We're to go over. He's worried."

"He sounded as if he was acting the goat or something," said Coombe.

"That's right," said Fox. "Worried. Come on, you chaps."

Detective-Sergeants Bailey and Thompson, carrying their kit, accompanied him to the Island. Coombe showed them the way, saw them off and returned to his office.

They walked in single file over the causeway. Alleyn saw them from his window, picked up his raincoat and went down the steps to meet them. They had attracted a considerable amount of attention.

"Quite a picturesque spot," said Mr. Fox. "Popular, too, by the looks of it. What's the story, Mr. Alleyn?"

"I'll tell you on the way, Br'er Fox."

They had their suitcases with them. Alleyn gave a likely-looking boy five shillings to take them up to the hotel. Numbers of small boys had collected and were shaping up to accompany them. "Move along," said Mr. Fox majestically. "Shove along, now. Right away. Clear out of it."

They backed off.

"You'm Yard men, be'ant you, mister?" said the largest of the boys.

"That's right," Alleyn said. "Push off or we'll be after you."

They broke into peals of derisive but gratified laughter and scattered. One of them started a sort of chant but the others told him to shut up.

Alleyn took his own kit from Fox and suggested that they all walked round the arm of Fisherman's Bay and up by Wally's route to the enclosure. On the way he gave them a résumé of the case.

"Complicated," Mr. Fox remarked when Alleyn had finished. "Quite a puzzle."

"And that's throwing roses at it."

"Which do you favour, Mr. Alleyn? Mistaken identity or dead on the target?"

"I don't want to influence you—not that I flatter myself I can—at the outset. The popular theory with Coombe is the first. To support it this wretched boy says he saw Miss Pride arrive, leave and return. She herself saw *him*. Down on the road we're coming to in a minute. So did Dr. Maine. Now the second figure, of course, must have been Miss Cost, not Miss Pride. But between the departure of Miss Pride and the arrival of Miss Cost, Barrimore went to the gates and chucked away the notice. Who replaced it? The murderer? Presumably. And when did Wally let himself into the enclosure? If he did? It must have been before Miss Cost appeared or she would have seen him. So we've got to suppose that for some reason Wally *did* go in and *did* hide behind the boulder, after Miss Pride had left, and avoiding Barrimore who didn't see him. I don't like it. It may be remotely possible but I don't like it. And I'm certain he wouldn't replace the notice. He hasn't got the gumption. Anyway the timetable barely allows all this."

"He'd hardly mistake the deceased for Miss Pride, silly and all as he may be, if he got anything like a fair look at her."

"Exactly, Br'er Fox. As for the galloping Major: he swims round in an alcoholic trance. Never completely drunk. Hardly ever sober. And reputed, incredibly enough, to have had a brief fling with Miss Cost at about the same time as Wally's warts vanished. He is thought to have proved fickle and to have aroused her classic fury. She also set her bonnet, unsuccessfully, it seems, at the doctor, the Rector and the Mayor. Barrimore's got a most beautiful and alluring wife who is said to be bullied by him. She showed signs of acute distress after she heard the news. She's the original Green

Lady. It's all in the notes—you can have a nice cosy read anytime you fancy."

"Thanks."

"That's Wally's Cottage. We are about to climb Wally's Way and that is Wally's mama, another alcoholic, by the by, leering over the back fence. His father is ferryman at hightide and general showman in between. The whole boiling of them, the Barrimores, the parson, the doctor, the Major, the Treherns, Miss Cost herself, with pretty well everybody else in the community, stood to lose by Miss Pride's operations. Apart from arousing the cornered fury of a hunted male, it's difficult to discover a motive for Miss Cost's murder. Good evening, Mrs. Trehern," Alleyn shouted and lifted his hat.

"Yoo-hoo!" Mrs. Trehern wildly returned, clinging to her back fence. "Lock 'er up. Bloody murderess."

"Who's she mean?" asked Fox.

"Miss Pride."

"Bless my soul! *Quelle galère!*" Fox added, cautiously.

"You must meet Miss Pride, Br'er Fox, she's a top authority on French as she should be spoke."

"Ah!" said Fox, "To be properly taught from the word go! That's the thing. What does she think of the gramophone method?"

"Not much."

"That's what I was afraid of," said Fox with a heavy sigh.

Mrs. Trehern gave a screech, not unlike one of her son's and tacked into the cottage. Alleyn went over to the fence and looked into the back garden. The clothes-line had been removed.

They climbed up Wally's Way to the enclosure. One of Coombe's men was standing a little way along the hotel path.

Alleyn said to Bailey: "The whole area was trampled over when the rain came down. From below, up to the boulder, it's thick broken bracken and you won't get results, I'm afraid. On the shelf above the pool where the deceased was crouched, leaning forward, you'll find her prints superimposed over others. Above that, behind the boulder, is the area where our man, woman or child is thought to have hidden. There's a clear indication of the place where the rock was prised up and signs that some effort was made to scrape out the footprints. All this, on top of the mess left by the crowd. And to add to your joy, Superintendent Coombe and Dr. Maine were up there this morning. Their prints ought to be fairly easy to cut out. The Super was wearing his regulation issue and the doctor's are ripple-soled. Thompson, give us a complete coverage, will you? And we'll need casts, Bailey. Better take them as soon as possible." He looked up at the sky. Heavy clouds were rolling in from the north-west and a fresh wind had sprung up. The sea was no longer calm. "Anyone notice the forecast?"

"Yes," said Fox. "Gales and heavy rain before morning."

"Damn."

He produced Coombe's key for the wire cage which had been locked over the slot machine.

"Notice this, Br'er Fox, would you? It was installed at Miss Cost's insistence to baffle courting couples after dark, and not often used. I think it might be instructive. Only Coombe and The Boy-and-Lobster had keys. You can get out of the enclosure by the other gate, which is on a spring and is self-locking on the inside. You could go in by this turnstile and, if you used a length of string, pull the padlock, on the slack of its chain, round to the netting and lock yourself in."

"Any reason to think it's been done?"

"Only this: there's a fragment of frayed string, caught in the groove of the wire. Get a shot of it, Thompson, will you, before we take possession."

Thompson set up his camera. Alleyn unlocked the cage. He gave each of the others a disc and, in turn, they let themselves in. The shelf and the area above it, round the boulder, had been covered with tarpaulins. "Laid on by Coombe's chaps," Alleyn said. "He's done a good job, never mind his great boots." He stood there for a moment and watched the movement of the welling pool, the sliding lip of water, its glassy fall and perpetual disappearance. Its voices, consulting together, filled the air with their colloquy.

"Well," Alleyn said. "Here you are, Bailey. We'll leave you to it. I'd better have a word with the local P.C.'s. Here are my notes, Fox. Have a look at them for what they're worth."

Mr. Fox drew out his spectacle case and seated himself in the lee of the hillside. Bailey, a man of few words, at once began work and in a minute or two, Thompson joined him. Alleyn returned to the gates and let himself out. He stood with his back to the enclosure where Miss Emily had hung her notice. He looked down Wally's Way to the spot where Wally himself had waved and shouted at her and, beyond that, to the back of the Treherns' cottage and the jetty in Fisherman's Bay. He was very still for a moment. Then he called to Fox who joined him.

"Do you see what I see?" he asked.

Fox placidly related what he saw.

"Thank you," Alleyn said. "Bear it in mind, Br'er Fox, when you digest those notes. I'm going along to that blasted outcrop." He did so and was met by the constable on duty. The wind was now very strong and much colder. Clouds, inky dark and blown ragged at their edges, drove swiftly in from the sea which had turned steely and was whipped into broken corrugations. The pleasure boats, all heading inshore, danced and bucketed as they came. Portcarrow front was deserted and a procession of cars crawled up the road to the downlands. The hotel launch was discharging a load of people for whom a bus waited by the village jetty. "There goes the Major's drink-cheque," thought Alleyn.

"'Evening," he said to the constable. "This doesn't look too promising, does it? What are we in for?"

"A dirty spell, sir, by all tokens. When she bears in sudden and hard like this from the nor'west there's only one way of it. Rain, high seas and a gale."

"Keep the trippers off, at least. Have you had much trouble?"

"A lot of foolish inquiries, sir, and swarms of they nippers from down along."

"Where's your mate? Round the point there?"

"Yes, sir. Nobody's come past the point, though there was plenty that tried. Sick ones and all."

"Anyone you knew?"

"Two of the maids from The Boy-and-Lobster, sir, giggling and screeching after their silly fashion. The Major came. One of his visitors had dropped a ring, they reckoned, behind that rock, and he wanted to search for it. Us two chaps took a look but it warn't thereabouts. We kept off the ground, sir. So did he, though not best pleased to be said by us."

"Good for you. Sergeant Bailey will deal with it in a minute and we'll get some pictures. Did Major Barrimore leave any prints, did you notice?"

"So he did, then, and us reckons they'm the dead spit-identicals for the ones that's there already."

"You use your eyes, I see, in this division. What's your name?"

"Carey, sir."

"I'll come along with you."

They went to the outcrop where Carey's mate, P.C. Pomeroy, kept a chilly watch. Alleyn was shown the Major's footprints where he had pushed forward to the soft verge. He measured them and made a detailed comparison with those behind the outcrop.

"Good as gold," he said. "We'll get casts. You've done well, both of you."

They said, "Thank you, sir," in unison and glanced at each other. Alleyn asked if they could raise another tarpaulin for the area and Pomeroy said he'd go down to Fisherman's Bay and borrow one.

They returned with him to the enclosure and found Fox in argument with James Trehern who was wearing an oilskin coat and looked like a lifeboat hero who had run off the rails. His face was scarlet and his manner both cringing and truculent.

"I left my launch in charge of my mate," he was saying, "to come up yurr and get a fair answer to a fair question which is: What the hell's going on in these parts? I got my good name to stand by, mister, and my good name's being called in question. Now."

Fox, who had his notebook in his palm, said: "We'll just get this good name and your address, if you please, and then find out what seems to be the trouble."

"Well, Mr. Trehern," Alleyn said, "what *is* the trouble?"

Pomeroy gave Trehern a disfavouring look and set off down the road. Trehern pulled at the peak of his cap and adopted a whining tone. "Not to say, sir," he said to Alleyn, "as how I'm out to interfere with the deadly powers of the law. Us be lawful chaps in this locality and never a breath of anything to the contrary has blowed in our direction. Deny that if you've got the face to, Bill Carey!" he added turning on that officer.

"Address yourself," Carey said stuffily, "to them that's axing you. Shall I return to my point, sir?"

"Yes, do, thank you, Carey," Alleyn said and received a salute followed by a smart turn. Carey tramped off along the path.

"Now," Alleyn said to Trehern. "Give Inspector Fox your name and address and we'll hear what you've got to say."

He complied with an ill grace. "I've no call to be took down in writing," he said.

"I thought you were lodging a complaint. Didn't you, Mr. Fox?"

"So I understood, sir. *Are* you?" Fox asked Trehern, and looked placidly at him over the top of his spectacles. "We may as well know, one way or the other, while we're about it."

"Just for the record," Alleyn agreed.

"Not to say a complaint," Trehern temporised. "Don't put words into my mouth, souls. No call for that."

"We wouldn't dream of it," Fox rejoined. "Take your time."

After an uneasy silence, Trehern broke into a long, disjointed plaint. People, he said, were talking. Wally, he inferred, had been taken aside and seduced with icecream. Anybody would tell them that what the poor little lad said was not to be relied upon since he was as innocent as a babe unborn and was only out to please all and sundry, such being his guileless nature. They let him ramble on disconsolately until he ran out of material. Fox took notes throughout.

Alleyn said: "Mr. Trehern, we meant to call on you this evening but you've anticipated us. We want to search your house and have a warrant to do so. If it suits you we'll come down with you, now."

Trehern ran the tip of his tongue round his mouth and looked frightened. "What's that for?" he demanded. "What's wrong with my property? I be'ant got nothing but what's lawful and right and free for all to see."

"In that case you can have no objection."

"It's a matter of principle, see?"

"Quite so."

Trehern was staring through the wire enclosure at the Spring where Bailey and Thompson had begun to pack up their gear. "Yurr!" he said. "What's that! What be they chaps doing up there? Be they looking fur footprints?"

"Yes."

"They won't find our Wal's then! They won't find his'n. Doan't 'ee tell me they will, mister. I know better."

"He was there yesterday."

"Not up to thicky shelf, he warn't. Not up to the top neither."

"How do you know it matters where he may have been? Do you know how Miss Cost was killed?"

Trehern gaped at him.

"Well," Alleyn said, "do you feel inclined to tell us, Mr. Trehern?"

He said confusedly that everyone was talking about stones being thrown.

"Ah," Alleyn said. "You're thinking of the night you encouraged Wally to throw stones at Miss Pride, aren't you?"

Trehern actually ducked his head as if he himself was some sort of target. "What's the lad been telling you?" he demanded. "He's silly. He'll say anything."

Alleyn said: "We'll leave it for the moment and go down to the house."

He called through the gate for Bailey and Thompson to follow and led the way down. Trehern looked at his back and opened and shut his hands.

"Will you move along, Mr. Trehern?" Fox invited him. "After you."

Trehern walked between them down to his cottage.

There were no visitors. The nets were half blown off the fence. The hollyhocks along the front path bent and sprang back in the wind, and the sign rattled.

Trehern stopped inside the gate. "I want to see thick. I want to see the writing."

Alleyn showed him the warrant. He examined it with a great show of caution and then turned to the door.

Alleyn said, "One moment."

"Well? What then?"

"It will save a great deal of time and trouble if you will let us see the thing we're most interested in. Where have you put the clothes-line?"

"I don't have to do nothing," he said, showing the whites of his eyes. "You can't force me."

"Certainly not. It's your choice." He looked at Fox. "Will you take the outhouses? We can go round this way."

He led the way round to the backyard.

Fox said pleasantly: "This'll be the shed where you keep all your gear, won't it? I'll just take a look round, if you please."

It was crammed with a litter of old nets, broken oars, sacking, boxes, tools and a stack of empty gin bottles. Alleyn glanced in and then left it to Fox. There was a hen coop at the far end of the yard with a rubbish heap nearby that looked as if it had been recently disturbed.

"Give me that fork, would you, Fox?" he said and walked down the path with it. Trehern started to follow him and then stood motionless. The first of the rain drove hard on their backs.

The clothesline had been neatly coiled and buried under the rubbish. Alleyn uncovered it in a matter of seconds.

"Shall we get under shelter?" he said and walked back past Trehern to the shed. He wondered, for a moment, if Trehern would strike out at him but he fumbled with his oilskin coat and stayed where he was.

"All right, Fox," Alleyn said. "First time lucky. Here we are."

He gave Fox the coil and took from his pocket the piece of trip-wire from Coombe's office. They held the ends together. "That's it," said Fox.

Alleyn looked at Trehern. "Will you come here for a moment?" he asked.

He thought Trehern was going to refuse. He stood there with his head lowered and gave no sign. Then he came slowly forward, lashed now, by the rain; a black shining figure.

"I am not going to arrest you at this juncture," Alleyn said, "but I think it right to warn you that you are in a serious position. It is quite certain that the wire which, two days ago, was stretched across the way up to the shelf above the Spring, has been cut from this line. Photography and accurate measurements of the strands will prove it. Is there anything you want to say?"

Trehern's jaw worked convulsively as if he were chewing gum. He made a hoarse indeterminate sound in his throat: like a nervous dog, Alleyn thought. At last he said: "Whosumdever done them tricks was having no more than a bit of fun. Boy-fashion. No harm in it."

"You think not?"

"If it was my Wal, I'll have the hide off of him."

"I shouldn't go in for any more violence if I were you, Mr. Trehern. And Wally didn't rig the trip-wire. It was done by a man who knows how to use his hands and it was done with a length of your clothes-line which you've tried to conceal. Will you make a statement about that? You are not compelled to do so. You must use your own judgment."

"A statement! And be took down in writing? Not such a damned fool. Lookie-yurr! What's these silly larks to do with Elspeth Cost? It's her that's laying cold, be'ant it? Not t'other old besom."

"Of course," Alleyn said, swallowing the epithet. After all, he'd thrown one or two himself, at Miss Emily. "So you don't think," he said, "that Miss Cost was mistaken for Miss Pride?"

"I do not, mister. Contrariwise. I reckon one female done it on t'other."

"What were *you* doing at half past seven this morning?"

"Asleep in my bed."

"When did you wake?"

"How do I know when I woke? Hold on, though."

"Yes?"

"Yes, b'God!" Trehern said slowly. "Give a chap time to think, will you? I disremembered but it's come back, like. I heered the lad, banging and hooting about the place. Woke me up, did young Wal, and I hollered out to him to shut his noise. He takes them fits of screeching. Por lil' chap." Trehern added with a belated show of parental concern. "Gawd knows why, but he does. I look at the clock and it's five past eight. I rouse up my old woman which is a masterpiece of a job, she being a mortal heavy slumberer, and tell 'er to wet a pot of tea. Nothing come of it. She sunk back in her beastly oblivyan. So I uprose myself and put the kettle on and took a look at the weather which were mucky."

"Was Wally still in the house?"

"So 'e were, then, singing to hisself after his simple fashion and setting in a corner."

"Did you see anybody about when you looked out-of-doors?"

Trehern peered sidelong at him. He waited for a moment and then said: "I seed the doctor, in 'is launch. Putting out across the gap to go home, he was, having seen Bessy

Trethaway, over the way, yurr, come to light with another in this sinful vale of tears."

"Is your clock right?"

"Good as gold," he said quickly. "Can't go wrong."

"Can I see it?"

He looked as if he might refuse but in the end, lurched into the house, followed by Fox, and returned with a battered alarm clock. Alleyn checked it by his watch.

"Six minutes slow," he said.

Trehern burst out angrily: "I don't have no call for clocks! I'm a seafaring chap and read the time of day off of the face of nature. Sky and tides is good enough for me and my mates in the bay'll bear me out. Six minutes fast or six minutes slow by thicky clock's no matter to me. I looked outer my winder and it wur dead water and dead water come when I said it come and if that there por female was sent to make the best of 'erself before 'er Maker, when I looked outer my winder she died at dead water and that's an end of it."

"Trehern," Alleyn said, "what are you going to make of this? Mrs. Trethaway's baby was born at seven-thirty and Dr. Maine left in his launch about ten minutes later. You're a full half hour out in your times."

There was a long silence.

"Well?" Alleyn said. "Any comment?"

He broke into a stream of oaths and disjointed expostulations. Did they call him a liar? Nobody called Jim Trehern a liar and got away with it. If they weren't going to believe him why did they ask? There was talk against him in the bay. Jealousy seemed to be implied. His anger modulated through resentfulness and fear into his familiar occupational whine. Finally he said that a man could make mistakes, couldn't he? When Alleyn asked if he meant that he'd mistaken the time, Trehern said he didn't want his words taken out of his mouth and used against him. He could scarcely have made a more dubious showing. He was joined briefly by his spouse who emerged from the interior, stood blinking in the back doorway, and was peremptorily ordered back by her husband. Inside the cottage, actors could be heard, galloping about on horses and shouting, "C'm' on. Let's go," to each other. Wally, Alleyn supposed, was enjoying television.

Trehern suddenly bawled out: "You boy! Wal! Come yurr! Come out of it when you're bid!"

Wally shambled into the back porch, saw Alleyn and smiled widely.

"Come on!" his father said and took him by the arm. Wally began to whimper.

"Now then. Tell truth and shame the devil. You been chucking rocks?"

"No. No, I be'ant."

"No, and better not. Speak up and tell these yurr gents. Swear if you hope you won't get half-skinned for a liar as you never chucked no rocks at nobody."

"I never chucked no rocks, only stones," Wally said, trembling. "Like you said to."

"That'll do!" his father said ferociously. "Get in." Wally bolted.

Alleyn said: "You'd better watch your step with that boy. Do you thrash him?"

"Never raise a hand to him, mister. Just a manner of speaking. He don't understand nothing different. Never had no mother-love, poor kid: I have to pour out sufficient for both and a heavy job it is."

"You may find yourself describing it to the welfare officer, one of these days."

"Them bastards!"

"Now, look here, Trehern, you heard what the boy said. 'No rocks, only stones, like you said to.' Hadn't you better make the best of that statement and admit he threw stones at Miss Pride and you knew it. Think it out."

Trehern made a half-turn, knocked his boot against an old tin and kicked it savagely to the far end of the yard. This, apparently, made up his mind for him.

"If I say he done it in one of his foolish turns meaning no harm and acting the goat—all right—I don't deny it and I don't axcuse it. But I do deny and will, and you won't shift me an inch, he never heaved no rock at Elspeth Cost. I'll take my Bible oath on it and may I be struck dead if I lie."

"How can you be so sure? Miss Pride saw the boy in the lane at about twenty to eight. So did Dr. Maine. You weren't there. Or were you?"

"I was not. *By God I was not*, and I'll lay anyone cold that says different. And how can I be so sure?" He advanced upon Alleyn and thrust his face towards him. His unshaven jowls glittered with raindrops. "I'll tell you flat how I can be so sure. That boy never told a lie in his life, mister. He'm too simple. Ax anybody. Ax his teacher. Ax parson. Ax his mates. He'm a truth-speaking lad, por little sod, and for better or worse, the truth's all you'll ever get out of our Wal."

Alleyn heard Jenny Williams's voice: "He's an extraordinarily truthful little boy. He never tells lies—never." He looked at Trehern and said: "All right. We'll let it go at that, for the moment. Good evening to you."

As they walked round the side of the house Trehern shouted after them: "What about the female of the speeches? Pride? Pride has to take a fall, don't she?"

There was a wild scream of laughter from Mrs. Trehern and a door banged.

"That will do to go on with," Alleyn said to Fox, and aped Wally's serial: "C'm. Let's go."

CHAPTER EIGHT

The Shop

THEY FOUND BAILEY and Thompson outside, locked in their mackintoshes with an air of customary usage and with their gear stowed inside waterproof covers. Rain cascaded from their hat brims.

"We'll go back to the pub," Alleyn said. "In a minute."

The Trethaways' cottage was across the lane from the Treherns'. Alleyn knocked at the back door and was invited in by the proud father: an enormous grinning fellow. The latest addition was screaming very lustily in the bedroom. Her father apologised for this drawback to conversation.

"'Er be a lil' maid, 'er be," he said, "and letting fly with 'er vocal powers according."

They stood by the kitchen window which looked up the lane towards the Spring. Seeing this, Alleyn asked him if he'd happened to notice Wally in the lane at about the time the baby was born or soon after and was given the reasonable answer that Mr. Trethaway's attention was on other matters. The baby had indeed been born at seven-thirty and Dr. Maine had in fact left very soon afterwards.

Alleyn congratulated Trethaway, shook his hand, rejoined his colleagues and told them what he'd gleaned.

"So why does Trehern say he saw the doctor leave at about five past eight?" Fox asked. "There's usually only one reason for that sort of lie, isn't there? Trying to rig the time, so that you look as if you couldn't have been on the spot. That's the normal caper."

"So it is then," Alleyn agreed with a reasonable imitation of the local voice. "But there are loose ends here. Or are there?"

"Well yes," Fox said. "In a way."

"Bailey, what did you get? Any fisherman's boots superimposed on the general mess? Or boy's boots? I couldn't find any."

"Nothing like that, Mr. Alleyn. But as you said yourself, this flat slice of stone's been used to cut out recent prints. We've picked up enough to settle that point," Bailey said grudgingly, "not much else. The only nice jobs are the ones left after this morning's rain by a set of regulation tens and another of brogues or gentleman's country shoes, size nine-and-a-half ripple soles and in good repair."

"I know. The Super and the doctor."

"That's right, sir, from what you've mentioned."

"What about the stuff near the outcrop and behind it?"

"What you thought, Mr. Alleyn. They match. Handsewn, officer's type. Ten-and-a-half but custom-made. Worn but well-kept."

"In a sense you might be describing the owner. Did you tell Carey he could go off duty?"

"Yes, sir. There seemed no call for him to stay. We've got all the casts and photographs we want. I used salt in the plaster, seeing how the weather was shaping. It was O.K. Nice results."

"Good. It's getting rougher. Look at that sea."

In the channel between Island and village, the tide now rolled and broke in a confusion of foam and jetting spray. Out at sea there were white horses everywhere. The horizon was dark and broken. The causeway was lashed by breakers that struck, rose, fell across it and withdrew, leaving it momentarily exposed and blackly glinting in what remained of the daylight. The hotel launch bucketed and rolled at the jetty. A man in oilskins was mounting extra fenders. Above the general roar of sea and rain, the thud of the launch's starboard side against the legs of the jetty could be clearly heard.

Light shone dimly behind the windows of Miss Cost's Giffte Shoppe.

"P.C. Pender's locked up in there with Miss Cissy Pollock on the switchboard," Alleyn muttered. "I'll just have a word with him." He tapped on the door. After a moment, it was opened a crack and Mr. Pender said, "Be'ant no manner of use pestering—" and then saw Alleyn. "Beg pardon, sir, I'm sure," he said. "Thought you was one of they damned kids come back." He flung open the door. Alleyn called to Fox and the others and they went in.

The shop smelt fustily of cardboard, wool and gum. In the postal section, Miss Cissy Pollock bulged at a switchboard: all eyes and teeth when she saw the visitors.

Pender said that a call had come through for Alleyn from Dunlowman. "Sir James Curtis, it were, sir," he said with reverence. Curtis was the Home Office pathologist. "Wishful to speak with you. I intercepted the call, sir, and informed the station and The Boy-and-Lobster."

"Where was he?"

"Dunlowman mortuary, sir, along with the body and the doctor. I've got the number."

"Aw, dear!" Miss Pollock exclaimed. "Be'ant it shocking though!" She had removed her headphones.

Alleyn asked if she could put him through. She engaged to do so and directed him to an instrument in a cubbyhole.

The mortuary attendant answered and said Sir James was just leaving but he'd try to catch him. He could be heard pounding off down a concrete passage. In a minute or two the great man spoke.

"Hullo, Rory, where the devil have you been? I've done this job for you. Want the report?"

"Please."

It was straightforward enough. Death by drowning following insensibility caused by a blow on the head. The piece of rock was undoubtedly the instrument. Contents of stomach, Sir James briskly continued, showed that she'd had a cup of tea and a biscuit about an hour and three-quarters before she died. On Dr. Maine's evidence he would agree that she had probably been dead about an hour when Alleyn found her. Sir James had another case more or less on the way back to London and would like to get off before he himself was drowned. Would Alleyn let him know about the inquest? Dr. Maine would tell him anything else he wanted to hear and was now on his way back to Portcarrow. "I'm told you're on an island," said Sir James, merrily. "You'll be likely to stay there if the weather report's to be trusted. What book will you choose if you can only have one?"

"*The Gentle Art of Making Enemies,*" said Alleyn and hung up.

He told Pender that he and Fox would return after dinner and asked him what he himself would do for a meal. Pender said that there was a cut loaf and some butter and ham in Miss Cost's refrigerator, and would it be going too far if he and Cissy made sandwiches? There was also some cheese and pickle. They could, he said, be replaced.

"You can't beat a cheese and pickle sandwich," Fox observed, "if the cheese is tasty."

Alleyn said that under the circumstances he felt Pender might proceed on the lines indicated and left him looking relieved.

They climbed the hotel steps, staggering against the gale, and entered The Boy-and-Lobster. It was now five minutes to eight.

Alleyn asked the reception clerk if he could find rooms for his three colleagues and learnt that the guests had dwindled to thirty. All incoming trains and buses had been met at Dunlowman and intending visitors told about the situation. Accommodation had been organised with various establishments over a distance of fifteen miles and, in view of the weather forecast and the closure of the Spring, most of the travellers had elected, as the clerk put it, to stay away. "We can be cut off," he said, "if it's really bad. It doesn't often happen but if this goes on, it might." The guests in residence had all come by car and were now at dinner.

Alleyn left the others to collect their suitcases and arranged to meet them in the dining-room. He went to his own room, effected a quick change and called on Miss Emily who was four doors away.

She was finishing her dinner. She sat bolt upright, peeling grapes. A flask of red wine was before her and a book was at her elbow with a knife laid across to keep it open. She was perfectly composed.

"I've only looked in for a moment," he said. "We're running late. How are you, Miss Emily? Bored to sobs, I'm afraid."

"Good evening, Roderique. No, I am not unduly bored, though I have missed taking my walk."

"It's no weather for walking, I assure you. How are they treating you?"

"This morning the chambermaid's manner was equivocal and at luncheon I found the waiter impertinent. Tonight, however, there is a marked change. It appears that I am, or was, suspected of murder," said Miss Emily.

"What makes you think so?"

"Before taking my siesta I ventured out on the balcony. There was a group of children on the steps leading to the hotel. When they saw me they began to chant. I will not trouble you with the words. The intention was inescapable."

"Little animals."

"Oh, perfectly. It was of no moment."

There was a tap on the door and a waiter came in.

"Thank you," said Miss Emily. "You may clear."

Alleyn watched the man for a moment and then said: "I'd like a word with you, if you please."

"With me, sir?"

"Yes. I am a Superintendent of Scotland Yard, in charge of investigations into the death of Miss Elspeth Cost. I think perhaps the staff of the hotel should be informed that this lady is associated with me in the case and may be regarded as an expert. Do you understand?"

"Yes, sir. Certainly, sir. I'm sure I hope madam has no complaints, sir."

"I hope so, too. She hasn't made any but I shall do so if any more idiotic nonsense is circulated. You may say so to anybody that is interested."

"Thank you, sir," said the waiter and withdrew.

"*Chose remarquable!*" said Miss Emily. "So now, it appears I am a detectrice."

"It'll be all over the hotel in five minutes and Portcarrow will have it by morning. About your transport to Dunlowman—"

"Do not trouble yourself. The young man—Patrick— has offered to drive us," Miss Emily said with an air of amusement.

"I see. It may be pretty rough going across to the village, if this weather persists."

"No matter."

"Before I go, would you mind very much if we went over one incident: the few minutes, round about twenty to eight, when you hung your notice by the Spring?"

"Certainly," Miss Emily said. She repeated her story. She had seen Wally down on the road. He had whooped, chanted, waved his arms and afterwards disappeared. She had seen nobody else and had returned to the hotel with her umbrella between herself and the prospect.

"Yes," he said. "I know. I just wanted to hear it again. Thank you, Miss Emily. You don't ask me how the case progresses, I notice."

"You would tell me, no doubt, if you wished to do so."

"Well," he said. "I always think it's unlucky to talk at this stage, but it does progress."

"Good. Go and have your dinner. If you are not too fatigued I should be glad if you would call upon me later in the evening."

"When do you retire?"

"Not early. I find I am restless," said Miss Emily.

They fell silent. The wind made a sudden onslaught on her windows. "Perhaps it is the storm," she said.

"I'll see if there's a light under your door. *Au revoir*, then, Miss Emily."

"*Au revoir*, my dear Roderique. Enjoy, if that is not too extravagant a word, your dinner. The dressed crab is not bad. The *filet mignon*, on the other hand, is contemptible."

She waved her hand and he left her.

Fox, Bailey and Thompson were already in the dining-room. Alleyn had been given a table to himself. As there was not room at theirs, he took it, but joined them for a minute or two before he did so.

Everyone else had gone except Jenny and Patrick who sat at the family table, nursing balloon glasses. They had an air of subdued celebration and as often as they looked at each other, broke into smiles. When Jenny saw Alleyn, she waggled her fingers at him.

Alleyn said: "Afraid it's a case of pressing on, chaps. We'll meet in the hall, afterwards, and go down to the shop. Have you ordered drinks?"

"Not so far, Mr. Alleyn."

"Well, have them with me. What shall it be? Waiter!"

They settled for beer. Alleyn went to his own table and was fawned upon by Miss Emily's waiter. Jenny and Patrick passed by and Jenny paused to say: "We're going to try and whip up a bit of *joie de vivre* in the lounge, like they do in ships. Patrick's thought up a guessing game. Come and help."

"I'd love to," Alleyn said, "but I'm on a guessing game of my own, bad luck to it." He looked at Patrick. "I hear you've offered to do the driving tomorrow. Very civil of you. Miss Emily's looking forward to it."

"It's going to be a rough crossing if this keeps up."

"I know,"

"Will she mind?"

"Not she. At the age of sixty, she was a queen-pin in the *Résistance* and hasn't noticed the passage of time. Get her to tell you how she dressed up a couple of kiwis as nuns."

"Honestly!" Jenny exclaimed.

"It's quite a story."

The waiter came up to say that Dr. Maine had arrived and was asking for him.

"Right," Alleyn said. "I'll come."

"In the writing-room, sir."

It was a small deserted place off the entrance hall. Dr. Maine had removed his mackintosh and hung it over the back of a chair. He was shaking the rain off his hat when Alleyn came in. "What a night!" he said. "I thought I wouldn't make it."

"How did you cross?"

"In my launch. Damned if I know how she'll take it going back. The causeway's impossible. Sir James thought you'd like to see me and I had to come over, anyway, to a patient."

Alleyn said: "I'm glad to see you. Not so much about the P.M.! Curtis made that clear enough. I wanted to check up one or two points. Have a drink, won't you?"

"I certainly will. Thank you."

Alleyn found a bell-push. "I hope you won't mind if I don't join you," he said. "I've had my allowance and I've got a night's work ahead of me."

"I suppose you get used to it—like a G.P."

"Very much so, I imagine. What'll you have?"

Dr. Maine had a whisky and soda. "I thought I'd take a look at Miss Pride while I'm here," he said. "She's recovered, of course, but she had quite a nasty cut in her neck. I suppose I mustn't ask about the police view of that episode. Or doesn't it arise?"

"I don't see why you shouldn't. It arises in a sort of secondary way, if only to be dismissed. What do you think?"

"On the face of it, Wally Trehern. Inspired by his father, I daresay. It's Miss Pride's contention and I think she may well be right."

"I think so, too. Does it tie up with the general pattern of behaviour—from your point of view?"

"Oh, yes. Very characteristic. He gets overexcited and wildish. Sometimes this sort of behaviour is followed up by an attack of *petit mal*. Not always, but it's quite often the pattern."

"Can't anything be done for the boy?"

"Not much, I'm afraid. When they start these attacks in early childhood, it's a poorish prospect. He should lead a quiet, regular life. It may well be that his home background, and all the nonsense of producing him as a showpiece, is bad for him. I'm not at all sure," Dr. Maine said, "that I shouldn't have taken his case up with the child-welfare people but there's been no marked deterioration and I've hesitated. Now, well—now, one wonders."

"One wonders—*what* exactly?"

"(A), if he shouldn't, in any case, be removed to a suitable institution and (B), whether he's responsible for heaving that rock at Miss Cost."

"If he did heave it, it must have been about half an hour after you saw him doing his stuff on Wally's Way."

"I know. Sir James puts the death at about eight o'clock, give and take twenty minutes. I wish I'd watched the boy more closely but of course there was no reason to do so. I was swinging the launch round."

"And it *was* about seven-forty, wasn't it?"

"About that, yes. Within a couple of minutes, I should say."

"You didn't happen to notice Miss Pride? She was in the offing too, and saw Wally."

"*Was* she, by George! No, I didn't see her. The top of the wheel-house would cut off my view, I fancy."

"What *exactly* was Wally doing? Sorry to nag on about it, but Miss Pride may have missed some little pointer. We need one badly enough, Lord knows."

"He was jumping about with his back towards me. He waved his arms and did a sort of throwing gesture. Now that you tell me Miss Pride *was* up by the gates, I should think his antics were directed at her. I seem to remember that the last thing I saw him do was to take a run uphill. But it was all quite momentary, you know."

"His father says Wally was in the house at five past eight."

Dr. Maine considered this. "It would still be possible," he said. "There's time, isn't there?"

"On the face of it—yes. Trehern also says that at five past eight or soon afterwards, he saw you leave in your launch."

"Does he, indeed! He lies like a flat-fish," said Dr. Maine. He looked thoughtfully at Alleyn. "Now, I wonder just why," he said thoughtfully. "I wonder."

"So do I, I assure you." They stared meditatively at each other. Alleyn said: "Who do you think was the original Green Lady?"

Dr. Maine was normally of a sallow complexion but now a painful red blotted his lean face and transfigured it. "I have never considered the matter," he said. "I have no idea. It's always been supposed that he imagined the whole thing."

"It was Mrs. Barrimore."

"You can have no imaginable reason for thinking so," he said angrily.

"I've the best possible reason," said Alleyn. "Believe me. Every possible reason."

"Do you mean that Mrs. Barrimore herself told you this?"

"Virtually, yes. I am not," Alleyn said, "trying to equivocate. I asked her and she said she supposed she must congratulate me."

Dr. Maine put his glass down and walked about the room with his hands in his pockets. Alleyn thought he was giving himself time. Presently he said: "I can't, for the life of me, make out why you concern yourself with this. Surely it's quite beside the point."

"I do so because I don't understand it. Or am not sure that I understand it. If it turns out to be irrelevant I shall make no more of it. What I don't understand, to be precise, is why Mrs. Barrimore should be so distressed at the discovery."

"But, good God, man, of course she's distressed! Look here. Suppose—I admit nothing—but suppose she came across that wretched kid, blubbing his eyes out because he'd been baited about his warts. Suppose she saw him trying to wash them off and on the spur of the moment, remembering the history of wart-cures, she made him believe they would clear up if he thought they would. Very well. The boy goes home and they do. Before we know—she knows—where she is, the whole thing blows up into a highly publicised nine-days-wonder. She can't make up her mind to disabuse the boy or disillusion the people that follow him. It gets out of hand. The longer she hesitates, the harder it gets."

"Yes," Alleyn said. "I know. That all makes sense and is perfectly understandable."

"Very well, then!" he said impatiently.

"She was overwhelmingly anxious that I shouldn't tell her husband."

"I daresay," Dr. Maine said shortly. "He's not a suitable subject for confidences."

"Did she tell you? All right," Alleyn said, answering the extremely dark look Dr. Maine gave him. "I know I'm being impertinent. I've got to be."

"I am her doctor. She consulted me about it. I advised her to say nothing."

"Yes?"

"The thing was working. Off and on; as always happens in these emotional—these faith-cures, if you like—there are authentic cases. With people whose troubles had a nervous connotation, the publicising of this perfectly innocent deception would have been harmful."

"Asthma, for one?"

"Possibly."

"Miss Cost, for instance?"

"If you like."

"Was Miss Cost a patient of yours?"

"She was. She had moles that needed attention; she came into my nursing home and I removed them. About a year ago, it would be."

"I wish you'd tell me what she was like."

"Look here, Alleyn, I really do not see that the accident of my being called out to examine the body requires me to disregard my professional obligations. I do not discuss my patients, alive or dead, with any layman."

Alleyn said mildly: "His Worship the Mayor seems to think she was a near-nymphomaniac."

Dr. Maine snorted.

"Well, was she?"

"All right. All right. She was a bloody nuisance, like many another frustrated spinster. Will that do?"

"Nicely, thank you. Do you imagine she ever suspected the truth about the Green Lady?"

"I have not the remotest idea but I should think it most unlikely. She, of all people! Look at that damn' farce of a show yesterday. Look at her shop! Green Ladies by the gross. If you want my opinion on the case which I don't suppose you do—"

"On the contrary I was going to ask for it."

"Then, I think the boy did it, and I hope that, for his sake, it will go no further than finding that he's irresponsible and chucked the rock aimlessly or at least with no idea of the actual damage it would do. He can then be removed from his parents, who are no good to him anyway, and given proper care and attention. If I'm asked for an opinion at the inquest that will be it."

"Tidy. Straightforward. Obvious."

"And you don't believe it?"

"I would like to believe it," said Alleyn.

"I need hardly say I'd be interested to know your objections."

"You may say they're more or less mechanical. No," Alleyn said, correcting himself. "That's not quite it, either. We'll just have to press on and see how we go. And press on I must, by the same token. My chaps'll be waiting for me."

"You're going out?"

"Yes. Routine, you know. Routine."

"You'll be half-drowned."

"It's not far. Only to the shop. By the way, did you know we're moving Miss Pride in the morning? She's going to the Manor Park Hotel outside Dunlowman."

"But why? Isn't she comfortable here?"

"It's not particularly comfortable to be suspected of homicide."

"But—oh, good *Lord!*" he exclaimed disgustedly.

"The village louts shout doggerel at her and the servants have been unpleasant. I don't want her to be subjected to any more Portcarrow humour in the form of practical jokes."

"There's no chance of that, surely. Or don't you think Miss Cost inspired that lot?"

"I think she inspired them, all right, but they might be continued in her permanent absence; the habit having been formed and Miss Pride's unpopularity having increased."

"Absolute idiocy!" he said angrily.

"I think, as a matter of fact, I've probably stopped the rot but it's better for her to get away from the place."

"You know, I very much doubt if the channel will be negotiable in the morning. This looks like being the worst storm we've had for years. In any case it'll be devilishly awkward getting her aboard the launch. We don't want a broken leg."

"Of course not. We'll simply have to wait and see what the day brings forth. If you're going to visit her, you might warn her about the possibility, will you?"

"Yes, certainly."

They were silent for a moment. A sudden onslaught of the gale beat against The Boy-and-Lobster and screamed in the chimney. "Well, good night," Alleyn said.

He had got as far as the door when Dr. Maine said: "There *is* one thing you perhaps ought to know about Elspeth Cost."

"Yes?"

"She lived in a world of fantasy. Again, with women of her temperament, condition and age, it's a not unusual state of affairs, but with her its manifestations were extreme."

"Was she in consequence a liar?"

"Oh, yes," he said. "It follows on the condition. You may say she couldn't help it."

"Thank you for telling me," Alleyn said.

"It may not arise."

"You never know. Good night, then, Maine."

When they were outside and the hotel doors had shut behind them, they were engulfed in a world of turbulence: a complex uproar into which they moved, leaning forward, with their heads down. They slipped on concrete steps, bumped into each other and then hung on by an iron rail and moved down crabwise towards the sea. Below them, riding-lights on the hotel launch tipped, rose, sank and shuddered. A single street lamp near the jetty was struck across by continuous diagonals of rain. On the far side, black masses heaved and broke against the front, obscured and revealed dimly lit windows and flung their crests high above the glittering terrace. As the three men came to the foot of the steps they were stung and lashed by driven spume.

Miss Cost's shop window glowed faintly beyond the rain. When they reached it they had to bang on the door and yell at Pender before he heard them above the general clamour. It opened a crack. "Easy on, souls," Pender shouted, "or she'll blow in." He admitted them, one by one, with his shoulder to the door.

The interior fug had become enriched by a paraffin heater that reeked in Miss Cissy Pollock's corner and by Pender who breathed out pickled onions. Miss Pollock, herself a little bleary-eyed now, but ever-smiling, still presided at the switchboard.

"Wicked night," Pender observed, bolting the door.

"You must be pretty well fed up, both of you," Alleyn said.

"No, sir, no. We be tolerably clever, thank you. Cissy showed me how her switchboard works. A simple enough matter to the male intelligence, it turned out to be, and I took a turn at it while she had a nap. She come back like a lion refreshed and I followed her example. Matter of fact, sir, I was still dozing when you hammered at the door, wasn't I, Ciss? She can't hear with they contraptions on her head. A simple pattern of a female, she is, sir, as you'll find out for yourself, if you see fit to interrogate her, but rather pleased than otherwise to remain." He beamed upon Miss Pollock who giggled.

Fox gravely contemplated Sergeant Pender. He was a stickler for procedure.

Alleyn introduced Pender to his colleagues. They took off their coats and hats and he laid down a plan of action. They were to make a systematic examination of the premises.

"We're not looking for anything specific," he said. "I'd like to find out how she stood, financially. Correspondence, if any. It would be lovely if she kept a diary and if there's a dump of old newspapers, they'll have to be gone over carefully. Look for any cuts. Bailey, you'd better pick up a decent set of prints if you can find them. Cashbox—tooth-glass—she had false teeth—take your pick. Thompson, will you handle the shelves in here? You might work the back premises and the bedroom, Fox. I'll start on the parlour."

He approached Cissy Pollock who removed her headphones and simpered.

"You must have known Miss Cost very well," he began. "How long have you been here with her, Miss Pollock?"

A matter of a year and up, it appeared. Ever since the shop was made a post office. Miss Cost had sold her former establishment at Dunlowman and had converted a cottage into the premises as they now stood. She had arranged for a wholesale firm to provide the Green Ladies, which she herself painted, and for a regional printer to reproduce the rhyme-sheets. Cissy talked quite readily of these activities and Miss Cost emerged from her narrative as an experienced businesswoman. "She were proper sharp," Cissy said appreciatively. When Alleyn spoke of yesterday's Festival she relapsed briefly into giggles but this seemed to be a token manifestation, obligatory upon the star performer. Miss Cost had inaugurated a Drama Circle of which the Festival had been the first fruit and Cissy herself, the leading light. He edged cautiously towards the less public aspects of Miss Cost's life and character. Had she many close friends? None that Cissy knew of, though she did send Christmas cards. She hardly got any herself, outside local ones.

"So you were her best friend, then?"

"Aw well," said Cissy and shuffled her feet.

"What about gentlemen friends?"

This produced a renewed attack of giggles. After a great deal of trouble he elicited the now familiar story of advance and frustration. Miss Cost had warned Cissy repeatedly of the gentlemen and had evidently dropped a good many dark hints about improper overtures made to herself. Cissy was not pretty and was no longer very young. He thought that, between them, they had probably indulged in continuous fantasy and the idea rather appalled him. On Major Barrimore's name being introduced in a roundabout fashion, she became uncomfortable and said, under pressure, that Miss Cost was proper set against him, and that he'd treated her bad. She would say nothing more under this heading. She remembered Miss Cost's visit to the hospital. It appeared that she had tried the Spring for her moles but without success. Alleyn ventured to ask if Miss Cost liked Dr. Maine. Cissy, with a sudden burst of candour, said she fair worshipped him.

"Ah!" said Sergeant Pender who had listened to all this with the liveliest attention. "So, she did then, and hunted the poor chap merciless, didn't she, Ciss?"

"Aw, you do be awful, George Pender," said Cissy, with spirit.

"Couldn't help herself, no doubt, and not to be blamed for it," he conceded.

Alleyn again asked Cissy if Miss Cost had any close women friends. Mrs. Carstairs? Or Mrs. Barrimore, for instance?

Cissy made a prim face that was also, in some indefinable way, furtive. "She weren't terrible struck on Mrs. Barrimore," she said. "She didn't hold with her."

"Oh? Why was that, do you suppose?"

"She reckoned she were sly," said Cissy and was not to be drawn any further.

"Did Miss Cost keep a diary, do you know?" Alleyn asked, and as Cissy looked blank, he added, "A book. A record of day-to-day happenings?"

Cissy said Miss Cost was always writing in a book of an evening but kept it away careful-like, she didn't know where. Asked if she had noticed any change in Miss Cost's behaviour over the last three weeks, Cissy gaped at Alleyn for a second or two and then said Miss Cost had been kind of funny.

"In what way, funny?"

"Laughing," said Cissy. "She took fits to laugh, sudden-like. I never see nothing to make her."

"As if she was—what? Amused? Excited?"

"Axcited. Powerful pleased too. Sly-like."

"Did you happen to notice if she sent any letters to London?"

Miss Cost had on several occasions put her own letters in the mailbag but Cissy hadn't got a look at them. Evidently, Alleyn decided, Miss Cost's manner had intrigued her assistant. It was on these occasions that Miss Cost laughed.

At this juncture, Cissy was required at the switchboard. Alleyn asked Pender to follow him into the back room. He shut the door and said he thought the time had come for Miss Pollock to return to her home. She lived on the Island, it appeared, in one of the Fisherman's Bay cottages. Alleyn suggested that Pender had better see her to her door as the storm was so bad. They could be shown how to work the switchboard during his absence.

When they had gone, Alleyn retired to the parlour and began operations upon Miss Cost's desk which, on first inspection, appeared to be a monument to the dimmest kind of disorder. Bills, dockets, trade-leaflets and business communications were jumbled together in ill-running drawers and overcrowded pigeonholes. He sorted them into heaps and secured them with rubber bands.

He called out to Fox, who was in the kitchen: "As far as I can make out she was doing very nicely indeed, thank you. There's a crack-pot sort of day-book. No outstanding debts and an extremely healthy bank statement. We'll get at her financial position through the income-tax people, of course. What've you got?"

"Nothing to rave about," Fox said.

"Newspapers?"

"Not yet. It's a coal range, though."

"Damn."

They worked on in silence. Bailey reported a good set of impressions from a tumbler by the bed and Thompson, relieved of the switchboard, photographed them. Fox put on his mackintosh and retired with a torch to an outhouse, admitting, briefly, the cold and uproar of the storm. After an interval he returned, bland with success, and bearing a coal-grimed, wet, crumpled and scorched fragment of newsprint.

"This might be something," he said and laid it out for Alleyn's inspection.

It was part of a sheet from the local paper from which a narrow strip had been cleanly excised. The remainder of a headline read: "—to Well-known Beauty Spot" and underneath: "The Natural Amenities Association. At a meeting held at Dunlowman on Wednesday it was resolved to lodge a protest at the threat to Hatcherds Common where it is proposed to build—" "That's it, I'm sure," Alleyn said. "Same type. The original messages are in my desk, blast it, but one of them reads 'Threat' (in these capitals), 'to close You are warned': a good enough indication that she was responsible. Any more?"

"No. This was in the ash-bin. Fallen into the grate, most likely, when she burnt the lot. I don't think there's anything else but I'll take another look by daylight. She's got a bit of a darkroom rigged up out there. Quite well-equipped, too, by the look of it."

"Has she now? Like to take a slant at it, Thompson?"

Thompson went out and presently returned to say it was indeed a handy little job of a place and he wouldn't mind using it. "I've got that stuff we shot up at the Spring," he said. "How about it, sir?"

"I don't see why not. Away you go. Good. Fox, you might penetrate to the bedchamber. I can't find her blasted diary anywhere."

Fox retired to the bedroom. Pender came back and said it was rougher than ever out-of-doors and he didn't see himself getting back to the village. Would it be all right if he spent the rest of the night on Miss Cost's bed? "When vacant, in a manner of speaking," he added, being aware of Fox's activities. He emerged from a pitchpine wardrobe, obviously scandalised by Sergeant Pender's unconventional approach, but Alleyn said he saw nothing against the suggestion and set Pender to tend the switchboard and help Thompson.

He returned to his own job. The parlour was a sort of unfinished echo of the front shop. Rows of plastic ladies, awaiting coats of green, yellow and pink paint, smirked blankly from the shelves. There were stacks of rhyme-sheets and stationery and piles of jerkins, still to be sewn up the sides. Through the open door he could see the kitchen table with a jug and sugar-basin and a dirty cup with a sodden crust in its saucer. Miss Cost would have washed them up, no doubt, if she had returned from early service and not gone walking through the rain to her death.

In a large envelope he came across a number of photographs. A group of village maidens, Cissy prominent among them, with their arms upraised in what was clearly intended for corybantic ecstasy. Wally, showing his hands. Wally with his mouth open. Miss Cost herself, in a looking-glass with her thumb on the camera trigger and smiling dreadfully. Several snapshots, obviously taken in the grounds of the nursing home, with Dr. Maine caught in moments of reluctance shading into irritation. Views of the Spring and one of a dark foreign-looking lady with an intense expression.

He heard Fox pull a heavy piece of furniture across the wooden floor and then give an ejaculation.

"Anything?" Alleyn asked.

"Might be. Behind the bed-head. A locked cupboard. Solid, mortise job. Now, where'd she have stowed the key?"

"Not in her bag. Where do spinsters hide keys?"

"I'll try the chest of drawers for a start," said Fox.

"You jolly well do. A favourite cache. Association of ideas. Freud would have something to say about it."

Drawers were wrenched open, one after another.

"By gum!" Fox presently exclaimed. "You're right, Mr. Alleyn. Two keys. Here we are."

"Where?"

"Wrapped up in her combs."

"In the absence of a chastity belt, no doubt."

"What's that, Mr. Alleyn?"

"No matter. Either of them fit?"

"Hold on. The thing's down by the skirting board. Yes. Yes, I do believe—here we are."

A lock clicked.

"Well?"

"Two cash boxes, so far," Fox said, his voice strangely muffled.

Alleyn walked into the bedroom and was confronted by his colleague's stern, up-ended beneath an illuminated legend which read:

"Jog on, jog on the footpath way
And merrily hent the stile-a."

This was supported by a bookshelf on which the works of Algernon Blackwood and Dennis Wheatley predominated.

Fox was on his knees with his head to the floor and his arm in a cupboard. He extracted two japanned boxes and put them on the unmade bed, across which lay a rumpled night-gown embroidered with lazy daisies.

"The small key's the job for both," he said. "There you are, sir."

The first box contained rolled bundles of banknotes and a well-filled cashbag; the second, a number of papers. Alleyn began to examine them. The top sheet was a carbon copy with a perforated edge. It showed, in type, a list of dates and times covering the past twelve months:

The Spring.
15th August   8:15 p.m.
21st   "   8:20 "
29th   "   8:30 "

There were twenty entries. Two, placed apart from the others, and dated the preceding year, were heavily underlined. "22nd July, 5 p.m." and "30th September, 8.45."

"From a duplicating book in her desk," Alleyn said, "a page has been cut out. It'll be the top copy of this one."

"Typewritten," Fox commented.

"There's a decrepit machine in the parlour. We'll check but I think this'll be it."

"Do the dates mean anything to you, Mr. Alleyn?"

"The underlined item does. Year before last. July 22nd, 5 p.m. That's the date and time of the Wally's Warts affair. Yesterday was the second anniversary."

"Would the others be notes of later cures? Was any record kept?"

"Not to begin with. There is now. The book's on view at Wally's Cottage. We can check, but I don't think that's the answer. The dates are too closely bunched. They give—let's see; they give three entries for August of last year, one for September, and then nothing until 27th April of this year. Then a regular sequence over the last three months up to—yes, by George!—up to a fortnight ago. What do you make of it, Br'er Fox? Any ideas?"

"Only that they're all within licensing hours. Very nice bitter, they serve up at The Boy-and-Lobster. It wouldn't go down too badly. Warm in here, isn't it?"

Alleyn looked thoughtfully at him. "You're perfectly right," he said. He went into the shop. " Pender," he called out, "who's the bartender in the evenings at The Boy-and-Lobster?"

"In the old days, sir, it were always the Major hisself. Since these yurr princely extensions, however, there be a barmaid in the main premises and the Major serves in a little wee fancy kind of a place behind the lounge."

"Always?"

"When he'm capable," said Pender dryly, "which is pretty well always. He'm a masterpiece for holding his liquor."

Pender returned to the shop. "There's one other thing," Alleyn said to Fox. "The actual times she's got here grow later as the days grow longer."

"So they do," Fox said. "That's right. So they do."

"Well, let it simmer. What's next? Exhibit two."

It was an envelope containing an exposed piece of film and a single print. Alleyn was about to lay the print on Miss Cost's pillow. This bore the impress of her head and a single grey hair. He looked at it briefly, turned aside, and dropped the print on her dressing-table. Fox joined him.

It was a dull, indifferent snapshot: a tangle of bracken, a downward slope of broken ground and the top of a large boulder. In the foreground out of focus was the image of wire-netting.

"Above the Spring," Alleyn said. "Taken from the hillside. Look here, Fox."

Fox adjusted his spectacles. "Feet," he said. "Two pairs. Courting couple."

"Very much so. Miss Cost's anathema. I'm afraid Miss Cost begins to emerge as a progressively unattractive character."

"Shutter-peeping," said Fox. "You don't get it so often among women."

Alleyn turned it over. Neatly written across the back was the current year and "17th June. 7:30 p.m."

"Last month," Alleyn said. "Bailey!" he called out. "Here, a minute, would you?" Bailey came in. "Take a look at this. Use a lens. I want you to tell me if you think the man's shoes in this shot might tally with anything you saw at the Spring. It's a tall order, I know."

Bailey put the snapshot under a lamp and bent over it. Presently he said: "Can I have a word with Thompson, sir?" Sergeant Thompson was summoned from outer darkness. "How would this blow up?" Bailey asked him. "Here's the neg."

"It's a shocking neg," Thompson said, and added grudgingly, "she's got an enlarger."

Alleyn said: "On the face of it, do you think there's any hope of a correspondence, Bailey?"

Bailey, still using his lens, said: "Can't really say, sir. The casts are in my room at the pub."

"What about you, Thompson? Got your shots of the prints?"

"They're in the dish now."

"Well, take this out and see what you make of it. Have you found her camera?"

"Yes. Lovely job," Thompson said. "You wouldn't have expected it. Very fast." He named the make with reverence.

"Pender," Alleyn said, re-entering the shop. "Do you know anything about Miss Cost's camera?"

Pender shook his head and then did what actors call a double-take. "Yes, I do, though," he said. "It was give her in gratitude by a foreign lady that was cured of a terrible bad rash. She was a patient up to hospital and Miss Cost talked her into the Spring."

"I see. Thompson, would it get results round about seven-thirty on a summer evening?"

"Certainly would. Better than this affair, if properly handled."

"All right. See what you can do."

Bailey and Thompson went away and Alleyn rejoined Fox in the bedroom.

"Fox," Alleyn said distastefully, "I don't know whose feet the male pair may prove to be but I'm damn' sure I've recognised the female's."

"Really, Mr. Alleyn?"

"Yes. Very good buckskin shoes with very good buckles. She wore them to the Festival. I'm afraid it's Mrs. Barrimore."

"Fancy!" said Fox, after a pause, and he added with his air of simplicity: "Well, then, it's to be hoped the others turn out to be the Major's."

❀ ❀ ❀

There were no other papers and no diary in either of the boxes.

"Did you reach to the end of the cupboard?" Alleyn asked Fox.

"No, I didn't. It's uncommonly deep. Extends through the wall and under the counter in the shop," Fox grumbled.

"Let me try."

Alleyn lay on the bedroom floor and reached his long arm into the cupboard. His fingers touched something—a book. "She must have used her brolly to fish it out," he grunted. "Hold on. There are two of them—no, three. Here they come: I think—yes. Yes. Br'er Fox. This is *it*."

They were large commercial diaries and were held together with a rubber band. He took them into the parlour and laid them out on Miss Cost's desk. When he opened the first he found page after page covered in Miss Cost's small skeleton handwriting. He read an entry at random:

"...sweet spot, so quaint and *unspoilt*. Sure I shall like it. One feels the *tug* of earth and sea. The 'pub' (!) is *really* genuine and goes back to smuggling days. Kept by a *gentleman*.

Major B. I take my noggin 'of an evening' in the taproom and listen to the wonderful 'burr' in the talk of the fisherfolk. All v. friendly... Major B. kept looking at me. 'I know your sort,' sez I. Nothing to object to, *really*. Just an awareness. The wife is rather peculiar: I am not altogether taken. A *man's* woman in every sense of the word, I'm afraid. He doesn't pay her v. much attention."

Alleyn read on for a minute or two. "It would take a day to get through it," he said. "This is her first visit to the Island. Two years ago."

"Interesting?"

"Excruciating. Where's that list of dates?"

Fox put it on the desk.

Alleyn turned the pages of the diary. References to Major B., later K., though veiled in unbelievable euphemisms, became more and more explicit. In this respect alone, Alleyn thought, the gallant Major had a lot to answer for. He turned back to the entry for the day after Wally's cure. It was ecstatic.

"I have always," wrote Miss Cost, "believed in fairies. The old magic of water and the spoken rune! The Green Lady! He *saw* her, this little lad *saw* her and obeyed her behest. Something *led* me to this Island." She ran on in this vein for the whole of the entry. Alleyn read it with a sensation of exasperated compassion. The entry itself was nothing to his purpose. But across it, heavily inked, Miss Cost on some later occasion had put down an enormous mark of interrogation and, besides this, had added a note: "30th Sept. 8:45."

This was the second of the two underlined dates on the paper. He turned it up in the diary.

"I am shocked and horrified and *sickened* by what I have seen this evening. My hand shakes. I can hardly bring myself to write it down. I *knew*, from the moment I first set eyes on her, that she was unworthy of him. One *always* knows. Shall not tell K. It would serve him right if I did. All these months and he never guessed. But I won't tell him. Not yet. Not unless— But I must *write* it. Only so can I rid myself of the horror. I was sitting on the hill below the Spring, thinking so happily of all my plans and so glad I have settled for the shop and ordered my lovely Green Ladies. I was *feeling* the magic of the water. (Blessed, blessed water. *No* asthma, now, for *four* weeks.) And then I heard them. Behind the boulder, laughing. I shrank down in the bracken. And then *she* came out from behind the boulder in her green dress and stood above the pool. She raised her arms. I could hear the man laughing still but I couldn't see him. I *knew*. I *knew*. The wicked desecration of it! But I won't believe it. I'll put it out of my mind forever. She was mocking— pretending. I *won't* think anything else. She went back to him. I waited. And then, suddenly, I couldn't bear it any longer. I came back here…"

Alleyn, looking increasingly grim, went over the entries for the whole list; throughout two summers, Miss Cost had hunted her evening quarry with obsessive devotion and had recorded the fruits of the chase as if in some antic game-book—time, place and circumstances. On each occasion that she spied upon her victims, she had found the enclosure padlocked and had taken up a point of vantage on the hillside. At no stage did she give the names of the lovers but their identity was inescapable. "Mrs. Barrimore and Dr. Maine," Alleyn said. "To hell with this case!"

"Awkward," observed Fox.

"My dear old Fox, it's dynamite. And it fits," Alleyn said, staring disconsolately at his colleague. "The devil of it is, it fits."

He began to read the entries for the past month. Dr. Maine, Miss Cost weirdly concluded, was not to blame. He was a victim, caught in the toils, unable to free himself and there- fore unable to follow his nobler inclination towards Miss Cost herself. Interlarded with furious attacks upon Miss Emily and covert allusions to the anonymous messages, were notes on the Festival, a savage comment on Miss Emily's visit to the shop and a distracted reference to the attack of asthma that followed it. "The dark forces of evil that emanate from this woman" were held responsible. There followed a number of cryptic asides:

("Trehern agrees. It's *right*. I *know* it's right.")

"'It is the Cause, it is the Cause, my soul,'" Alleyn muttered, disconsolately. "The old, phoney argument."

Fox, who had been reading over his shoulder, said: "It'd be a peculiar thing if she'd worked Trehern up to doing the job and then got herself mistaken for the intended victim."

"It sounds very neat, Br'er Fox, but in point of fact, it's lousy with loose ends. I can't take it. Just let's go through the other statements now."

They did this and Fox sighed over the result. "I suppose so," he said and added, "I like things to be neat and they so seldom are."

"You're a concealed classicist," Alleyn said. "We'd better go back to this ghastly diary. Read on."

They had arrived at the final week. Rehearsals for the Festival. Animadversions upon Miss Emily. The incident of the Green Lady on Miss Emily's desk. "He did it. K. I'm certain. And I'm *glad*, glad. *She*, no doubt, suspects *me*. I refused to go. She finds she can't order *me* about. To sit in that room with *her* and the two she has ruined! *Never*."

Alleyn turned a page and there, facing them, was the last entry Miss Cost was to make in her journal.

"Yesterday evening," Alleyn said. "After the debacle at the Spring."

The thunderstorm, he was not surprised to find, was treated as a judgment. Nemesis, in the person of one of Miss Cost's ambiguous deities, had decided to touch up the unbelievers with six of the cosmic best. Among these offenders Miss Emily was clearly included but it emerged that she was not the principal object of Miss Cost's spleen. "Laugh at your peril," she ominously wrote, "at the Great Ones." And, as if stung by this observation she continued, in a splutter of disjointed venom, to threaten some unnamed persons. "At last," she wrote. "After the agony of months, the cruelty and now, the final insult, *at last* I shall speak. I shall face both of them with the facts. I shall tell *her* what was between us. And I shall show that other one how I know. He—both—all of them shall suffer. I'll drag their names through the papers. Now. Tonight. I am determined. It is the end."

"And so it was," Fox said, looking up over his spectacles. "Poor thing. Very sad, really, these cases. Do you see your way through all this, Mr. Alleyn?"

"I think I do, Br'er Fox. I'm afraid I do. And I'll tell you why."

He had scarcely begun, when Bailey, moving rather more quickly than he was wont, came through from the shop.

"Someone for you, sir. A Miss Williams. She says it's urgent."

Alleyn went to the telephone.

Jenny sounded as if it was very urgent indeed.

"Mr. Alleyn? Thank God! Please come up here, quickly. Please do. Miss Emily's rooms. I can't say anything else." Alleyn heard a muffled ejaculation. A man shouted distantly and a woman screamed. There was a faint but unmistakable crash of broken glass… "Please come," said Jenny.

"At once," Alleyn said. And to Fox: "Leave Pender on the board and you others follow as quick as you can. Room 35 to the right of the stairhead on the first floor."

Before they had time to answer he was out of the shop and had plunged, head down, into the storm outside.

CHAPTER NINE

Storm

It was not raining now but the night was filled with so vast an uproar that there was no room for any perception but that of noise: the clamour of wind and irregular thud and crash of a monstrous tide. It broke over the foreshore and made hissing assaults on the foot of the steps. Alleyn went up them at a sort of shambling run, bent double and feeling his way with his hands. When he reached the last flight and came into range of the hotel windows, his heart pounded like a ram and his throat was dry. He beat across the platform and went in by the main entrance. The night porter was reading behind his desk. He looked up in astonishment at Alleyn who had not waited to put on his mackintosh.

"Did you get caught, sir?"

"I took shelter," Alleyn said. "Good night."

He made for the stairs and when he was out of sight, waited for a moment or two to recover his wind. Then he went up to the first floor.

The passage had the vacant look of all hotel corridors at night. A wireless blared invisibly. When he moved forward he realised the noise was coming from Miss Emily's room. A brass band was playing "Colonel Bogey."

He knocked on the door and was not answered. He opened it and went in.

It was as if a tableau had been organised for his benefit; as if he had been sent out of the room while the figures arranged themselves to their best effect. Miss Emily stood on the hearthrug very pale and grand, with Jenny in support. Margaret Barrimore, with her hands to her mouth, was inside the door on his left. He had narrowly missed striking her with it when he came in. The three men had pride of place. Major Barrimore stood centre with his legs straddled and blood running from his nose into his gaping mouth. Dr. Maine faced him and frowned at a cut across the knuckles of his own well-kept doctor's hand. Patrick, dishevelled, stood between them, like a referee who had just stopped a fight. The wireless bellowed remorselessly. There was a scatter of broken glass in the fireplace.

They all turned their heads and looked at Alleyn. They might have been asking him to guess the word of their charade.

"Can we switch that thing off?" he asked.

Jenny did so. The silence was deafening.

"I did it to drown the shouting," she said.

"Miss Emily," Alleyn said. "Will you sit down?" She did so.

"It might be as well," he suggested, "if everyone did."

Dr. Maine made an impatient noise and walked over to the window. Barrimore sucked his moustache, tasted blood and got out his handkerchief. He was swaying on his feet. Alleyn pushed a chair under him and he collapsed on it. His eyes were out of focus and he reeked of whisky. Mrs. Barrimore moved towards Dr. Maine. Jenny sat on an arm of Miss Emily's chair and Patrick on the edge of the table.

"And now," Alleyn said, "what has happened?"

For a second or two nobody spoke and then Jenny said: "I asked you to come so I suppose I'd better explain."

"You better hold your tongue," Barrimore mumbled through his bloodied handkerchief.

"That'll do," said Patrick dangerously.

Alleyn said to Jenny, "Will you, then?"

"If I can. All right. I'd come in to say good night to Miss Emily. Patrick was waiting for me downstairs, I think. Weren't you?"

He nodded.

"Miss Emily and I were talking. I was just going to say good night when—when Mrs. Barrimore came in."

"Jenny—no! No!" Margaret Barrimore whispered.

"Don't stop her," Miss Emily said quietly, "it's better not to. I am sure of it."

"Patrick?" Jenny appealed to him.

He hesitated, stared at his mother and then said, "You'd better go on, I think. Just the facts, Jenny."

"Very well. Mrs. Barrimore was distressed and—I think—frightened. She didn't say why. She looked ill. She asked if she could stay with us for a little while and Miss Emily said yes. We didn't talk very much. Nothing that could matter."

Margaret Barrimore said rapidly: "Miss Pride was extremely kind. I wasn't feeling well. I haven't been well lately. I had a giddy turn: I was near her room. That's why I went in."

Dr. Maine said: "As Mrs. Barrimore's doctor I must insist that she's not troubled by any questioning. It's true that she is unwell." He jerked a chair forward and touched her arm. "Sit down, Margaret," he said gently and she obeyed him.

"'As Mrs. Barrimore's doctor,'" her husband quoted and gave a whinnying laugh. "That's wonderful! That's a superb remark."

"Will you go on, please?"

"O.K. Yes. Well, that lasted quite a long time—just the three of us here. And then Dr. Maine came in to see Miss Pride. He examined the cut on her neck and he told us it would probably be too rough for us to cross the channel tomorrow. He and Mrs. Barrimore were saying good night when Major Barrimore came in."

So far Jenny had spoken very steadily but she faltered now, and looked at Miss Emily. "It's—it's then that—that things began to happen. I—"

Miss Emily, with perfect composure, said: "In effect, my dear Roderique, there was a scene. Major Barrimore made certain accusations. Dr. Maine intervened. A climax was reached and blows were exchanged. I suggested, aside to Jenny, that she solicit your aid. The fracas continued. A glass was broken. Mrs. Barrimore screamed and Mr. Patrick arrived upon the scene. He was unsuccessful and, after a renewal of belligerency, Major Barrimore fell to the floor. The actual fighting came to a stop but the noise was considerable. It was at this juncture that the wireless was introduced. You entered shortly afterwards."

"Does everybody agree to this?"

There was no answer.

"I take it that you do."

Dr. Maine said: "Will you also take it that whatever happened has not the remotest shade of bearing upon your case? It was an entirely private matter and should remain so." He looked at Patrick and, with disgust, at Major Barrimore. "I imagine you agree," he said.

"Certainly," Patrick said shortly.

Alleyn produced his stock comment on this argument. "If it turns out that there's no connection, I assure you I shall be glad to forget it. In the meantime, I'm afraid I must make certain."

There was a tap at the door. He answered it. Fox, Bailey and Thompson had arrived. Alleyn asked Fox to come in and the others to wait.

"Inspector Fox," he said, "is with me on this case."

"Good evening, ladies and gentlemen," Fox said.

They observed him warily. Miss Emily said, "Good evening, Mr. Fox. I have heard a great deal about you."

"Have you, ma'am?" he rejoined. "Nothing to my discredit, I hope." And to Alleyn: "Sorry to interrupt, sir."

Alleyn gave him a brief summary of the situation and returned to the matter in hand.

"I'm afraid I must ask you to tell me what it was that triggered off this business," he said. "What were Major Barrimore's accusations?"

Nobody answered. "Will you tell me, Miss Emily?"

Miss Emily said: "I cannot. I am sorry. I—I find myself unable to elaborate upon what I have already said." She looked at Alleyn in distress. "You must not ask me," she said.

"Never mind." He glanced at the others. "Am I to know?" he asked and, after a moment, "Very well. Let us make a different approach. I shall tell you instead, what we have been doing. We have, as some of you know, been at Miss Cost's shop. We have searched the shop and the living quarters behind it. I think I should tell you that we have found Miss Cost's diary. It is a long, exhaustive, and in many places, relevant document. It may be put in evidence."

Margaret Barrimore gave a low cry.

"The final entry was made last night. In it she suggests that as a result of some undefined insult she is going to make public certain matters which are not specifically set out in that part of the diary but will not, I think, be difficult to arrive at when the whole document is reviewed. It may be that after she made this last entry, she wrote a letter to the Press. If so, it will be in the mailbag."

"Has it gone out yet?" Patrick asked sharply.

"I haven't inquired," Alleyn said coolly.

"It must be stopped."

"We don't usually intercept Her Majesty's mail."

Barrimore said thickly: "You can bloody well intercept this one."

"Nonsense," said Dr. Maine crisply.

"By God, sir, I won't take that from you. By God!" Barrimore began, trying to get to his feet.

"Sit down," Alleyn said. "Do you want to be taken in charge for assault? Pull yourself together."

Barrimore sank back. He looked at his handkerchief, now drenched with blood. His face was bedabbled and his nose still ran with it. "Gimme 'nother," he muttered.

"A towel, perhaps," Miss Emily suggested. Jenny fetched one from the bathroom.

"He'd better lie down," Dr. Maine said impatiently.

"I'll be damned if I do," said the Major.

"To continue," Alleyn said, "the facts that emerge from the diary and from the investigations are these. We now know the identity of the Green Lady. Miss Cost found it out for herself on 30th September of last year. She saw the impersonator repeating her initial performance for a concealed audience of one. She afterwards discovered who this other was. You will stay where you are, if you please, Major Barrimore. Miss Cost was unwilling to believe this evidence. She began, however, to spy upon the two persons involved. On 17th June of this year she took a photograph at the Spring."

Dr. Maine said, "I can't allow this," and Patrick said, "No, for God's sake!"

"I would avoid it if I could," Alleyn said. "Mrs. Barrimore, would you rather wait in the next room? Miss Williams will go with you, I'm sure."

"Yes, darling," Jenny said quickly. "Do."

"Oh, no," she said. "Not now. Not now."

"It would be better," Patrick said.

"It would be better, Margaret," Dr. Maine repeated.

"No."

There was a brief silence. An emphatic gust of wind battered at the window. The lights flickered, dimmed and came up again. Alleyn's hearers were momentarily united in a new uneasiness. When he spoke again, they shifted their attention back to him with an air of confusion.

"Miss Cost," he was saying, "kept her secret to herself. It became, I think, an obsession. It's clear from other passages in her diary that some time before this discovery, she had conceived an antagonism for Major Barrimore. The phrases she uses suggest that it arose from the reaction commonly attributed to a woman scorned."

Margaret Barrimore turned her head and for the first time looked at her husband. Her expression, one of profound astonishment, was reflected in her son's face and Dr. Maine's.

"There is no doubt, I think," Alleyn said, "that during her first visit to the Island their relationship, however brief, had been of the sort to give rise to the later reaction."

"Is this true?" Dr. Maine demanded of Barrimore.

He had the towel clapped to his face. Over the top of it his eyes, prominent and dazed, narrowed as if he were smiling. He said nothing.

"Miss Cost, as I said just now, kept her knowledge to herself. Later, it appears, she transferred her attention to Doctor Maine and was unsuccessful. It's a painful and distressing story and I shan't dwell on it except to say that up to yesterday's tragedy we have the picture of a neurotic who has discovered that the man upon whom her fantasy is now concentrated, is deeply attached to the wife of the man with whom she herself had a brief affair that ended in humiliation. She also knows that this wife impersonated the Green Lady in the original episode. These elements are so bound up together, that if she makes mischief, as her demon urges her to do, she will be obliged to expose the truth about the Green Lady and that would be disastrous. Add to this, the proposal to end all publicity and official recognition of the Spring and you get some idea, perhaps, of the emotional turmoil that she suffered and that declares itself in this unhappy diary."

"You do, indeed," said Miss Emily abruptly and added: "One has much to answer for, I perceive. I have much to answer for. Go on."

"In opposing the new plans for the Spring, Miss Cost may have let off a head of emotional steam. She sent anonymous messages to Miss Pride. She was drawn into the companionship of the general front made against Miss Pride's intentions. I think there is little doubt that she conspired with Trehern and egged on ill feeling in the village. She had received attention. She had her Festival in hand. She was somebody. It was, I daresay, all rather exciting and gratifying. Wouldn't you think so?" he asked Dr. Maine.

"I'm not a psychiatrist," he said. "But, yes. You may be right."

"Now this was the picture," Alleyn went on, "up to the time of the Festival. But when she came to write the final entry in her diary, which was last night, something had happened— something that revived all her sense of injury and spite, something that led her to write, 'Both—all of them—shall suffer. I'll drag their names through the papers. Now. Tonight. I am determined. It is the end'."

Another formidable onslaught roared down upon The Boy-and-Lobster and again the lights wavered and recovered.

"She doesn't say, and we can't tell, positively, what inflamed her. I am inclined to think that it might be put down to aesthetic humiliation."

"What!" Patrick ejaculated.

"Yes. One has to remember that all the first-night agonies that beset a professional director are also visited upon the most ludicrously inefficient amateur. Miss Cost had produced a show and exposed it to an audience. However bad the show, she still had to undergo the classic ordeal. The reaction among some of the onlookers didn't escape her notice."

"Oh, dear!" Jenny said. "Oh, *dear!*"

"But this is all speculation and a policeman is not allowed to speculate," Alleyn said. "Let us get back to hard facts, if we can. Here are some of them. Miss Cost attended early service this morning and afterwards walked to the Spring to collect a necklace. It was in her hand when we found her. We know, positively, that she encountered and spoke to three people: Mrs. Carstairs and Dr. Maine before church; Major Barrimore afterwards."

"Suppose I deny that?" Barrimore said thickly.

"I can't, of course, make any threats or offer any persuasion. You might, on consideration, think it wiser, after all, to agree that you met and tell me what passed between you. Major Barrimore," Alleyn explained generally, "has already admitted that he was spying upon Miss Pride who had gone to the enclosure to put up a notice which he afterwards removed."

Miss Emily gave a sharp ejaculation.

"It was later replaced." Alleyn turned to Barrimore and stood over him. "Shall I tell you what I think happened? I think hard words passed between you and Miss Cost and that she was stung into telling you her secret. I think you parted from her in a rage and that when you came back to the hotel this morning, you bullied your wife. You had better understand at once, that your wife has not told me this. Finally, I believe that Miss Cost may even have threatened to reveal your former relationship with herself. She suggests in her diary that she has some such intention. Now. Have you anything to say to all this?"

Patrick said: "You had better say nothing." He walked over to his mother and put his arm about her shoulders.

"I didn't do it," Barrimore said. "I didn't kill her."

"Is that all?"

"Yes."

"Very well. I shall move on," Alleyn said and spoke generally. "Among her papers we have found a typewritten list of dates. It is a carbon copy. The top copy is missing. Miss Cost had fallen into the habit of sending anonymous letters. As we know only too well, this habit grows by indulgence. It is possible, having regard for the dates in question, that this document has been brought to the notice of the person most likely to be disturbed by it. Possibly with a print of the photograph. Now, this individual has, in one crucial respect, given a false statement as to time and circumstance and because of that—"

There was a tap at the door. Fox opened it. A voice in the passage shouted: "I can't wait quiet-like, mister. I got to see 'im." It was Trehern.

Fox said: "Now then, what's all this?" And began to move
out. Trehern plunged at him, head down, and was taken in
a half-nelson. Bailey appeared in the doorway. "You lay your
hands off of me," Trehern whined. "You got nothing against
me."

"Outside," said Fox.

Trehern, struggling, looked wildly round the assembled
company and fixed on Alleyn. "I got something to tell you,
mister," he said. "I got something to put before all of you. I got
to speak out."

"All right, Fox," Alleyn said and nodded to Bailey, who
went out and shut the door. Fox relaxed his hold. "Well,
Trehern, what is it?"

Trehern wiped the back of his hand across his mouth and
blinked. "I been thinking," he said.

"Yes?"

"I been thinking things over. Ever since you come at me
up to my house and acted like you done and made out what you
made out, which is not the case. I be'ant a quick-brained chap,
mister, but the light has broke and I see me way clear. I got to
speak and speak public."

"Very well. What do you want to say?"

"Don't you rush me now, mister. What I got to say is a
mortal serious matter and I need to take my time."

"Nobody's rushing you."

"No, nor they better not," he said. His manner was half
truculent, half cringing. "It concerns this yurr half-hour in time
what was the matter, which you flung in my teeth. So fur so
good. Now. This yurr lady," he ducked his head at Miss Emily,
"tells you she seen my lil' chap in the road round about twenty
to eight on this yurr fatal morning. Right?"

"Certainly," said Miss Pride.

"Much obliged. And I says, so she might of then, for all I
know to the contrariwise, me being asleep in my bed. And I
says I uprose at five past eight. Correct?"

"That's what you said, yes."

"And God's truth if I never speak another word. And my lil' chap was then to home in my house. Right. Now then. Furthermore to that, you says the doctor saw him at that same blessed time, twenty to eight, which statement agrees with the lady."

"Yes."

"Yes. And you says, don't rush me, you says the doctor was in his launch at that mortal moment."

Alleyn glanced at Maine. "Agreed?" he asked.

"Yes. I saw Wally from the launch."

Trehern moved over to Dr. Maine. "That's a bloody lie, Doctor," he said. "Axcusing the expression. I face you out with it, man to man. I seen you, doctor, clear as I see you now, moving out in thicky launch of yourn at five to ten bloody minutes past eight and by God, I reckon you'm not telling lies for the fun of it. I reckon as how you got half an hour on your conscience, Doctor Maine, and if the law doesn't face you out with it I'm the chap to do the law's job for it."

"I have already discussed the point with Superintendent Alleyn," Maine said, looking at Trehern with profound distaste. "Your story is quite unsupported."

"Is it?" Trehern said. "Is it, then? That's where you're dead wrong. You mind me. And you t'other ladies and gents and you, mister." He turned back to Alleyn. "After you shifted off this evening, I took to thinking. And I remembered. I remembered our young Wal come up when I was looking out of my winder and I remembered he said in his por simple fashion, 'Thicky doctor's launch, be'ant she?' You ax him, mister. You face him up with it and he'll tell you."

"No doubt!" said Maine. He looked at Alleyn. "I imagine you accept my statement," he said.

"I haven't said so," Alleyn replied. "I didn't say so at the time, if you remember."

"By God, Alleyn!" he said angrily and controlled himself. "This fellow's as shifty as they come. You must see it. And the boy! Of what value is the boy's statement if you get one from him. He's probably been thrashed into learning what he's got to say."

"I never raised a hand—" Trehern began but Alleyn stopped him.

"I was coming to this point," he said, "when we were interrupted. It may as well be brought out by this means as any other. There are factors, apart from those I've already discussed, of which Trehern knows nothing. They may be said to support his story." He glanced at Miss Emily. "I shall put them to you presently but I assure you they are cogent. In the meantime, Dr. Maine, if you have any independent support for your own version of your movements, you might like to say what it is. I must warn you—"

"*Stop.*"

Margaret Barrimore had moved out into the room. Her hands writhed together, as they had done when he saw her in the garden, but she had an air of authority and was, he thought, in command of herself.

She said: "Please don't go on, Mr. Alleyn. There's something that I see I must tell you."

"Margaret!" Dr. Maine said sharply.

"No," she said. "No. Don't try to stop me. If you do I shall insist on seeing Mr. Alleyn alone. But I'd rather say it here. In front of you all. After all, everybody knows now, don't they? We needn't pretend anymore. Let me go on."

"Go on, Mrs. Barrimore," Alleyn said.

"It's true," she said. "He didn't leave the bay in his launch at half past seven or whenever it was. He came to the hotel to see me. I said I had breakfast alone. I wasn't alone. He was there. Miss Cost had told him she was going to expose—everything. She told him when they met outside the church so he came to see me and ask me to go away with him. He wanted us to make a clean break before it all came out. He asked me to meet him in the village tonight. We were to go to London and then abroad. It was all very hurried. Only a few minutes. We heard somebody coming. I asked him to let me think, to give me a breathing space. So he went away. I suppose he went back to the bay."

She walked over to Maine and put her hand on his arm. "I couldn't let you go on," she said. "It's all the same now. It doesn't matter, Bob. It doesn't matter. We'll be together."

"Margaret, my dear," said Dr. Maine.

There was a long silence. Fox cleared his throat.

Alleyn turned to Trehern.

"And what have you to say to that?" he asked.

Trehern was gaping at Mrs. Barrimore. He seemed to be lost in some kind of trance.

"I'll be going," he said at last. "I'll be getting back along." He turned and made for the door. Fox stepped in front of it.

Barrimore had got to his feet. His face, bedabbled with blood, was an appalling sight.

"Then it's true," he said very quietly. "She told me. She stood there, grinning and jibbering. She said she'd make me a public laughing stock. And when I said she could go to hell she—d'you know what she did?—she spat at me. And I—I—"

His voice was obliterated by a renewed onslaught of the gale: heavier than any that had preceded it. A confused rumpus broke out. Some metal object, a dustbin perhaps, racketed past the house and vanished in a diminishing series of irregular clashes, as if it bumped down the steps. There was a second monstrous buffet. Somebody, Margaret Barrimore, Alleyn thought, cried out, and at the same moment the lights failed altogether.

The dark was absolute and the noise intense. Alleyn was struck violently on the shoulder and cannoned into something solid and damp: Fox. As he recovered, he was hit again and putting out his hand, felt the edge of the door.

He yelled to Fox, "Come on!" and snatching at the door, dived into the passage. There, too, it was completely dark. But less noisy. He thought he could make out the thud of running feet on carpet. Fox was behind him. A flashlight danced on a wall. "Give it me," Alleyn said. He grabbed it and it displayed for an instant the face of Sergeant Bailey. "Out of my way," he said. "Come on, you two. Fox—get Coombe."

He ran to the stairhead and flashed his torch downwards. For a split second it caught the top of a head. He went downstairs in a controlled plunge, using the torch, and arrived in the entrance hall as the front door crashed. His flashlight discovered, momentarily, the startled face of the night porter who said: "Here, what's the matter?" and disappeared, open-mouthed.

The door was still swinging. He caught it and was once more engulfed in the storm.

It was raining again, heavily. The force of the gale was such that he leant against it and drove his way towards the steps in combat with it. Two other lights, Bailey's and Thompson's, he supposed, dodged eccentrically across the slanting downpour. He lost them when he reached the steps and found the iron rail. But there was yet another lancet of broken light beneath him. As Alleyn went down after it, he was conscious only of noise and idiot violence. He slipped, fell and recovered. At one moment, he was hurled against the rail.

"These bloody steps," he thought. "These bloody steps." When he reached the bottom flight he saw his quarry, a dark, foreshortened, anonymous figure, veer through the dull light from Miss Cost's shop window. "Pender's got a candle or a torch," Alleyn thought.

The other's torch was still going: a thin erratic blade. "Towards the jetty," Alleyn thought. "He's making for the jetty." And down there were the riding lights of the hotel launch, jauncing in the dark.

Here at last, the end of the steps. Now he was in seawater, sometimes over his feet. The roar of the channel was all-obliterating. The gale flattened his lips and filled his eyes with tears. When he made the jetty, he had to double-up and grope with his left hand, keeping the right, with Fox's torch still alive, held out in front—he was whipped by the sea.

He had gained ground. The other was moving on again, doubled up, like Alleyn himself, and still using a torch. There were no more than thirty feet between them. The riding-lights danced near at hand and shuddered when the launch banged against the jetty.

The figure was poised—it waited for the right moment. A torchlight swung through the rain and Alleyn found himself squinting into the direct beam. He ducked and moved on, half-dazzled but aware that the launch rose and the figure leapt to meet it. Alleyn struggled forward, took his chance, and jumped.

He had landed aft, among the passengers' benches; had fallen across one of them and struck his head on another. He hung there, while the launch bucketed under him and then he fell between the benches and lay on the heaving deck, fighting for breath and helpless. His torch had gone and he was in the dark. There must have been a brief rent in the night sky because a company of stars careened across his vision, wheeled and returned. The deck tilted again and he saw the hotel windows, glowing. They curtsied and tipped. "The power's on," he thought, and a sudden deadly sinking blotted everything out. When he opened his eyes he thought with astonishment: "I was out." Then he heard the engine and felt the judder of a propeller racing above water. He laid hold of a bench and dragged himself to his knees. He could see his opponent, faintly haloed by light from the wheelhouse, back towards him, wrestling with the wheel itself. A great sea broke over them. The windows along Portcarrow front lurched up and dived out of sight again.

Alleyn began to crawl down the gangway between rows of fixed seats, clinging to them as he went. His feet slithered. He fell sideways and, propping himself up, managed to drag off his shoes and socks. His head cleared and ached excruciatingly. The launch was now in mid-channel, taking the seas full on her beam and rolling monstrously. He thought, "She'll never make it," and tried to remember where the lifebelts should be.

Did that other, fighting there with the wheel, know he was aboard? How had the launch been cast off? Were the mooring-lines freed from their cleats and was she now without them? Or had they been loosed from the bollards while he was unconscious? What should he do? "Keep observation!" he thought sourly. An exquisite jab of pain shot through his eyeballs.

The launch keeled over and took in a solid weight of sea. He thought, "Well, this is it," and was engulfed. The iron legs of the bench bit into his hands. He hung on, almost vertical, and felt the water drag at him like an octopus. It was disgusting. The deck kicked. They wallowed for a suspended moment and then, shuddering, recovered and rose. The first thing he saw was the back of the helmsman. Something rolled against his chest. He unclenched his left hand and felt for it. The torch.

Street lamps along the front came alive and seemed dramatically near at hand. At the same time the engine was cut. He struggled to his feet and moved forward. He was close now, to the figure at the wheel. There was the jetty. Their course had shifted and the launch pitched violently. His left hand knocked against the back of a seat and a beam of light shot out from the torch and found the figure at the wheel. It turned.

Maine and Alleyn looked into each other's faces.

Maine lurched out of the wheelhouse. The launch lifted prodigiously, tilted, and dived, nose down. Alleyn was blinded by a deluge of saltwater. When he could see again, Maine was on the port gunwale. For a fraction of time he was poised, a gigantic figure against the shore lights. Then he flexed his knees and leapt overboard.

The launch went about and crashed into the jetty. The last thing he heard was somebody yelling high above him.

He was climbing down innumerable flights of stairs. They were impossibly steep—perpendicular—but he had to go down. They tipped and he fell outwards and looked into an abyss laced with flashlights. He lost his hold, dropped into nothing, and was on the stairs again, climbing, climbing. Somebody was making comfortable noises. He looked into a face.

"Fox," he said, with immense satisfaction.

"There now!" said Inspector Fox.

Alleyn went to sleep.

When he woke, it was to find Troy nearby. Her hand was against his face. "So there you are," he said.

"Hallo," said Troy and kissed him.

The wall beyond her was dappled with sunshine and looked familiar. He puzzled over it for a time and, because he wanted to lay his face closer to her hand, turned his head and was stabbed through the temples.

"Don't move," Troy said. "You've taken an awful bash."

"I see."

"You've been concussed and all."

"How long?"

"About thirty-four hours."

"This is Coombe's cottage."

"That's right, but you're meant not to talk."

"Ridiculous," he said and dozed off again.

Troy slid her hand carefully from under his bristled jaw and crept out of the room.

Superintendent Coombe was in his parlour with Sir James Curtis and Fox. "He woke again," Troy said to Curtis, "just for a moment."

"Say anything?"

"Yes. He's—" Her voice trembled. "He's all right."

"Of course he's all right. I'll take a look at him."

She returned with him to the bedroom and stood by the window while Curtis stooped over his patient. It was a brilliant morning. The channel was dappled with sequins. The tide was low and three people walked over the causeway: an elderly woman, a young man and a girl. Five boats ducked and bobbed in Fisherman's Bay. The hotel launch was still jammed in the understructure of the jetty and looked inconsequent and unreal, suspended above its natural element. A complete write-off, it was thought.

"You're doing fine," Curtis said.

"Where's Troy?"

"Here, darling."

"Good. What happened?"

"You were knocked out," Curtis said. "Coombe and two other chaps managed to fish you up."

"Coombe?"

"Fox rang him from the hotel as soon as you'd set off on your wild goose chase. They were on the jetty."

"Oh, yes. Yelling. Where's Fox?"

"You'd better keep quiet for a bit, Rory. Everything's all right. Plenty of time."

"I want to see Fox, Curtis."

"Very well, but only for one moment."

Troy fetched him.

"This is more like it now," Fox said.

"Have you found him?"

"We have, yes. Yesterday evening, at low tide."

"Where?"

"About four miles along the coast."

"It was deliberate, Fox."

"So I understand. Coombe saw it."

"Yes, well now, that's quite enough," said Curtis.

Fox stepped back.

"Wait a minute," Alleyn said. "Anything on him? Fox? Anything on him?"

"All right. Tell him."

"Yes, Mr. Alleyn, there was. Very sodden. Pulp almost, but you can make it out. The top copy of that list and the photograph."

"Ah!" Alleyn said. "She gave them to him. I thought as much."

He caught his breath and then closed his eyes.

"That's right," Curtis said. "You go to sleep again."

"My sister, Fanny Winterbottom," said Miss Emily, two days later, "once remarked with characteristic extravagance (nay, on occasion, vulgarity), that, wherever I went, I kicked up as much dust as a dancing dervish. The observation was inspired more by fortuitous alliteration than by any degree of accuracy. If, however, she were alive today, she would doubtless consider herself justified. I have made disastrous mischief in Portcarrow."

"My dear Miss Emily, aren't you, yourself, falling into Mrs. Winterbottom's weakness for exaggeration? Miss Cost's murder had nothing to do with your decision on the future of the Spring."

"But it *had*," said Miss Emily, smacking her gloved hand on the arm of Superintendent Coombe's rustic seat. "Let us have logic. If I had not persisted with my decision, her nervous system, to say nothing of her emotions (at all times unstable), would not have been exacerbated to such a degree that she would have behaved as she did."

"How do you know?" Alleyn asked. "She might have cut up rough on some other provocation. She had her evidence. The possession of a dangerous instrument is, in itself, a danger. Even if you had never visited the Island, Miss Emily, Barrimore and Maine would still have laughed at the Festival."

"She would have been less disturbed by their laughter," said Miss Emily. She looked fixedly at Alleyn. "I am tiring you, no doubt," she said. "I must go. Those kind children are waiting in the motor. I merely called to say *au revoir*, my dear Roderique."

"You are not tiring me in the least and your escort can wait. I imagine they are very happy to do so. It's no good, Miss Emily. I know you're eaten up with curiosity."

"Not curiosity. A natural dislike of unexplained detail."

"I couldn't sympathise more. Which details?"

"No doubt you are always asked when you first began to suspect the criminal. When did you first begin to suspect Dr. Maine?"

"When you told me that, at about twenty to eight, you saw nobody but Wally on the road down to Fisherman's Bay."

"And I should have seen Dr. Maine?"

"You should have seen him pulling out from the bay jetty in his launch. And then Trehern, quite readily, said he saw the doctor leaving in his launch about five past eight. Why should he lie about the time he left? And what, as Trehern pointed out, did he do in the half-hour that elapsed?"

"Did you not believe that poor woman when she accounted for the half-hour?"

"Not for a second. If he had been with her she would have said so when I first interviewed her. He has a patient in the hotel and she could have quite easily given that as a reason and would have wanted to provide him with an alibi. Did you notice his look of astonishment when she cut in? Did you notice how she stopped him before he could say anything? No, I didn't believe her and I think he knew I didn't."

"And that, you consider, was why he ran away?"

"Partly that, perhaps. He may have felt," Alleyn said, "quite suddenly, that he couldn't take it. He may have had his moment of truth. Imagine it, Miss Emily. The blinding realisation that must come to a killer: the thing that forces so many of them to give themselves up or to bolt or to commit suicide. Suppose we had believed her and they had gone away together. For the rest of his life he would have been tied to the woman he loved by the most appalling obligation it's possible to imagine."

"Yes," she said. "He was a proud man, I think. You are right. Pray go on."

"Maine had spoken to Miss Cost outside the church. She was telling Mrs. Carstairs she would go to the Spring after the service and collect the necklace that had been left on the shelf. She ran after Maine and Mrs. Carstairs went into church. We don't know what passed between them but I think she may, poor creature, have made some final advance and been rebuffed. She must have armed herself with her horrid little snapshot and list of dates and been carrying them about in her bag, planning to call on him, precipitate a final scene and then confront him with her evidence. In any case she forced them on him and very likely told him she was going to give the whole story to the Press."

"Did she—?"

"Yes. It was in the mailbag."

"You said, I think, that you did not normally intercept Her Majesty's mail."

"I believe I did," said Alleyn blandly. "Nor do we. Normally."

"Go on."

"He knew she was going to the Spring. He was no doubt on the lookout as he washed his hands at the sink in the Trethaways' cottage. He saw Wally. He probably saw you pin up your notice. He saw Barrimore tear it down and go away. He went up and let himself in. He had admittance discs and used one when we sent for him. He hid behind the boulder and waited for Miss Cost. He knew of course that there were loose rocks up there. He was extremely familiar with the terrain."

"Ah, yes."

"When it was over he scraped away his footprints. Later on, when we were there, he was very quick to get up to the higher level and walk over it. Any prints that might be left would thus appear to be innocuous. Then he went back in his launch at ten minutes past eight and waited to be sent for to examine the body."

"It gives me an unpleasant *frisson* when I remember that he also examined mine," said Miss Emily. "A cool, resourceful man. I rather liked him."

"So did I," Alleyn said. "I liked him. He intended us, of course, to follow up the idea of mistaken identity but he was too clever to push it overmuch. If we hadn't discovered that you visited the Spring, he would have said he'd seen you. As it was he let us find out for ourselves. He hoped Wally would be thought to have done it and would have given evidence of his irresponsibility and seen him bestowed in a suitable institution, which, as he very truly observed, might be the best thing for him, after all."

"I shall do something about that boy," said Miss Emily. "There must be special schools. I shall attend to it." She looked curiously at Alleyn. "What would you have done if the lights had not failed, or if you had caught up with him?"

"Routine procedure, Miss Emily. Asked him to come to Coombe's office and make a statement. I doubt if we had a case against him. Too much conjecture. I hoped, by laying so much of the case open, to induce a confession. Once the Wally theory was dismissed, I think Maine would have not allowed Barrimore or anyone else, to be arrested. But I'm glad it turned out as it did."

Fox came through the gate into Coombe's garden.

"*Bon jour, Mademoiselle,*" he said laboriously. "*J'espère que vous êtes en bonne santé ce matin.*"

Miss Emily winced. "Mr. Fox," she said in slow but exquisite French. "You are, I am sure, a very busy man, but if you can spare an hour twice a week, I think I might be able to give you some assistance with your conversation. I should be delighted to do so."

Fox asked her if she would be good enough to repeat her statement and, as she did so, blushed to the roots of his hair.

"*Mademoiselle,*" he said, "*c'est bonne,* no blast—*pardon— bien aimable de vous*—I mean—*de votre part.* Would you really? I can't think of anything I'd like better."

"*Alors, c'est entendu,*" said Miss Emily.

Patrick and Jenny sat in his car down by the waterfront. Miss Emily's luggage and Jenny's and Patrick's suitcases were roped into the open boot. Miss Emily had settled to spend a few days at the Manor Park Hotel and had invited them both to be her guests. Patrick felt he should stay with his mother but she was urgent for him to go.

"It made me feel terribly inadequate," he said. "As if somehow I must have failed her. And yet, you know, I thought we got on awfully well together, always. I'm fond of my mama."

"Of course you are. And she adores you. I expect it's just that she wants to be by herself until—well, until the first ghastly shock's over."

"By herself? With him there?"

"He's not behaving badly, Patrick. Is he?"

"No. Oddly enough, no." He looked thoughtfully at Jenny. "I knew about Bob Maine," he said. "Of course I did. I've never been able to make out why I didn't like it. Not for conventional reasons. If you say Oedipus Complex I shall be furious."

"I won't say it then."

"The thing is, I suppose, one doesn't like one's mama being a *femme fatale*. And she is, a bit, you know. I'm so sorry for her," he said violently, "that it makes me angry. Why should that be? I really don't understand it at all."

"Do you know, I think it's impossible for us to take the idea of older people being in love. It's all wrong, I expect, and I daresay it's the arrogance of youth or something."

"You may be right. Jenny, I do love you with all my heart. Could we get married, do you think?"

"I don't see anything against it," said Jenny.

After a longish interval, Jenny said: "Miss Emily's taking her time, isn't she? Shall we walk up to the cottage and say goodbye to that remarkable man?"

"Well—if you like."

"Come on."

They strolled along the seafront, holding hands. A boy was sitting on the edge of the terrace, idly throwing pebbles into the channel.

It was Wally.

As they came up he turned and, when he saw them, held out his hands.

"All gone," he said.